"Be thankful that even though
I threw you in the dungeon yesterday,
I will also lay down my life for you, for
this I have pledged to my lord to do."

Clara would not be lured away by the sudden
turn of his temper. Scoffing, she tossed up her
bandaged hand. "What nonsense! I am but
a Saxon midwife. You make me sound like a
precious princess to be protected."

"I know nothing of fine ladies and fancy
princesses," Kenneth answered. "I only know that
I will protect you."

A part of her leaped inside, but she would not be
like a young girl taken by charming words. "Until
Lord Taurin arrives."

"Thanks to your stubbornness, woman, Lord
Taurin may be on his way here right now! Led
here by the townsfolk of Colchester. *Your* people."

She stilled, then swallowed. Aye, she'd pledged
to keep Rowena safe, and her baby with her, and
aye, she'd die in order to keep such a pledge,
but what if Taurin was on his way? What would
happen then?

Books by Barbara Phinney

Love Inspired Historical

Bound to the Warrior
Protected by the Warrior ✓

Love Inspired Suspense

Desperate Rescue
Keeping Her Safe
Deadly Homecoming
Fatal Secrets ✓
Silent Protector

BARBARA PHINNEY

was born in England and raised in Canada. She has traveled throughout her life, loving to explore the various countries and cultures of the world. After she retired from the Canadian Armed Forces, Barbara turned her hand to romance writing. The thrill of adventure and the love of happy endings, coupled with a too-active imagination, have merged to help her create this and other wonderful stories. Barbara spends her days writing, building her dream home with her husband and enjoying their fast-growing children.

Protected by the Warrior

BARBARA PHINNEY

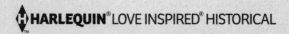

™ LOVE INSPIRED BOOKS

Recycling programs
for this product may
not exist in your area.

ISBN-13: 978-0-373-28276-0

PROTECTED BY THE WARRIOR

Copyright © 2014 by Barbara Phinney

Printed in U.S.A.

Jesus looked at them and said, "With man this is impossible, but with God all things are possible."
—*Matthew* 19:26

Dedicated to those who enjoy Love Inspired Historicals.

Aim to make the future better, and live in the present, but keep your heart in the past, for there lies the clues to who you are. B.P.

This author acknowledges the hard work of the late Pam Strickler. Rest in Peace.

Chapter One

Essex County, 1068 AD

"Push, milady, push!"

Though Clara had been the midwife in Dunmow, a small keep and village west of Colchester, for a few weeks only, she'd already learned Lady Ediva's determined personality. But at this point in milady's labor, the mother-to-be definitely needed strong encouragement. "Push harder! Harder!"

Lady Ediva scrunched up her face and glared down from the birthing chair. "I'm pushing as hard as I can! Stop shouting at me!" Her words ended with a growl and another hard push.

Already situated at milady's feet, Clara gave her forehead a fast wipe with her forearm. She had long since pulled back her own thick red hair and now felt it start to slip free, but could do nothing at that moment. The babe's head had crowned, and with deft movements, and more bearing down on the new mother's part, she soon assisted in delivering a healthy son. "It's a boy!"

Lady Ediva fell back against the chair. Clara knew their work was not yet complete, but for a few minutes they could revel in the joy of new life.

Clara prepared the babe for his mother, even though they weren't finished with the birthing yet. All the while, Lady Ediva's maid, Margaret, wiped her mistress's face. Tears of joy streamed down each woman's cheeks. Clara stopped a moment to admire the beautiful, squalling child in her arms.

Praise God! A new babe! New life when lately she had felt only the threat of death.

A surge of excitement washed over Clara as the indignant howl of the healthy babe bounced off the thick oak door of the solar. She knew that beyond, in the corridor, the father waited impatiently, along with his men.

As Margaret tended to Lady Ediva, Clara swaddled the babe in a soft cloth, snuggling him close as she walked over and opened the door.

Closer to the door, Kenneth d'Entremont, sergeant at arms for Dunmow Keep, whirled. Behind him, Lord Adrien stopped his pacing. Each man's face split into a broad smile at the sight of the child in her arms.

"'Tis a good day, Lord Adrien!" Kenneth announced to the new father.

"Aye. Nothing can spoil it."

Both men stepped toward Clara, a question on each face. "A boy or a girl?" Kenneth asked.

Adrien waved his hand. "I care not, but by the sound of that lusty wail, it's a boy!"

They laughed together. Clara smiled tiredly as she pulled back the wrap to reveal the babe's scrunched-up face. "You have a fine son, Lord Adrien." Behind her, Margaret approached, and Clara handed her the child.

"Your wife is ready to see you. Go spend time with your family."

"I will!" Adrien turned to Kenneth. "The keep is yours, d'Entremont, as we discussed. Guard it well, for I do not wish to be disturbed."

"You have my pledge," Kenneth answered solemnly before Adrien disappeared into the solar. Clara smiled as she shut the door to stop any draft. 'Twas good to see a new father so eager to spend time with his wife while she recuperated. She hadn't seen such devotion before. She would give them this moment of privacy before she returned to check on Lady Ediva. The birthing process was not quite finished.

Then came the sound of swift, pounding feet. Clara spun at the urgent tattoo, noticing Kenneth's hand resting lightly on his blade as he stepped in front of her. It may have been the finest day for Lord Adrien, and one during which he would cast all other cares aside, but Clara knew Kenneth would not lower his guard. Not when he'd just given his promise to Adrien to mind the keep.

A man approached. 'Twas a courier, Clara noticed, a man who wore the crest of the Baron of Colchester—Lord Adrien's brother—on his short, travel-worn tunic. His face ruddy, his leggings and surcoat splattered with mud from a hard, fast ride, he slowed his approach.

"I have a missive for the master of the keep," the man panted out. "'Tis urgent, I've been told."

Kenneth held out his hand. "I have control of this keep."

The courier handed Kenneth the communiqué and departed. With only the dim, morning glow from a slit window in which to read the missive, Kenneth frowned as he held it close to scan the words.

In front of the closed door, Clara watched a black expression spreading across the young sergeant's features. She swallowed. 'Twas not good news. Was someone sick?

Kenneth looked up, his mouth thinning as he drilled a brittle stare into her. "Are you finished with Lady Ediva?"

Clara frowned. "Aye, for now. Margaret has my complete confidence. She will care for mother and babe until I am needed again."

"Good." His jaw tightened. "Because you are headed for the dungeon."

Stunned, Clara gaped at Kenneth, starting when he grabbed her arm. "The dungeon! Are you mad? Why should I go there?"

Kenneth called out and a guard met them on the curved stone stairs that led to the main floor.

"Let go of me!" Clara twisted, but to no avail.

Kenneth's grip tightened. "Nay, woman. Not after what you've done!"

"I've done nothing wrong! I demand you release me!"

"You have no right to make any demands!"

Clara barely had time to lift her cyrtel to prevent tripping on it as he dragged her down the stairs into the kitchen and down more steps to the darkness below. With the door to the dungeon ahead, she fought back more fiercely and, for her effort, was pushed hard down the short corridor. She struggled to keep her balance in the murky maw around her.

The guard proceeded to unlock the solitary door. Clara tilted up her chin and threw back her shoulders.

A thick wooden door, secured by long hinges and an iron lock, would soon imprison her. With her mouth pressed into a thin line, she told herself not to do something foolish.

And not to be scared.

She wrenched her arm free and turned to Kenneth. "Why am I here? I should be upstairs and available, for Lady Ediva's birthing is not done! You had no right to drag me down here! What was in that missive that has prompted this ridiculous act?"

"'Twas from Colchester, where you lived before coming to our keep. I would think you know exactly what the warning says."

Her voice lowered and quivered as she struggled to stand tall. Fatigue was robbing her not only of balance but thought, as well. "I am nearly too tired to stand, let alone think, so please, Kenneth, reconsider your actions. Or at least tell me why I'm here."

His expression softening only slightly, Kenneth took a step over the threshold, only to stop when he caught sight of the soldier beside him. "If you are so tired, mayhap a nice rest in isolation for a day or two will clear your head and return your memory."

She shook her head, tossing away the cobwebs that exhaustion had draped across her thoughts. She surged forward. "Nay, you're a fool! I can't be imprisoned! Not now! You know nothing of women in confinement, or of babes and all the dangers that can befall them! 'Tis a perilous time for Lady Ediva!"

The soldier shoved her back, hard, and Kenneth grabbed the man's hand as Clara struggled to remain standing.

"'Tis a perilous warning from Colchester, also, so mayhap keeping you from Lady Ediva is warranted!"

Clara felt the blood drain from her face. The cold left in its wake sent a shiver through her. *No. Please, no.* Had the guild masters in Colchester finally told their baron, Lord Eudo, why they'd insisted she be sent here to replace the midwife who'd died? This tiny village and isolated keep would never have been her choice of home. Had Lord Eudo suspected something was amiss from her departing look that day a month ago, and finally gleaned the truth from the guild masters on whom he'd bestowed far too much control? She shivered again. Or had that evil Lord Taurin finally arrived to claim what he had no right to possess? Did Taurin have enough influence to take her into custody, as well? Nay, she would fight this, for more than just her life was at stake.

Worry bit into her. All she knew was that Lord Eudo had seen fit to warn his brother of something he'd learned. She swallowed the hard lump in her throat.

Nay. She would not be frightened. She had done what was right and true in her eyes and would do so again. The guild masters, and indeed, all the townsfolk of Colchester, had no right to toss her out, and Kenneth had no right to imprison her for what she'd done there!

Through the dimness, she peered at Kenneth, recalling how they'd met. A month ago, he'd ridden to Colchester to escort her here. During the majority of the time they'd spent traveling, his looks had been cold enough to freeze the North Sea solid. She'd bristled, and still stinging from the town's rejection, she'd lashed back at Kenneth by correcting his sloppy equestrian habits. The ride here had been awkward and unpleasant.

"You are a brutish race of people," she whispered

harshly. "All of you Normans are, coming to our land, taking what you see fit and discarding us when we are of no more use!"

Kenneth ordered the guard away. When they were alone, he stepped forward into the dank, stinking room. With his dark tunic and leggings, he immediately blended into the shadows around them. "I can tell by your expression you know exactly why you're here." Triumph lit his face at her guilty surprise. "See, you *do* know the reason, don't you? Then you should be imprisoned."

She snapped her head to the right to hide her expression. All the worries of the past spring flooded back. The weak, frightened voice begging her for asylum, her desperation to keep safe a frail young mother and her newborn son, whom no one here would even know, much less care for. Aye, all her own fears and that of the young woman's washed back over her.

But Clara had pledged with her life to allow no harm to come to the helpless pair. And that included never revealing their location. She'd told only one person and she was far away from Colchester. 'Twas needed, for the lives of mother and son depended on it.

If time in this horrible room, with its stink of mold and filth from drunken soldiers who'd needed to sober up, was part of the cost of her personal integrity, 'twas a cost she was willing to pay. She would *never* reveal where mother and child were, no matter who ordered it. The guild masters and the townsfolk in Colchester, even her own father, God rest his soul, should he return and demand she divulge their location, would never learn it.

Should Lord Taurin find Rowena and the babe, 'twould be disastrous, for he had been brutal when he'd bought her as a slave and brutal in fathering the child against her will. The Good Lord had designed that Clara help Rowena through her childbirth and then hide the pair away when Taurin's men arrived looking for them.

Since coming to Dunmow, she'd secreted Rowena and her infant to another hiding place, one closer by. It had taken a whole night and part of an early morning to travel the few leagues from the first hiding spot to the other, but Rowena was safe for now. And she would stay that way, no matter what the cost to Clara in keeping the secret.

Kenneth leaned toward her, his voice softening. "So, Clara, save yourself. Tell me where they are. Tell me all about them."

Never. Revealing their new location would surely sign a death warrant for the mother, and Clara had long since pledged to save lives, not take them. Only God should take lives.

She squared her shoulders as her eyes finally adjusted to the dimness and her nose to the stench. Her mouth thinned further as she folded her arms. Whatever Kenneth had read meant nothing, and she would not dignify his curiosity with an answer.

"Fine," Kenneth said, apparently reading her determined stance. "We'll sort out your stubbornness after you've had time to chew on it. I'm thinking you'll find your decision as tough as old shoe leather."

Clara watched as Kenneth grabbed the ring of the heavy plank door to slam it shut. At the last moment, she raced forward, hoping to say that Lord Adrien should hear her explanation, not just his brother's message. But when her hands connected with damp wood, she knew it was too late. Slowly, she sank to the dirt and rubble at her feet, her hands dragging down the roughly planed door. Something sharp stabbed into her left palm as she crumpled into a ball, worried and desperate—yet not surprised. She'd known this day was coming.

Lord Adrien and Sergeant Kenneth d'Entremont were both Normans, like that filthy baron who'd caused this trouble for Rowena. They would likely never believe the tales of brutality that had Rowena fearing for her life if she stayed with her master. Lord Adrien was a good man, but would any Norman care about a poor Saxon mother as Clara did?

Her head shot up. But they would care for Lady Ediva upstairs! When Kenneth had grabbed her arm a few moments ago, she hadn't even been given a chance to call out instructions to Margaret on how to care for her mistress and the new babe. Surely they would see that she was needed!

Please, Lord, keep Ediva and her child safe! Clara bit her lip through the prayer. There was so much that could happen. Things that could easily end their lives. She jumped up and smacked the hard, mold-darkened wood with her stinging palm. "Nay! I must return to Lady Ediva! Kenneth, you must let me return to her! Kenneth, she could die! Think of your lady! Think of her babe!"

But her cries bounced around the dark room to no avail, and her hands pained from pounding on the door. She could feel blood splatter onto her cheek from the injury in her hand. Ignoring it, she called out her plea to consider Lady Ediva, but no one, save herself and whatever creatures scurried within the cell, heard her voice.

With one last soft cry on her lips, she fell to the floor again.

* * *

Kenneth paused at the base of the narrow stairs that led down to this filthy place from the kitchen. His gaze moved from the guard posted at the top to the door he'd just slammed shut on the midwife. Clara pounded on it, crying out to him to think of Lady Ediva. Even the guard looked down at him, a question in his eyes.

Kenneth strode up the stairs. Of course he was thinking of the lady of the keep. Who knew what Clara would do if allowed to return to the new mother? He'd read that missive. She was not to be trusted and had even put her own stubbornness ahead of the well-being of a whole town. Lord Taurin was an influential man. When he had sent troops to Colchester to find his slave and child, they had carried the weight of his heavy authority. Little wonder that in the aftermath, the guild masters, not known for their bravery, had been quick to evict the treacherous midwife from their midst. Lord Eudo's letter had warned of the consequences that could fall upon Lord Adrien and his keep if the midwife were not made to cooperate with Lord Taurin's demands.

As he reached the main floor, Clara's cries suddenly stopped. Immediately, he paused. Was she hurt?

Nay, she was just realizing that the truth of her treachery was coming to light. Ahead of him, one of the young maids cried out something in English. Kenneth looked over into the kitchen to see her near a pot of boiling water while shaking her hand. She'd scalded herself. The old cook told her to plunge it into cold water. He swallowed. What would the village do without a midwife and healer?

Slowly, he left the kitchens. In the corridor, he stopped again. What would Lady Ediva do? And her newborn son, the heir to Dunmow Keep? Sadly, 'twas far too common for babes to depart this world soon after birth, and a healthy howl at the start of life did not mean all was well and good for him.

Kenneth glanced up the stairs that led to the solar. Both mother and babe *needed* Clara. But he'd read that warning. Clara could not be trusted.

Immediately, several maids charged past him into the kitchen, calling for buckets of steaming water and herb satchels. Kenneth barely managed to jump out of their way in time. He glanced up to find Margaret reaching the bottom of the steps, not bothering to disguise the fearful look in her eyes.

"What's wrong?" he demanded.

"Milady has collapsed," she whispered tightly. "Where is Clara?"

"In the dungeon."

"Dungeon! What on earth for?"

"For past crimes. 'Tis of no concern to you."

"I only pray that you know what you've done, for surely as the sun rises, 'tis a dangerous business birthing without a midwife's help, even after the main part's done." She sniffed and rushed back up the stairs.

A few treads up, she turned. "I don't know why you jailed her, but it had best be a good reason. 'Tis one command you'll have to answer for!"

Kenneth stiffened. No one had read the missive except him. Would they still censure him if they knew how dangerous Clara could be?

He swallowed. Was she really that dangerous? She'd worked hard for Lady Ediva, stayed in that solar for more than a day, laboring with her mistress. He had seen no sign that she wished either mother or child to come to any harm.

Nay, he would not risk Lady Ediva's life! He plowed back into the bowels of the keep. There, he fumbled with the keys, hating how his hands had begun to shake as he struggled to unlock the door.

Clara blinked at the sudden light. She stood in the center of the cell, her arms wrapped around her torso as if to keep at bay the filth and fear only the dungeon could create. Kenneth heard the scurry of some unseen creature behind her.

"Milady has collapsed," he grated out as he grabbed her upper arm. "I will take you to her, but be warned. If she dies, I will hold you personally responsible, for you've made poor decisions so far with new mothers and their babes."

As Kenneth dragged Clara through the keep, he heard her call over her shoulder, "I want the broth I ordered when her confinement began. Milady needs the strength in it!" She added to that order herbs, more hot water and water with spirits in it to cleanse the dungeon from her hands.

"Aye, mistress, we have it all!" a young female voice answered.

As if only then fully realizing the danger now happening, Clara broke free of Kenneth's grip and bolted up the stairs.

All Kenneth could do was race after her, a prayer on his lips.

Chapter Two

As soon as Kenneth learned that all was well with Lady Ediva and the new child, he approached Lord Adrien in his private chamber. The Baron of Dunmow had left his wife to sleep. "Milord, we need to speak."

Kenneth swallowed. He needed to confess his part in how Clara had disappeared so soon after Ediva had delivered, then suddenly reappeared when milady needed her help.

"Hmm?" Distracted, Lord Adrien looked up from his mindless task. He held his oiling cloth in his shaking hand. 'Twas the job of that young squire, Harry, to oil and care for Lord Adrien's chain mail, but Kenneth knew the baron took pride in keeping his own armor in order. Mayhap something to keep himself busy?

The man looked tired, as if battle worn, and Kenneth set aside his confession for the time being. "Come, my lord. Let's get you some refreshment. You have stayed up as long as Lady Ediva has. She's resting, as you should be also." Kenneth took charge and stepped out into the corridor to order Harry to provide some food and drink.

Watching the young squire dash off, he could hear

the sounds of supper preparation. 'Twas late in the day, and the evening meal had been delayed until word came down from the solar that mother and babe were safe from the dangers of delivery for the time being. Though his stomach growled, Kenneth ignored his hunger and returned to Adrien's chamber. The pallet bed Adrien had used when he first arrived was shoved into one corner, its original space now occupied by a large desk and several chairs, a wardrobe and several trunks. Dropping his oiling cloth on the desk, Adrien leaned back heavily in his seat. The meal came, and Kenneth encouraged his baron to eat.

Adrien looked up and blew out a sigh. "My thanks to you, Sergeant. Your quick actions saved Lady Ediva."

Kenneth straightened. "Nay," he admitted tightly. "Clara saved her, milord. I merely retrieved her. I had—"

Adrien carried on as if he hadn't heard Kenneth. "Ediva was doing fine, smiling, feeding the babe, and suddenly, she paled and fell back onto the pillows. Our son nearly rolled off the bed when she went limp. Margaret caught him just in time. I don't know what would have happened if Clara hadn't returned so soon." He straightened quickly. "She stepped out of the chamber after the delivery. Where did she go?"

Kenneth swallowed. "I sent her to the jail below the stairs."

Lord Adrien's brows shot up. "The dungeon? You threw her in the dungeon? What did she do wrong?"

Kenneth pulled the missive from the pocket of his surcoat. Adrien took it. Standing, he read aloud,

Dear brother, I greet you in the name of our Lord and pray for your health. My new and dear wife does well in her pregnancy and I enjoy each day with her. I hope Ediva is also fine.

But this is not a social letter. Only today have I discovered the true reason for the offer of Clara, the midwife, to you, by my guild masters, when I asked for someone to replace yours. Though I had sensed Clara's reluctance to leave Colchester, I assumed 'twas due to nervousness on her part. She was, after all, moving by herself to an unknown place to fill a position vacated by a death. Now I suspect she had no wish to leave but was given no other recourse by those in town.

However, the reason the guild masters recommended her is enough for me to write this letter. It began last year when Taurin, Duke of Evreux, took a mistress, a destitute farm girl whom he purchased as a slave from her parents shortly after arriving in England, because his wife is barren. The slave girl conceived, and in her seventh month of pregnancy she fled Lord Taurin's grasp. I am told that she made her way to Colchester. Clara took care of the woman and eventually assisted as she delivered a boy. The child was born two months ago. Clara kept the mother and child in her home.

Shortly after the child was born, while I was in London at King William's request, some of Lord Taurin's men arrived here to search for the mother and son. They went to my sergeant at arms, who refused to assist them in their search, for they came without writ or summons. These men eventually approached the guild masters, who retrieved Clara, but by this time, she had hidden mother and child and refused to reveal where they were.

After that, my sergeant forced Taurin's troops to leave empty-handed.

When I returned, your request for a midwife was waiting for me and I sought out the advice of the guild masters, who immediately offered Clara, so I sent her right away. You must understand that I had not yet been debriefed by my sergeant.

Later, when Clara's younger sister was discovered living alone in Clara's old house, I investigated this matter more fully and discovered the real reason why the guild masters had recommended Clara. Fearing Taurin himself would come to Colchester with more troops and the king's summons, the guild masters sought to thrust their problem onto you and your village.

I will deal with the guild masters and their trickery myself, but I cannot guarantee anyone's safety should Lord Taurin come for his mistress. I can, however, warn you of Clara's dangerous secret and stubborn character. I trust you will act wisely when dealing with her. She will bring only trouble for you and the people under your protection if she doesn't reveal the mother and babe's location.

But, as you probably have realized now, dear brother, I am also sending you Clara's younger sister. The guild masters suspect that this girl, Brindi, may know where the slave is hidden. I cannot say whether that is true—she refused to answer the question when it was put to her. Regardless, she cannot be allowed to live here alone, nor can she be returned to her aged mother.

Be careful, Adrien. Taurin is not to be trifled with. He is as crafty as the guild masters here

are. Be cautious dealing with him and with your
midwife.
Your brother in blood and in Christ,
Eudo

Adrien looked up at Kenneth. "Her sister is here?
How old is this girl?"

"She's about ten years of age," Kenneth answered as
he folded his arms. "After Clara returned to Lady Ediva,
I found her in the bailey and sent her to the kitchen. The
cook can always use an extra set of hands, though I did
not see the girl there later."

"Such trickery." Adrien inhaled deeply, then sighed.
"Should Lord Taurin arrive here, I want to be ready for
him."

"Aye. And it sounds like the guild masters in Colchester would be quite happy to tell Lord Taurin where
to look, especially since it would take him away from
their town."

"True. They're a devious lot."

Kenneth studied Lord Adrien. "Do *you* know Lord
Taurin, milord?"

"I know only of him. He did not fight at Hastings.
Regardless, his family has enough influence with King
William to earn him an estate without military service.
His land is to the west, I believe." He paused. "All this
trouble over a runaway slave."

*Who is too foolish to realize her child would be bet-
ter off with his father,* Kenneth thought. Lord Taurin
had wealth from Normandy. Couldn't the mother see
that the father would be able to give his son far more
than she could?

Giving up the child may save her own life, too. And

it would spare the town from Lord Taurin's anger. Nay, for the sake of Dunmow, 'twould be best if the child was found and handed over to Taurin. Even a blind person could see this.

Kenneth stood tall. "We need to find this girl and her child immediately," he stated. "'Tis best for Dunmow if we hand the child over to Lord Taurin as soon as he arrives." Adrien nodded his agreement. "But," Kenneth continued, "what punishment should be laid upon the midwife who brought this trouble to us?"

Adrien stood and rubbed his cheek. "As much as I would like to punish Clara for her secrecy, I cannot forget she has saved my wife's life. I will address her deceit, but in my own time."

Of course. Kenneth suspected that Adrien would keep her handy until his wife and son were well out of danger. He couldn't blame the man, for Adrien loved his wife with a powerful love that Kenneth secretly envied. Not for love's sake, but for the peace and happiness such love gave his baron.

"What are we to do with Clara in the meantime?"

Adrien sighed. "As much as I am grateful to her for saving Ediva's life, I won't have the woman near my wife or child unless she's absolutely needed. Escort her to her hut and watch her closely. Indeed, you *must* guard her well. Who knows what Lord Taurin will do should he find his way here. I won't lose Dunmow's only healer."

Adrien scrubbed his face with his hands, then rotated his arms as if to loosen stiff muscles. Kenneth frowned. Lord Adrien had pledged to Lady Ediva that he would keep all of the people in the keep and the village of Little Dunmow safe. He grimaced. That meant even Clara of Colchester, for all the trouble she'd brought.

"I wonder where she's hidden the pair," Adrien finally mused.

"We'll find out soon enough. Clara will eventually reveal their location, either by accident or by traveling there herself. She's been with Lady Ediva for days now, so she'll want to check on them soon. Though not tonight, I suspect. She's far too tired. But when she does, I will follow and bring the child here." Kenneth steeled his spine. "'Twill be an easy task."

Adrien nodded. "Do whatever is necessary to keep everyone safe. 'Tis a dangerous time for Saxons who defy Norman law, and our king will not be discriminatory with his punishment if he takes Lord Taurin's side."

Kenneth silently agreed. King William could easily provide Lord Taurin with a writ allowing him to do whatever he felt necessary with his slave girl and the babe—and take whatever degree of justice he saw fit against those who had hidden them, willingly or no. After all, wasn't the king illegitimate himself, and hadn't he earned his place in history by being recognized as his father's heir? Aye, King William could easily mete out heavy punishment to many Saxons should they refuse to turn over the slave and her child.

But hadn't the king abolished slavery? Aye, but that wasn't the issue. 'Twas not even the issue that Lord Taurin had purchased a slave in the first place. Nay, disobedience was the issue. "I'll discover the location of the child, my lord. I promise."

Kenneth turned to leave, but Adrien stopped him. "Sergeant, be careful. We both know that Clara is a good healer, but should she learn what you plan to do, I doubt her thoughts will stay on healing. She appears to be full of guile."

"Indeed, milord, but I am no fool." At the door, however, Kenneth hesitated. He'd fought at Hastings, defended his king and his baron with his life, and was not afraid of dying. But he knew Clara. He'd been sent to Colchester to deliver her here and had found her temper and disposition matched her fiery hair perfectly. Aye, fighting a woman whose scorn could sear meat would make the battle for England's crown seem like a squabble between kittens.

Clara continued to work with Lady Ediva, encouraging her to take some strong broth and nettle tea. That done, she helped the babe to suckle properly.

Ediva cringed. "I ache all over, Clara. He hurts me."

While Ediva's tone was weak and petulant, Clara knew 'twas more from fatigue than personality. Ediva had already decided she wanted to feed her own babe and not hand him over to a nurse. "Aye," Clara agreed softly. "He will until you get used to him, but 'tis just for a short time, and then you can rest. Remember how I said that ladies who refuse to nurse often waste away?"

Ediva obeyed, and after, Clara showed Margaret how to rub some herbed oil on her mistress. Finally, all was cleaned up, and Clara tucked Lady Ediva into her bed for some much-needed rest. The wide-eyed boy lay swaddled in a cradle between the bed and the well-stoked brazier, a sealed skin of warm water set beside him to keep the chill at bay. Margaret dozed on her pallet at the far end of the room while Clara guarded them all. Her hand throbbed where she'd slammed it into the dungeon door, but the dim light of evening made it impossible to deal with.

She was too agitated, anyway, her thoughts far away

from her own pain. Rowena and her child were safe. The only other person who knew of their new location was her small sister, Brindi, whom she'd told before sending her home. Should Lord Taurin—

A tear dropped down onto her lap as she rose. Nay, Brindi was safe and far away from Colchester. Clara had returned the girl to their aged mother, to their home near the seaside and away from the clutches of the guild masters who'd forced her out.

She fisted her hands and the left one stung sharply. She'd acquired a splinter from the door to the dungeon, and now that she wasn't busy, it throbbed. *Forget it.* She'd deal with it on the morrow when the light was better. The end of the day was fast approaching.

Clara paced to the window, anxious for some air to clear her mind. She quietly eased the vellum shutter from the window, wanting only a few breaths of fresh air before she blocked out the cool evening again.

She leaned forward. Having abandoned her wimple and veil earlier, the light breeze brushed over her neck and through her thick hair. Glad for it, as her cyrtel clung to her and was in need of laundering, she stretched out as far out as she could manage.

The window had a direct view of the village below, in particular, her small hut at the center. Her gaze automatically fell on it.

In the darkening evening, a shadow passed in front of her home, someone thin and stealthy. A breath or two later, the door, set at the side of the hut, opened. Then, as Clara stared hard, a lamp was lit, spilling light onto the small herb garden for a brief moment before the door shut tight.

She gasped. Someone was in her home.

A sharp rap cut through her and she jumped. After a glance around the solar, and noting all was as it had been a moment before, she heard the knock again. Someone was at the door. Quickly, she set the vellum frame back into place and hurried to crack the door open a tiny bit.

Kenneth stood at the threshold.

"'Tis time for you to return to your hut," he growled out softly.

She stepped out into the corridor. "And not to the dungeon? Have I earned a reprieve somehow? Oh, mayhap you've come to your senses and realized I have done nothing wrong!"

"Anyone who deliberately puts an entire town at risk should be imprisoned, but, nay, Lord Adrien pledged to Lady Ediva he would protect all in Little Dunmow. Apparently, that includes you. I will escort you home."

Did he think her a fool? She'd have to be addled not to realize that Kenneth would want Rowena's child given to his father and, as a result, would stay close to discover her location.

Ha! If Kenneth believed that by dogging her footsteps day and night she would, out of frustration, finally tell him where she'd hidden Rowena, he was sadly mistaken. She was the oldest of several children and had dealt with all her siblings' childish ways. She could easily outlast this one man's pestering.

But 'twas a moot point. "I am not ready to leave Lady Ediva yet."

"Is she still in danger?"

"Nay, but—"

"Is the babe safe? Is Margaret there to watch them?"

"Aye, but—"

"Then there's no reason for you to linger. By not resting, you risk your own health. Lord Adrien will come here soon, and with Margaret's help they will be fine dealing with Lady Ediva and her babe. Now, get your cloak."

Irritated that she'd been interrupted and annoyed even more that Kenneth was right, Clara pursed her lips.

"As I suspected, your stubbornness will be your downfall." He turned. "Stay, then. Lord Adrien will not be happy to see you after he ordered you home to sleep. I expect he'll suggest the dungeon instead. Or, just as unpleasant, the grand hall. By the way, all the soldiers have been celebrating the birth of Lord Adrien's son…."

"Fine," she snapped. She was not unreasonable. And, aye, she needed a good night's sleep. "Wait here."

She slipped back into the solar, carefully took her wimple and veil, and fitted them hastily on before throwing her cloak over her shoulders and returning to the corridor.

In the flickering torchlight, she noticed Kenneth's mouth turn up at the corners ever so slightly. She huffed as she marched past him and his smug insolence.

Downstairs and out in the bailey, they waited for the gatekeeper to open the small door within the larger gate, and Kenneth stepped out first, his hand on the hilt of his sword. Obviously satisfied that all was safe, he held out his hand to help her step through. She took it, finding it warmer and stronger than she expected. But as soon as she was safely on the path that wound down into the village, she tugged her hand back.

The late-spring night had turned colder than she'd expected. Clara looked up at the display of stars, bright because the quarter moon had yet to dominate the darkness. Clear skies always went with chilly nights. She pulled her long, dark blue cloak closer while darting a glance at Kenneth, noting that the cold didn't seem to bother him. He wore only a lightweight cloak tossed over his broad shoulders and a knee-length tunic over snug leggings. The leather thongs that secured them pressed against his sculpted muscles. Long and lean, he was the very essence of both ease and readiness.

Clara slowed as they approached her hut. Only a short time ago, she'd spied a stealthy figure enter her hut. Now, as they rounded the corner of her hut, she could see light bleeding from around the edges of the old, worn door. Her intruder was still there.

Was it Rowena? Had the young mother slipped into the village with her child? Clara swallowed. Was her babe sick? Was that why Rowena risked a visit?

Clara turned, determined to capture Kenneth's attention to keep it away from the door. "You have seen me home, Kenneth, and I thank you for it. Good night."

The man laughed, a noise that bore little resemblance to humor. "Do you expect me to depart? 'Tis not what will happen. Since we now know why you were sent here, don't you think 'twould be best if you were guarded? Surely you realize that your own life is at risk should Lord Taurin arrive."

"Then why didn't Lord Adrien insist I stay in the keep?"

Kenneth took her upper arm and continued to guide her up the short path toward her door. "No doubt he won't have you that close to his wife."

She steeled her spine and yanked back her arm. "I would never hurt Lady Ediva!"

He took her arm again, this time at the elbow. "Of course not. You aren't *that* foolish."

She pursed her lips into a thin, tight line, not willing to engage him in an argument if Rowena lingered behind her closed door. She knew Kenneth's type. Hidden strength came with those wiry muscles, so different from her clan of shorter, thicker Saxons. And she had no strength tonight to do anything save trudge to her door.

Still, her foolish tongue belied her fatigue. "You'll find it a waste of time to guard me. If you're hoping I'll slip away tonight, you'll be hoping in vain. I'm dead on my feet and I plan to do nothing but sleep."

"Good. It has been a long day for both of us."

She stalked up to the door, hoping her long cloak would block the thin light seeping under it. "Since you are so set on guarding me and there's only one way in and out of my home, I suggest you spend the night out here. I'm not the sort of woman who allows men in her home overnight."

"And I am not the sort of man to be enticed inside, woman, certainly not by so sly a female as you."

She shot him a blistering glare. "You have a lot of—"

A short, harsh clunk sounded within the hut. Before Clara could draw her next breath, Kenneth had shoved her behind him.

She heard his sword scrape free of its leather scabbard just as Kenneth's booted foot connected with the door.

Clara gasped. Kenneth was prepared to kill whoever was inside!

Chapter Three

Kenneth charged into the hut, a single thought slicing through his mind. *Protect Clara.* And he would do so even if it cost him his life—

A downward shot of dun-colored clothing met his glare and he stabbed at it in the dimly lit hut. A whimper, weak and childlike, reached up to him as his sword snagged a scrap of wool and tore it free from a small body. Another soft cry rent the air in front of him.

A child? Immediately, Kenneth pulled back and lowered his sword, accidentally elbowing Clara. Her fingers curled around his lower arm as if to hold him still. The cowering soul in front of them whimpered again.

"Wait!" Clara whispered in his ear as she leaned forward, so close he could feel her sharp gasp brush his neck. "Brindi?"

Kenneth blinked. The sister? He focused on the heap of pale clothes cornered in front of him, scarcely visible in the low lamp flame the intruder had kindled. The bundle moved and he saw how small it was. 'Twas indeed a child! He blew out his breath, trying to will his heart to stop racing at the horror that could have happened.

He'd nearly killed the little girl.

Clara shoved past him and dropped at her sister's huddled form. The small girl lifted her head as her whisper penetrated the hut. "Aye, Clara, 'tis me."

As Clara drew her sister to standing, Kenneth sheathed his sword and hastily turned up the wick on the old lamp on the table. The thin light strengthened to fill the room.

"How did you get here?" Clara exclaimed as she gave the girl a hard hug. "I sent you home to Mama!"

Brindi kept her head buried in her sister's cloak, and Kenneth could barely hear her answer. "Mama sent me to you. She was always angry at me, saying I ate too much. I didn't want to be there anymore."

Clara set her away from her to search her face. "When did she send you?"

The girl shrugged. "A few days ago."

"A few days ago! Have you been walking here since?"

"Nay, she sent me to Colchester."

"Didn't you remind Mama where I was sent?"

"Aye, but she kept forgetting. I hid in your old home, but the guild masters found me and told Lord Eudo. I said I didn't want to go home to Mama. She's too old now. But he said I was too young to live alone and I must go to you."

Clara glanced over at Kenneth.

"Lord Eudo's courier delivered her to the keep," he explained. "She was supposed to stay in the kitchen with the cook. Obviously, the child disobeys as easily as her sister."

Clara shot him a scathing glare, which he deflected immediately. Aye, her mother had pushed her own child out of her home, and his threatening her with a sword after the ordeal she'd already endured was harsh, but, he argued with himself irritably, if she'd stayed in the keep's kitchen as she'd been told to do, he wouldn't have nearly killed her just now.

"You knew Brindi was here and you didn't tell me?" Clara's voice was a mere breath of shock.

He stiffened. "You were in the dungeon. I would have seen she was cared for. I'm not a beast."

"But you knew she was at the keep all the time we were walking here? That she was brought here like a sack of grain?"

"Aye." He tightened his jaw. "In Lord Eudo's letter, he warned his brother that the guild masters feared a confrontation with Lord Taurin—"

Clara's brows shot up as she interrupted him to ask, "You know him?"

"Nay, I have not met him. But I read the missive that explains how Lord Eudo discovered the truth about why you were sent here." He shook his head. "You brought trouble to your people with your own stubbornness and refusal to reveal a slave girl's location. I suspect that once the townsfolk discovered Brindi, they feared the same of her and shipped her off to Lord Eudo. I don't blame them a jot."

Clara pulled her sister closer and covered the child's ears. Then, with a glower at him, she set Brindi down on one of the two benches, the child's back to him. She kept her hands on the girl's shoulders. "What do you know about Rowena?" she asked Kenneth over her sister's head.

So that was the slave's name? 'Twas a good start to finding her location. He kept his face impassive. "I know enough. You have no right to interfere with a Norman lord's personal affairs. And you certainly do not have any right to send fear through the town of Colchester or bring trouble to Dunmow."

"If I caused any fear, 'twas for good reason. And I have every right to help save a person's life."

"The girl and her child would not have been hurt!"

She let out a laugh. "I beg to differ! She has run away from a cruel man. If he catches her, he'll kill her!"

"How do you know what Lord Taurin will do? 'Tis clear he wishes to keep the child, and if so, 'twould hardly be in his best interests to kill the girl on whom the babe depends."

Her eyes flared. "What is the punishment for a slave running away?"

He shrugged, looking away, not wanting to tell Clara that slavery had been abolished. 'Twould have Clara heading to London to demand Rowena's release, right from King William. "A beating?"

"I doubt Rowena would be so fortunate," Clara answered. "Besides, as a new mother, would she survive a simple beating?"

He remembered Ediva's struggle in childbirth. Nay, this Rowena would not have survived a beating had it come directly after childbirth. But it had been at least a month since the child had been born. Surely Rowena had recovered sufficiently to bear her punishment now. He asked, "And you aiding her? What would your punishment be?" In Normandy, those who abetted runaway slaves were often punished more harshly than the slaves themselves. Though the king had abolished slavery, the Normans here would have brought their punishments with them. Aye, Clara was also in danger.

"My punishment is not important. I am pledged to save lives." She shook her head, flame-colored hair dancing like a fresh fire. "As a soldier, you wouldn't understand. You take lives. You don't save them."

He bristled, his teeth set on edge by her accusation. But he would not be drawn into a useless argument. There was nothing more sinister here than a child who'd slipped from the cook's supervision. "At least all is well, then."

She flung out her arm in the direction of the doorway. Her cyrtel, simple and faded, swished out with her. "Nay, all is *not* well! You've terrified my sister, and look what you've done to my door!" Her words, like her hand, sliced the air with alarm.

He turned and cringed briefly at the sight before him. He'd not meant to batter down the door, but 'twas an old thing, brittle with age and weather. The sun had beat down on it for too many years. Now it lay in splinters, good for nothing save kindling.

His heart sank. The surge of fight in him a moment ago had cost Clara much. Good solid wood was saved for the keep, for defenses and strongboxes. The most Clara could hope to purchase to replace her door, should she have the money, would be a mix of discarded pieces patched together, something that wouldn't hold up in any of the storms they'd see during the coming winter.

And even now, the night's chill rolled unhindered into the tiny hut, one draft fluttering the lamp's flame. He swallowed, then straightened. "I will replace it on the morrow."

"With solid, quality wood, reserved for the keep?"

He groaned inwardly, knowing the cost and his duty to pay for it. "Aye, solid wood."

"And what of tonight? 'Tis cold out."

"Burn the scraps we have here." He glanced around,

spying the worn yet laundered curtain the old midwife had used to separate her sleeping chamber on the far side of the hearth. He pointed to it. "Use that for a door tonight."

"And what about safety? You were quick to draw your sword, so you know of the dangers that night can bring."

He had been quick to draw his sword because he'd thought that someone had broken into her home. "Very well," he said. "You and Brindi build a fire and share the pallet in the other room. I will sleep in front of the door." He'd planned to do so, anyway. Nighttime would have been a perfect opportunity for her to slip out to visit Rowena. He had planned to use her table as a bed, as was the custom of many soldiers.

But considering what he'd just done to the door, 'twould be wiser, not to mention warmer, to set the table on end to block the nighttime draft. "I'll use the table as a door."

With a heavy sigh, Clara began to gather up the scraps of wood, cradling them in the crook of her left arm, but keeping her fingers curled. Brindi, with one eye on Kenneth lest he draw his sword again, reached out to snatch up a few pieces, also.

Kenneth sagged. 'Twas not the way this evening was meant to go. Aye, his few meetings with Clara today had not gone favorably at all, but if he was to discover where Rowena was, or to convince both Clara and Rowena that the child was better off with his father, acting as he had just now was the worst plan of action.

As Clara kindled the fire, he hefted up the table and blocked the doorway with it. Soon, the hut glowed with heat and light, a welcome sight for all three. Clara herded her sister into the other room. Then, with a cautious and oddly fearful look on her face, so different from what he'd seen on it when they met in Colchester a month ago, Clara drew closed the curtain that separated the rooms.

Had it only been a month? He'd gone to Colchester to escort Clara back. The tension in the town that day had been rife, but no one had said a word as to why. He'd just assumed it was Clara's fiery personality that had made the others eager for her departure, but of course, now he knew differently. Still, she could take a lesson or two from Lady Ediva, who, though strong-willed, was gracious and not given to flares of temper.

Once the makeshift door was set firmly in place, Kenneth turned. This hut seemed to be some combination of two buildings, with the hearth and its chimney wall shared by both rooms. The sound of Brindi's quiet whispers rolled through the space above the crackling fire. Kenneth could barely hear Clara's soft, soothing answers. Deciding to ignore them, he wrapped his cloak around him and stretched out in front of the upended table, his back to the fire and his heart heavy with the knowledge that he'd nearly killed the baby sister of the woman he was sent to guard.

After bedtime prayers, Clara tied her spare sleeping cap under Brindi's chin and settled her sister on the pallet. Just before curling under the furs they used for bedding, she peered furtively through the flames to Kenneth's back. With the exception of her family, never in her life had she had a man sleep in such proximity. And yet, she felt safe. Safer than she would have if they'd used the curtain as a door.

Any manner of beast could have wandered into her home. Bad enough that one of the stray cats had slipped in one morning a week ago and, after having been trapped inside for the whole day, had torn her home to shreds. And there were wild dogs and rodents and who knew what else out there in the night—

Goodness, though, Kenneth had broken down her door, then simply grabbed her table as if 'twere a child's toy! And before that, he had threatened her sister with his sword. He may be protection against wild beasts, but who would protect Clara and Brindi from *him?* Mayhap she should have insisted he sleep on the other side of the door.

Nay, she knew the night air was unhealthy. And she'd long ago decided that she would not cause harm to anyone. Her aunt, gone now two years, had been Colchester's best midwife and healer. She had insisted, when Clara made her decision to become one also, that she pledge to God that she would not harm anyone. Clara took that promise seriously and refused to dissolve it for anyone, even surly Norman soldiers.

She snuggled down against her sister, only now remembering the splinter in her palm. The throbbing heat in it told her it had begun to fester, but 'twas too late tonight to dig it out and cleanse the wound. And she was far too tired and cold to do so.

As with all children, Brindi was warm, and despite the circumstances, Clara was glad she had been found in Colchester and sent to Dunmow. Who knew what Lord Taurin would have done to Brindi had he found her?

She bit her lip. 'Twas an awful situation. And out there, hidden away, closer to Dunmow than Colchester, was Rowena. Clara would have to make sure that Taurin never found her. And never learned she and Brindi were here in Little Dunmow, despite there being only a day's journey on horseback between the two settlements.

Please, Father, don't let the guild masters tell Lord Taurin anything!

Daylight had begun to bleed into the sky when Clara, waking, eased herself back from her sleeping sister. Outside, in the coop, her rooster crowed, boldly announcing the new day.

She turned, sensing heat on her cheek. Surprisingly, a fire blazed in the hearth, its flames dancing around her best kettle, which hissed with steam.

She peered through the hearth to see the table righted and the doorway clear, with early-morning freshness rolling in to mix with the fire's warmth. But no one was in sight. Where was Kenneth?

Clara rose, slipped past the curtain and stepped outside. Long, dark shadows stretched from the forest behind her house, shading her garden. She spotted Kenneth to her right, easing up the hatch to her chicken coop at the far end of the garden. The hens inside cackled their disapproval.

Though he still wore his clothes from yesterday, they had been brushed and straightened. His dark tunic and lighter leggings fit him well. She could see strong muscles along his back as he reached into the coop.

"Shh, ladies," he cooed softly. "I just want a few eggs. You can spare them."

Clara shoved her hands on her hips. "But I cannot!"

The hatch slammed shut and Kenneth spun, his hand dropping to his sword. Clara rolled her eyes. Only a soldier would take his sword to the henhouse for eggs.

"I was going to coddle you some eggs, but your hens

are reluctant to move off their nests. I think I've upset them."

"They're fussy old women. I usually let them set for a while and come back when the sun is above the trees." She looked up. "The sky is still clear. Was it cold for you last night?"

"I've slept in colder spots."

She was glad to hear that, for all he'd had to keep him warm was his cloak, which was now tossed over his shoulders. Slipping past him, she lifted the hatch and propped it up with her shoulder to ease her hand under the hens' warm bodies for their eggs. One old bird pecked her in defense, and Clara hastily recoiled. Automatically, she reached out with her left hand and received a sharper peck that time.

"Ouch!" She jumped back quickly, and the hatch slammed shut on her festering hand. She cried out again.

She stepped away, curling her stinging hand and biting her lip. Her palm hurt far more than it should from a simple splinter, and seething with the pain, she marched away from the coop, toward the corner of her hut, where the sun's rays were reaching into the village and she could get a better look at her wound.

There, she peered down at her hand and sagged. The skin was red, shiny and open. The splinter site angrily announced that the wooden door to the dungeon had been filthy. Such filth had caused her flesh to fester. When she reached down to touch the skin with her finger, it felt smooth and hot.

"Let me see it." Kenneth came up behind her and took her arm.

She fisted her hand and pulled it closer to her chest. "'Tis nothing but a scratch. The hen startled me, 'tis all."

Kenneth shook his head. "If there is nothing there, then there is nothing to hide." He firmly turned her wrist, easing up only when he noticed her grimace. "But if you are injured, you will need to have it cared for."

"'Tis only a small cut."

Kenneth tilted his head and raised his brows. "You say you pledged to do no harm, but you're harming yourself. Therefore your word is about as healthy as that hand."

Reluctantly, hating his rationale, she opened her fist. Kenneth frowned. "I've seen worse, of course, but a wound like this must be cleaned before it can heal." His tone softened and he met her gaze with dark, unexpectedly warm eyes. "You're a midwife, Clara. You should know that."

"Aye, I do! Yesterday, 'twas not so bad, so I decided to wait until the light of day to pick out the wood. It has worsened overnight, unfortunately."

"And it's begun to fester. If you ignore it, 'twill cause a red streak up your arm and you will get very sick."

She looked up at him. He knew a lot about injuries for a soldier. He must have seen plenty of them. "I know about the blood fester. My aunt would have used a leech on it, which are plentiful in Colchester with the Colne River close by. But I have none here. I'll have to use that water you've heated to open the wound and dig out the splinter."

"Nay, I'll do it. You'll probably shake too much. Do you have any salve? Honey would be best, but I fear it's been in short supply lately and best saved for new cuts that have been cleaned."

She blew on the hot flesh. "You sound like you have experience. Aye, honey works best before a cut begins to fester. In a copper pot above the hearth is a salve. It smells awful, so I usually mix it with wintergreen, which also helps to cool wounds. That's in the clay pot beside it."

He looked around, spying a bench along the low front wall of the hut. "Sit down and I'll get what I need."

"My thanks." She sat. "But you're a sergeant at arms, not a healer. How do you know of these things?"

"I have had to stitch many a wound. I recently sewed up Lord Adrien's leg."

"He fought here before I came?"

"Not in a battle, but against those who had tried to take over the keep and kill Lady Ediva."

She bit her lip. "I had heard about a danger to Lady Ediva, but thought the old midwife had been responsible. Surely she hadn't stabbed Lord Adrien?"

He shook his head slowly. "Nay, I believe she sought to stop the fight and was murdered for it. I will tell you the whole tale another time. First we need to clean that wound."

Kenneth stopped at the corner and turned. "Your aunt was a healer and midwife, also?"

"Aye. My mother sent me to be with her years ago, and I learned the skills from her."

"Where did you live before?"

"By the sea. My father was a fisherman."

"Was?"

"He went out on his boat one day and didn't return. My mother had too many children to feed, so she sent me off to my aunt in Colchester."

"Is your aunt still there?"

Clara shook her head, not trusting her voice to explain. She'd tried her best to save her aunt's life, but in the end, had lost the woman who was more of a mother to her than her real mother.

Finally, she dared to speak. "She died several years ago, and I took over her home and the craft."

"Craft? You make it sound like midwifery should have its own guild."

Her eyes flared. "We should. Too many people think only the lowest class of woman should be a midwife or a healer. With a guild, we would have more protection."

"Healers with their own guild? What nonsense. 'Twill never happen." He disappeared around the corner before she could snap back that such *would* happen someday.

A short time later, she was settled on the bench and Kenneth was dribbling hot water on the wound. She sucked in her breath. It stung like a bouquet of nettles. But with the small blade from her healing kit, he deftly coaxed the filthy splinter from her tender flesh.

"Let me mix the salves." He returned a moment later with a dollop of mixed salves on a clean strip of linen. "You're right when you say that one stinks. It smells like cattle."

"'Tis ox gall. I found it in the old midwife's things. 'Tis very effective, so it must be quite fresh." She looked up at him. "Is Brindi still asleep?"

"Aye. She would have been exhausted, having traveled so far yesterday."

"She's used to riding, but I doubt they'd have given her a mount of her own. Poor thing, she must have been terrified. Clinging to the courier's clothing." Though the ride to Colchester took not quite a full day, it would have been long for a child.

Sitting down beside her, Kenneth dipped his forefinger into the salve and began to spread it on the wound, eliciting a quick indrawn breath from Clara. "Do you think she would have thought they were taking her to Lord Taurin?" he asked.

Clara pulled back her hand. "How much do you know of Lord Taurin and Rowena?"

"Only what I read in the message Lord Eudo sent. She was pregnant when she ran away. You took Rowena in for the rest of her confinement. The babe was delivered safely, and you have concealed the mother and child ever since. I'm sure if you asked Lord Adrien, he would allow you to read the missive, also. My lord is a fair man and believes that a person deserves the right to face his accusers."

"'Twould do no good to ask for that, for I cannot read."

Kenneth hesitated. "I saw labels on your pots, written in English. How did you know about this salve if you can't read the label?"

"'Twas the old midwife's labeling, not mine. She even had a book she wrote in."

"A book? Like a Bible?"

"Aye, though not as thick. It must be a record of her medicines." Clara shrugged. "Since I can't read it or the labels, I had to test the contents of each pot first to find out what each contained."

"How? By tasting? 'Tis dangerous." He sniffed the salve. "Not to mention quite disgusting."

"I know most healing substances by smell and texture."

Kenneth fell into a heavy silence as he continued his work. "What's wrong?" she asked.

"Nothing."

"Nay, I think there is. Your mouth tightened when I

mentioned the book." She studied him. "Why should it bother you?"

He paused in his ministrations and looked up at her. She drew in her breath. How did she get so close to him? Aye, he was handsome to look upon, and indeed she was tempted to reach out and stroke his cheek. To discover for herself if the burr of his short beard was as rough as it looked.

Nay! He was an unwelcome guest forced upon her. He said he was here to protect her. Only a part truth, she was sure, for she knew he would side with Taurin should the man arrive and demand Rowena. She'd dealt with this back in Colchester when the guilds had met and told her that Rowena's life was not worth the wrath of the Normans. Clara disagreed. If not for Lord Eudo's sergeant at arms ordering Taurin's men out of the town, she would have surely ended up jailed or in the stocks until she revealed the location.

Clearing her throat, she focused on Kenneth as he straightened the strip of linen. "What is so bad about that book?"

"I cannot say for certain. Lord Adrien and Lady Ediva were poisoned before you came. I think 'twas also why the old midwife was murdered." He paused. "The man knew she would reveal his guilt, for only he knew where to find the poisons in her stock of medicines." He looked directly into her eyes. "Where did you find that book? What have you done with it? We searched for proof the midwife stored poisons, but we couldn't find any. I suspect that Lord Adrien would prefer it be burned after all he and Lady Ediva endured."

"I found a box buried in the corner near the hearth.

I noticed the dirt was softer there." She shifted away. "When I saw that the ground was disturbed, I dug and found the box. In it was the book."

He was nearly done wrapping her palm, and he quickly finished. "Did she make this book herself?"

"Mayhap. Someone had cut parchment to small squares and sewed them along one edge. But 'tis only a few pages and is very old."

"What does it say? Is it a ledger?"

Clara yanked back her arm. "I told you that I cannot read." She looked down at the wound. It throbbed less now. Kenneth had done a good job and the wintergreen had cooled the site. She looked up at him. "My thanks. But you still have a door to replace."

"Aye, 'twill be done. I honor my pledges."

Noise sounded from within the hut, and Clara stood. She'd been altogether too close to Kenneth as he tended her wound and was now glad for the diversion. "Brindi's awake. We need to start this day. I have much to do, and you should return to the keep. I am sure Lord Adrien will need you."

"Nay, I'm staying with you, Clara. If Lord Taurin should come looking for the woman you've seen fit to hide, then you would be in the most danger. We both know the punishment for those who defy the king."

"Lord Taurin is not the king."

"But he has influence with him. King William could give him a writ to do whatever is necessary to find Rowena, because she has defied a Norman."

He wiped his hands on a portion of a remaining dressing he'd brought out with him. His voice then dropped as he shot a sidelong glance in her direction. "Of course, 'twould be best for all if you simply told me where Rowena is so I can deliver the son to his father for his own best interests."

Chapter Four

Clara flew to her feet, fury surging up with her. "How dare you even think I would simply blurt it out! Is that your true reason for being here?"

"Nay, I am here to protect you. Mayhap even from yourself!"

"You know nothing of this situation, save what was written in some Norman missive penned by a Norman. And his understanding of the situation was told to him by some treacherous guild masters! None of you know what Rowena has endured. And you think you can simply ask me to betray a woman I have pledged to keep safe? Are you addled?"

For the briefest of moments, Kenneth looked bewildered. Clara wondered if she'd switched languages. So far, their conversations had been totally in English, which he spoke well enough, albeit with a heavy accent.

Then the moment ended. Whatever Kenneth was thinking at that moment was gone. He rose, standing a full head above her, his long, lean form looking far stronger than she'd first realized. "I am not addled, woman," he ground out. "'Tis as obvious as the nose on your face that the son needs his father, and that the mother, with barely two coins to rub together, cannot provide for him properly. Even King William's mother knew enough to allow William to be raised by his father's people. Given to his father, Rowena's child would have food in his belly and clothes on his back!"

"Aye, food from a brutal father who would wrench mother and child apart, then kill the mother? I expect you feel 'tis fine for a man to use a woman, then kill her when she stands up for herself! And you think that a child only needs food and clothing? Nay, you know nothing of family life! Nothing!" Her voice cracked. "A child needs its mother. Believe me when I say that!"

She then threw up her hands. "Why am I even talking to you? You're a soldier who knows only encampments and battles and polishing mail for your master!"

He laughed, a hearty, bold outburst that proved he was genuinely enjoying himself! Immediately, she felt herself bristle, her face heating while humiliation burned inside of her. Her mother had often said that redheads had hot brains that caused their hair to be such a fiery color. Well, her brains were very hot right now!

Finally calming, Kenneth shook his head. "Oiling the mail of as fine knight as Lord Adrien is a privilege, not a duty for a fool. My lord has taught me too many important things, and I am privileged to pledge my life to him." His smile dissolved, replaced by a dark stare. "And be thankful that even though I threw you in the dungeon yesterday, I will also lay down my life for you, for this I have pledged to my lord to do."

She would not be lured away by the sudden turn of

his temper. Scoffing, she tossed up her bandaged hand. "What nonsense! I am but a Saxon midwife. You make me sound like a precious princess to be protected."

"I know nothing of fine ladies and fancy princesses," Kenneth answered. "I only know that *I will* protect you."

A part of her leaped inside, but she would not be like a young girl taken by charming words. "Until Lord Taurin arrives."

"Thanks to your stubbornness, woman, Lord Taurin may be on his way here right now! Led here by the townsfolk of Colchester. *Your* people."

She stilled, then swallowed. Aye, she'd pledged to keep Rowena safe, and her baby with her, and aye, she'd die in order to keep such a pledge, but what if Taurin *was* on his way? What would happen then? Her own people would have turned on her, leaving her to the mercy of Taurin and his men.

Her heart squeezed. Then the question would be, *could* she keep Rowena safe? What if Taurin attacked the keep? She'd pledged to save lives, not cause them to be lost in battle.

Dear Lord, guide me and keep Rowena and her babe safe.

Tears sprang to her eyes as she sank onto the bench. For a long moment, she just swallowed and thought and rethought all that was happening. Then she felt a soft hand on her shoulder and looked up to find not Kenneth offering sympathy, but Brindi. Through watery eyes, she saw Kenneth frown with curiosity behind the little girl.

"'Tis just her usual tears, sir," Brindi said, sitting down and putting her arms around Clara as if she were the older sister. "Ever since she offered her life to our

Lord and pledged to care for the sick, her heart has turned as soft as lamb's wool. Our aunt often said 'tis the price of having a heart for God and people."

Clara flushed. Enough of this. She wouldn't be exposing her heart to the man who would see Rowena punished for running away. Clara bustled to her feet and quickly swiped the wetness from around her eyes. She had no desire to lay bare her woolly, foolish heart in front of Kenneth. He'd only make her regret all she'd done so far and twist it to make her reveal where Rowena was.

Nay, she would not do such a thing, and no amount of fear for the consequences would change that.

She smoothed the skirt of her cyrtel. 'Twas her best one, and she should keep it good. That meant no tears to stain the material at her lap. "Never mind me. We will deal with the day as it comes. And I see it has already started. Brindi, we need to break our fast before we weed the garden, and you—" she leveled as firm a stare as possible at Kenneth "—you have a door to fix."

Kenneth tried the door one last time, satisfied that, finally, it closed firmly, without scraping or catching. And none too soon, for his patience with this expensive board was growing thin. He was a soldier, not a carpenter. Still, his handiwork was satisfactory.

Though Clara may find some fault in it. When he'd escorted her to Dunmow from Colchester, she'd corrected him several times on his equestrian abilities. Aye, she *was* skilled on a horse, more than most men, which was unusual, for she'd been a fisherman's daughter and then a midwife. But he would not ask her how she'd learned such talent. He refused to risk hearing even more pointers on how to ride a big horse properly.

He bent to gather the tools he'd borrowed from the smithy, a man who lived at the end of the road, beside the forest.

Not the safest place to live, but the smithy could easily defend his family, he was that strong. Kenneth's thoughts wandered to Rowena and her safety. Where had Clara hidden the young mother and her babe? There were leagues between here and Colchester, with few homes and even fewer inns. The fens to the east, where peat had once been cut and dried for fuel, were unlivable. And Clara would be a fool to hide her in the forest. Those Saxons who defied the law and lived in the king's forests were hardened men, criminals some. Not the safest place to hide a mother and child. Surely Clara would choose a hiding spot wisely. Perhaps to the west? A few abandoned sheep pens lay scattered about, but they would be just as unlivable.

Mayhap Clara was not wise. She'd been plucked from Colchester for her stubbornness, and the day he'd escorted her here he'd have had to have been blind to miss the fact that Clara didn't wish to leave the town. At the time, he'd assumed it was worry at the unknown, but could it have been she'd made a hasty and unwise decision as to where she'd hidden Rowena?

If only she could just see how foolish her ideas were. 'Twas clear she feared Taurin would mistreat Rowena, but on what did she base her fears? Rowena, a runaway slave, would likely have said anything to win Clara's sympathy and aid. Lord Taurin was not a soft man, but there was no reason to believe him to be brutal toward the mother of the child he clearly valued. Nay, Rowena would come to no serious harm if restored to Taurin's care.

Indeed, after her punishment was past, she would

likely find herself better off than she was now, with a good roof over her head and steady meals on her table. As for her child, the young son would be raised in privilege to take over a peerage and enjoy the favor of royalty. King William and his future heirs would reward strong Norman lords and their sons, legitimate or otherwise.

As he stooped to retrieve the final tool, he noticed a small section of the cloth on which he'd wiped the splinter fragments when ministering to Clara's hand.

It had been a nasty injury she'd had. She'd endured the pain of that festering wound with no tears, but at the mention of helping the sick, she had practically wept openly.

He paused as he shoved the tools into their leather pouch. She was as dedicated to what she saw as her duty as he was. And even more stubborn. Nay, she would never reveal where Rowena was.

Oddly, such determination sparked admiration in him. Lord Adrien would love to have such strength of character in his troops.

Nay, he needed to set aside all admiration. He'd pledged to find the slave woman and her child, and turn them over to Taurin.

Though some punishment was warranted, and 'twould be hard on the new mother, Taurin would be a fool to kill her. Who would feed the babe? It would cost him to hire a wet nurse.

Rolling closed the flap of the tool pouch, he tightened his jaw. Clara had to be exaggerating the danger. People lied when they tried to support a rash decision.

'Twas nearly suppertime when Kenneth returned to Clara's hut, having returned the tools and asked those

Clara had visited that day how long she'd stayed with them. Thankfully, he had earned the respect of most of the villagers, and thus discovered that Clara, with Brindi in tow, had not left the village all day.

Poor little Brindi. Like many a child, she was expected to work alongside her mother—or in this case, her sister—with never a moment to enjoy life.

Rowena's babe would end up as such, or worse, since he had no father figure to mentor him. Kenneth paused at the compact garden beside the hut. At least he might be able to do something for Brindi. For starters, he could teach her to read, and mayhap...

Mayhap he could make her a doll. Aye, she'd like a doll, he was sure, a toy to relieve the drudgery of work. He was a satisfactory carver, and if he found a knot of wood, or better still, a large apple, he could carve a head. With the apple, 'twould dry to imitate the features of a wrinkled old lady. Then he could ask Lady Ediva's maid, Margaret, if she could fashion a soft body for it, something filled with wool or fine straw and dressed like one of those princesses Clara scorned.

Aye, and such a gift would go a long way to changing Clara's attitude toward him.

As he approached the midwife's garden, the air offered the coaxing scents of supper. Evening meals were often just leftover broth and old bread, but this meal smelled rich and satisfying. He could hear Brindi singing softly inside the hut and, suddenly, the clear, stronger voice of Clara as she filled in the rest of the song.

He smiled. 'Twas good to hear. His sisters and mother often sang, especially when minstrels visited. They'd beg their visitors to teach them new songs, and one time his oldest sister even managed to convince their father to purchase a rebec from one of the minstrels. She did eventually master the strings on it, but it took years, and Kenneth had fled their home on more than one occasion when practice began.

He stepped into the hut, through the open door, for the day was warm. The song they sang carried on for a short time, allowing Kenneth to enjoy it.

Then Clara looked up at him, her song dying and her expression immediately turning guarded. He offered a controlled smile, but received only caution from her for the effort.

Brindi, however, smiled innocently. "Thank you for the new door, sir. It works better than the old one."

"I oiled the hinges and planed the edges to make it fit properly."

The girl brightened further. "'Tis good work, sir!"

"Enough chatter, Brindi. Set the table." Clara shot Kenneth a sharp look. "If we are to have a guard, he'll need to eat."

She lifted up a large quarter of cheese. "Lord Adrien sent this over, along with some meat and honeyed pastries. We'll eat well tonight."

"I can't wait for the pastries," Brindi chimed in.

He smiled at her. She was a pretty little thing, though not the stunning beauty her sister was, with that fiery hair, clear, pale skin and perfectly even features. Brindi's hair was light brown, a simple color, and braided deftly. Her nose was upturned and dusted with freckles. Clara's hair was wildly curly and obviously refusing to be restrained into braids. She opted to tie it back with a simple leather thong, barely seen amid the unruliness. She owned a wimple and veil, so where were they? Probably tossed on a pallet, for they would be too hot with all that thick hair. Not unlike his heavy chain mail and the helmet, with its annoying nosepiece.

As she turned, a thick lock of that hair found freedom and danced to her shoulder. A stray thought flitted through his mind that he'd love to plunge his hands through her mane and see it cascade down his arms. But he'd need an extra arm to deflect what would surely be Clara's firm fist from his face.

With a smile at his addled musing, Kenneth sat down. At the far end of the table sat a small leather-bound book. He looked up at Clara with a question on his face.

"I thought that since you said you can read, you could read this to me."

"You say it was hidden in the floor?"

"Aye. An odd place to put a book, but 'twas there."

Kenneth worked his jaw. The old midwife had been a crafty woman, and she'd always asked for payment in coin, instead of provisions. Was this where she kept her records? Did she hide this book so that when the king's men came for taxes, they wouldn't know what she'd earned? They would never know, now that she was gone.

He looked down at the script. "'Tis in English, which I don't read as well as French."

"I can help you pronounce the words if you start them off. I know all the medicines, but wish to know the old midwife's records of what she did with them. She opted to be paid in coinage, and I also want to know how much her healings cost, if that information is recorded within."

Kenneth opened the book carefully, as the stitches that held it together were old and fragile. "I can more than just read it to you. I can teach you how to read, if you like." Earning this woman's trust would go a long way to achieving his goal of finding the slave woman and her child.

Brindi gasped. "And me, too!"

"Hush, girl," Clara admonished her. "We'll decide that later. For now, I want to know what is written in this book."

Kenneth skimmed the earlier entries, dated many years ago. He turned the pages and found the few months leading up to the old midwife's death. Several in the keep had been poisoned last year, including both Lord Adrien and Lady Ediva. The midwife had been murdered in order to cover up the identity of the man who had committed the crime. It had been a terrible blow to everyone in Dunmow. Even now, there were still questions unanswered. Perhaps this book held the key.

'Twould be good to have this record opened and hopefully find the truth.

And then destroy the book. It served as a reminder of a dark and painful memory that still roamed through the rooms of the keep like a hungry wolf.

"Why not start reading now?" he suggested. "We can begin with a few simple words just to get you used to seeing them." He smiled at her hopefully. 'Twould be good to begin a lesson, not just for learning the secrets of this book, but to earn Clara's trust. Aye, that would be needed, for the sideways look she had just shot him spoke of her suspicion more than anything else.

He shoved the book to his right and then dusted off the bench beside him, inviting her to sit. Her cyrtel today was soft green and a lovely color, the color of moss in autumn, complementing her pale skin. But her vibrant hair demanded something more daring. Briefly, he considered what colors she should wear.

A smile hovered on his lips. Red. Aye, a bold red that no modest woman should wear and no redhead would consider. But she would never own a cyrtel like that, for the color was far too expensive, and if nothing else, Clara was practical.

Discarding his silly thoughts, he opened the book to the first page and devoted his attention to it. Cautiously, Clara sat down beside him. Brindi looked from the pastries to him. Her annoyance showed clearly on her face as she realized supper was being delayed for a silly reading lesson.

"This looks like a list of herbs the old midwife had one year," he commented as Clara leaned toward the book.

"It's set up differently than the next few pages," she said.

Kenneth turned the page. "This is a ledger of who bought what herb and what she charged for it. I can see the date here. 'Twas Michaelmas when she collected her fees."

Clara leaned forward. "Hopefully by then I will be able to read what I need to charge. But let's go back to the list of herbs. 'Tis best we start there."

Encouraged, Kenneth carefully flipped back a page. The leaves of parchment were stiff and he decided to hold the corner rather than press the page open at its spine and risk tearing the pages. "We will start at the list. See this letter? 'Tis an *N*." He made the sound as he traced the shape with his finger. His lessons as a youth, and even this past winter, were paying off. Holding open the page with his left forefinger, he took up Clara's right hand, closing all but the forefinger into a fist as he carefully showed her how to trace the letter. She would feel nothing on the parchment, but 'twas important to figure out how the letter was formed.

Clara stiffened, but he continued the task. "The next letter is an *E*. Eeee. Then the next two letters are *T*." He sounded out that letter, then put the word together so far. *"N-e-t-t."*

Relaxing, Clara allowed him to trace her finger along the four letters. 'Twas the easy part, for the cursive script flowed easily along. But Kenneth didn't know his herbs and Clara wasn't volunteering the word in English. "What word is this?" he asked her. *"Neet? Net?"*

Clara shrugged. "Neet? I'm not sure 'tis an herb at all."

"Nettle!" Brindi popped up between the pair, squeezing them apart as she cried out the word.

Glaring at her sister, Clara snapped, *"Nettle* has a different sound!" With a sharp glare, she shoved her sister's head back down, pushing the girl to the floor.

Kenneth snickered. "I think Brindi may be right. In English, the letter *E* has two sounds. And I know the last two letters have the 'le' sound."

On the floor, Brindi called out, "I told you so!"

"You were right, Brindi," Kenneth said, leaning over to speak to her. "The description says something about causing a rash, but the stingers dissolve when boiled." He looked at Clara. "Is that true?"

Clara opened her mouth, but her sister cut in before she could speak. "'Tis true!"

The tiniest of frowns creased between Clara's fine reddish eyebrows, and she swallowed. She looked slightly annoyed and almost hurt.

"Do you want to stop?" he asked her quietly.

"No!" she announced. "Brindi is young and smart, too smart sometimes, so she will learn quickly. But I need to learn this, and my sister is not going to better me."

"I don't want to stop, either!" Brindi called out, her back leaning against the bench as she sat on the floor below them.

Clara twisted about and shot her sister another fast glare. Kenneth felt the smile that hovered on his face melt away. Was Clara jealous of Brindi?

"I want you to show me the next letters," Clara announced.

Clearing his throat, Kenneth began on the next word, slowly pronouncing each letter. As they reached the last letter, having tried various forms of pronunciation, both he and Clara turned to peer down at Brindi, who looked up with curiosity.

"Are you going to guess this word, too?" he asked her.

Brindi looked over at her sister. Slowly, a soft, indulgent smile spread over Clara's face and she nodded. "Go on. Say the word."

"Tisane?" The little girl's eyes were wide with caution.

Clara nodded. "Aye, that's it."

Kenneth asked, "'Tis a tea, 'tisn't it?"

"Aye, but this word indicates you are to pound the herbs first. We also use this preparation for barley water. 'Tis good for babes, to prepare them for food."

She smiled at him, any insecurity she had from Brindi shouting out the words now gone. Brindi popped back up between them. "Please let me read, too, Clara. I won't be rude again, I promise."

Clara shifted away from Kenneth. "I doubt that promise, but you may listen in."

Brindi scrambled up between him and Clara, her attention focused on the worn book before them. She immediately asked which words they had pronounced.

Kenneth pointed to the two, and as the girl traced each scripted letter with great exaggeration, he looked across the top of her head to Clara.

She met his gaze, her smile hesitant.

"You will learn all of this, Clara. I promise."

She laughed. "Aah, another empty promise?" Abruptly, she sighed. "I know, but I was only thinking of how this must be what a real family is like in the evenings."

Kenneth felt his heart chill. How different her childhood must have been. Her father missing at sea, her mother unable to feed her children, shipping them off to other relatives, not being a mother at all. No wonder both sisters seemed to vie for his attention. His upbringing was far different. A strong family unit, separated only when his oldest sister decided she wanted to play that stringed instrument and drove her siblings from the house. He'd thought for many years that all childhoods were like his.

"Are we going to continue the lesson?" Clara cut into his thoughts.

The lesson had been meant to earn her trust so she would reveal Rowena's location. That single purpose suddenly soured in his stomach as guilt flooded him.

But 'twasn't the only reason, he told himself. He'd hoped to find a mention of the poison used on Lord Adrien and Lady Ediva. Still, what kind of honorable Christian man was he, that he would use this lesson time for his own purposes? He should just take this book and burn it, *now,* and never mention it to anyone in the keep.

Then what would he use to teach Clara? He didn't want to stop this lesson. Seeing Clara move from jealousy to love for her sister and wistfully describe her thoughts was as potent as any dose of medicine she could mix up. It warmed him and settled something restless deep within him.

But 'twas all a ruse, and suddenly, he hated it. He stood. "Nay, it's far too late, and I am hungry, as I am sure Brindi is, also."

"Aye!" Brindi agreed. "Time for our sup!"

Kenneth scooped up the book and set it on the mantel. When he turned back, Clara set a bowl of pottage down in front of him. Then she did the same for Brindi. After serving herself, they all bowed their heads and gave thanks. The grace was barely finished when Brindi dived into her meal with the gusto of youth.

"Is there something wrong?"

Kenneth looked blankly at Clara, realizing he'd been mulling over the past again. "Last year was a dark and dismal time for the keep. This book is a reminder of that. I'd rather we move on and forget it."

Then he lifted up his spoon to eat. As he swallowed his first delicious mouthful, a short scraping noise echoed in the quiet hut.

Kenneth's head snapped to his left, at the wall a few feet away, waiting for the odd sound to repeat.

The scratching began again.

From the corner of his eye, he noted Brindi, her small, carved horn spoon hovering below her mouth and her eyes as big as her bowl. Beside him, Clara ate as if the noise didn't exist. But her knuckles were white as she gripped her spoon.

He steadied his gaze on Brindi, whose look of horror grew with each passing heartbeat. Again, he looked to Clara. Her jaw was tight.

All three knew exactly who was outside.

Chapter Five

"Did you hear that?" Kenneth demanded.

Brindi paled. Clara swallowed her food and glanced at her sister before turning to him. Her expression was bland, but her knuckles remained white. "I heard nothing unusual. Mayhap 'twas a branch rubbing the wall. 'Tis windy and the hut sits close to the woods."

Ha! The wind was no harder now than last night or when he was repairing the door, and he had not heard that noise before.

It sounded again. Immediately, Kenneth bolted outside. He heard Clara gasp and rush out behind him, but he still charged around the back of the hut, past the coop to where the forest encroached on the small building. Indeed, the trees grew very close here, and some did brush the old, mildewed wall, but these branches were soft growth and what he'd heard was a harsh scrape.

He stopped, tense and listening, realizing as he did that he'd left his sword inside. A rustling answered his stillness, followed by a silence so loud, it rang in his ears. He held his breath, until, aye, he heard another rustle, and the sound of something, or someone, hastily plunging back into the thick forest beyond his sight.

From deep within in the woods, an indescribable cry came. Kenneth wasn't sure what had caused it.

"Brindi, get me my sword," Kenneth called out.

"Nay!" Clara stepped up beside him, holding up her sister's arm. "My sister is not your squire."

"There's someone in the woods."

"Likely an animal, probably a rabbit. You've scared it away," Clara announced over the disturbed clucking of the bothered hens. "Good for you. You'll be able to report back to Lord Adrien that you saved me from a vicious hare."

With that biting comment, she spun on her heel, dragging Brindi back toward the hut. Kenneth followed, angry that he hadn't been able to catch whoever had trespassed, for it surely was not an animal.

As he passed the coop, the rooster crowed and Kenneth jumped. A soft snicker slipped from Clara's mouth as she reached the door, and he berated himself at his nerves.

And for his earlier guilt. Nay, someone was out there. Be it Rowena or one of Lord Taurin's men sent to spy, he had no time for contrition about Clara's upbringing. Guilt and softness on his part would lead him do something foolish, like galloping out of the hut unarmed, as he'd just done.

As he reached the door, he slowed. That noise *was* caused by someone, for the scraping was methodical, and that cry he'd heard did not come from a hare. Aye, they cried when wounded, in fact they cried like a sick babe—

He stopped. A babe? Had Rowena come with her

child? Was that scratching noise some prearranged signal? Inside the hut, Brindi gobbled her meal, her furtive glance up at him almost too quick to catch. Did she know something, or was she afraid that her meal might be forfeit, to give to someone else?

Clara's back was to him and she seemed completely undisturbed by the noise.

He hesitated. Could he have been mistaken?

Nay. He'd honed his battlefield skills, and fighting alongside Lord Adrien had sharpened his intuition. He'd traveled in dangerous woods, where hearing and instinct were vital to fighting off robbers. He knew that something was amiss here.

But calling Clara on a lie would be fruitless. If she'd even lied at all. Thinking over her words, he realized that she'd tried to distract him from attributing the sound to a person, but she'd never actually denied it. Nor, he thought, would she easily admit it.

Slowly, he sat down beside Clara and continued his meal, but no longer did the savory pottage or sharp cheese taste well on his tongue.

"Should I go now, Clara?" Brindi whispered the next day as they pulled weeds from the garden to feed the hens.

"Not yet." Beside her, Clara whispered back, wincing as she used her injured left hand. "Be patient."

They continued their work, with Clara shooting a quick look at Kenneth as he worked on his chain mail nearby. He caught her glance, and Clara darted hers away. She grabbed a handful of weeds with her left hand, then yanked it back when the cut opened again.

"Give those weeds to the chickens, Brindi." She stood

and walked into her home to wipe away the blood and dab on some salve to seal the wound again.

"How is your cut?"

Not hearing Kenneth enter, Clara jumped. "It has opened again, from me working in the garden. I should have favored this hand a little longer, I'm afraid."

"Don't be afraid. You aren't that way with anything else."

She stole a fast look at him. A slight smile hovered on his face. Despite the stinging cut on her hand, she chuckled.

He walked closer. "Let me help you. I'm your healer, remember?" He took her hand in his, and with the clean cloth she'd found, he dabbed the wound. "'Tis not as bad as it looks. A day or so and 'twill be closed over completely." With that, he reached over her shoulder for the two pots of salve.

He was right, of course, Clara noted, feeling his proximity as he deftly applied the mixture. Though the wound had begun to heal and no longer felt hot, the mint in the salve still soothed. As did Kenneth's gentle touch. He was born to be a healer.

A pang of remorse for her plans to deceive him struck her belly but she ignored it. Kenneth had been ordered here to ensure her personal safety and no doubt discover Rowena's hiding place. He was not here to woo her, nor would she permit him to win her confidence. She would do what she must because she'd promised a young mother, and her promises were just as important as Kenneth's.

He wrapped a strip of cloth around her hand. "Let's keep it covered for one more day, shall we?"

Peeking around his elbow, for she was not tall enough

to peer over his shoulder, Clara spied Brindi standing at the threshold of the hut. The little girl bit her lower lip, and Clara glared the order for her sister to say nothing. Thankfully, the girl returned to her chore.

"Aye," she said, looking up at Kenneth. Her heart started to pound in her chest, but not from his warm hands on hers or from how close he was to her, she told herself. 'Twas from the ruse she must begin.

Like her sister, Clara bit her lip. Would Kenneth be punished when she slipped away from him?

She stepped back. "Thank you. I will favor it for the rest of the day." She set the pots of salve back on the old shelf above the fire. "Did you finish repairing your mail?"

"Aye."

"After we're done in the garden, I shall start a good stew for our midday meal. I've found a few stray vegetables. Whoever harvested the garden last year missed them and they must be eaten before they sprout again."

"Won't they give you new vegetables?"

Despite the tension gripping her, Clara smiled and shook her head. "Nay. These are root vegetables and will soon turn woody. Besides, they are misshapen and we only allow the best roots to go to seed." She tipped her head. "You've never gardened?"

"Nay. My sisters did that with my mother, but as soon as I was old enough, I went to Lord Adrien's family to page, then to squire for him. I've only trained for soldiering, not for keeping a home, I'm afraid."

"Don't be afraid," she mocked softly. "Keeping a home never killed anyone."

"Unlike soldiering?"

Her smile dropped. She hated everything that caused

death—fevers, fighting, even hard childbirth *and damp conditions for a newborn.*

She swallowed. The conversation was souring, so she lifted the skirt of her dark cyrtel with her good hand. This was her darkest outfit, for she needed to blend into the forest. "I should finish in the garden before I start that stew."

Back outside, Clara plunked down beside Brindi.

"We need to go," the girl whispered. "Rowena needs you!"

With the barest nod, Clara eased out a controlled sigh. "You'll know when."

Since that scraping noise, Brindi had been anxious to check on the woman. Only when Kenneth left the hut this morning to set up his armor—having had it delivered by young Rypan, the sweet boy whose aunt worked in the keep's kitchen—did Clara quietly work out their plan. They'd done it before, having slipped away from unwanted people. She'd already hidden a bundle of things she would need in the forest behind the village.

She peered over her shoulder. Kenneth had returned to the nearby bench to collect his things in sober silence.

Clara stood to toss more weeds into the coop and abruptly felt Kenneth's gaze upon her, heavy as a winter cloak. Like Brindi, she wanted badly to check on Rowena. For the woman to have come by last night, it must have been urgent. Mayhap the babe was sick?

But with Kenneth here, waiting for her to reveal the location, there would be no open trips to Rowena.

Brindi stood also. *Now?* she mouthed.

Nodding, Clara walked past Kenneth to retrieve the rake she'd left at the front of the hut. He watched her walk by. She grabbed the handle and turned to capture his stare with a mild one of her own, something suggesting complete innocence, she hoped.

She then shot her gaze from him to where Brindi had been standing. Immediately, Kenneth spun, catching a glimpse of the child as she slipped into the woods behind the hut.

In the next heartbeat, he raced after her.

Kenneth plunged into the thick undergrowth, his eyes capturing Brindi's darting movement as she tore through the forest. Her cyrtel had just enough color to stand out in the light green foliage. She wasn't going to be hard to follow.

Ahead, she let out a cry as she lost her footing and plunged forward. He raced toward her, crashing through the trees.

"Brindi!" he cried, stopping at the last minute to prevent himself from toppling on top of her as she lay in a shallow hollow. She lifted her head. Her eyes were as wide as they had been last night, her gaze cautious as she scanned their surroundings.

"Are you hurt?" he asked.

In a tiny voice, she answered, "I cannot tell. I'm too scared to move."

He scanned her frame, seeing her cyrtel was merely mussed. Her feet wiggled as she tried to sit up, and he could see she was quite unharmed. Children being children, they often imagined ailments for attention.

Still, he checked her for broken bones. "You'll be fine," he said soothingly. "Just a tumble. See, the hollow here has only leaves, and they cushioned your fall."

She nodded and sniffed.

But, he noted, there were no tears, just that cautious look again.

"Why did you race off? Were you going to Rowena?" He tried to keep his voice even and smooth, but wasn't completely successful.

She sniffed again. "Nay. I just wanted to play in the woods."

And as with all children, small lies came far too easily to their lips. He bristled, hating that he'd seen through it so quickly. "'Tis a sin to lie, girl. You know there is too little time to play, and just moments ago, you were quite content to pull weeds with your sister. Why did you run away? The truth this time!"

The girl looked away, her cheeks flushing. With a sigh, Kenneth helped her to her feet. "Can you walk, or would you like me to carry you? After all, you *think* you are injured."

Still hanging her head, she answered, "I can walk."

Kenneth followed her back the way they'd come. As he stepped over fallen forest debris, the same he'd galloped over after the girl—who had been on her way to Rowena, he was sure—he pondered how easily she'd changed her mind and returned with him. Surely, then, the trip to the escaped slave was not imperative, if she could give it up so easily. After all, had she truly been intent on reaching her goal, he knew he would have been hard-pressed to catch the girl, for smaller frames as hers could dart through thick woods more easily than men like him.

As soon as she realized she'd not hurt herself, she should have been off like a rabbit again.

Unless…

Biting back a growl of realization and of frustration, he caught Brindi's arm.

"'Twasn't you at all who was off to see Rowena, was it?"

Horror flashed in her features. The girl tore her arm free and bolted away, not in the direction of Clara's hut, but somewhere to the left, closer to the smithy's house at the edge of the village.

He let her go and broke into a gallop, crashing through the same undergrowth he'd just battled, until he broke free of the woods and nearly plowed into the chicken coop. The hens let out cackles of surprise.

No one was in the garden. "Clara!"

He tore into the hut, but found it empty. Smacking his hand down on the table, he hated that he'd been manipulated by these siblings. Brindi's dash had had him thinking she was off to Rowena, but 'twas a ruse. And a fairly good one, too.

He would dash off to intercept Clara, but he didn't even know which way to go. Instead, he sank down onto the bench, listening to the silence around him. No young Brindi outside, either. He doubted he'd see her again until nightfall. Clara would have instructed her to remain out of sight for fear he'd bully Rowena's location from her.

He would never hurt a child. Never! Hadn't he recently decided to make Brindi a doll, because she was facing a life of low means with little time to be a child?

And he would certainly never intimidate her or any child. Aye, young Harry, Lord Adrien's squire, was a handful and loved to be cheeky. The boy was young, and his impudence was part and parcel of who he was. But

Kenneth would never hurt him, just as he would never hurt the bright young Brindi.

His lips thin, he tidied up the morning's mess. Setting the full water kettle back on the hook to take advantage of the heat from the waning fire, Kenneth noticed a small bundle of cloths tucked behind the poker and shovel. He stooped and found the bundle heavy for its size. Unwrapping it, he found a large apple hidden inside.

An apple? 'Twas soft and obviously from last year's harvest, for the apples of this year were barely formed. How odd. Apples were mostly made into cider or eaten all winter to keep muscles from weakening and mouths fresh. Why had this one been left behind?

He weighed the fine piece of fruit in his hand. It was almost perfect, despite its softening. He turned it over. 'Twould make a fine doll's head.

With nothing else to do, he pulled out his knife and began to carve it. Clara may not trust him, and Brindi may have been told to vacate the house while she was gone, but he would stay and wait for them. And during that time, he would make the doll.

The head finished, Kenneth was about to set it above the hearth to dry, but stopped. Nay, the doll needed to be a surprise. He walked outside and reached up to nestle it in the thatched roof that saw the sun all day long. It should be safe there from both prying eyes and hungry birds.

Chomping on the skin, and still stewing over how he'd fallen for the ruse, Kenneth made his way to the keep. He would ask Margaret to fashion a body for the doll head.

Later, with that done, he returned to Clara's hut to wait for her.

Chapter Six

Clara reached the mossy hut before the sun hit its noon peak. Through the dappled woods and small but open peat bog before her, she confirmed again that she was alone and had not been followed. She'd prayed all the way here that Kenneth would not discover the ruse she and Brindi had planned until it was too late. And that he'd not hurt the girl once he realized he'd been tricked.

Stopping again, she peered around, analyzing the short, ancient walls of peat blocks, cut decades ago and left to dry. No one was hiding around them. Nothing moved.

She eased up to the darkened hut and tapped twice on the door. A moment later, it flew open and Rowena welcomed her with a relieved smile.

"Clara! I was so worried. I heard a man talking in your hut and saw a Norman bolt out of it a moment later!" The young woman pulled back her pale hair. 'Twas not warm and golden-yellow like Lady Ediva's, but silvery and thinner, as straight as an arrow and as wispy as a cobweb.

"He heard your tapping, though I confess I did not

catch it completely," Clara replied. "Brindi also heard it, and I suspect her reaction 'twas what made him bolt out."

"Who is he? I've only been to your new home once and didn't see him then."

"He's a Norman soldier that Lord Adrien has sent to guard me." Clara bit her lip. "'Tis nothing for you to worry about."

"To guard you? Why? How were you able to slip away?" Rowena's gaze shot to the door. "He's not outside, is he?"

"Nay!" Clara smiled and patted the young mother's hand as she closed the door. "I'm alone."

"Your hand is injured," Rowena noticed.

"Aye. But 'tis healing. The next time you see me, I'll be all better."

"Did Brindi tie the bandage for you?"

"Nay, the guard did." Clara pursed her lips at the young mother's abundant questions. She could not stay long and wished to learn quickly what had brought Rowena to her home. 'Twas a risk to come here, one she hadn't wanted to take, but the ruse had worked for them in the past.

Clara walked to the cradle to find the babe swaddled snugly and sleeping. "Now, tell me why you risked coming to see me."

"He's not been feeding well, and today he refuses to eat." Rowena came to stand over the simple cradle beside Clara. "All he does is sleep. I'm worried."

"I will check him out shortly. Let him sleep for a bit. I have some things for you."

Clara opened her parcel, unwrapping the cloth to reveal a portion of the cheese from the keep, fresh bread and some honey.

"Cheese! Honey!" Rowena cried. "Such wonderful things. But where did you get them? And how were you able to slip away from that guard?"

"Brindi helped to create a ruse. 'Twas necessary. Don't worry. He does not know Lord Taurin. My only concern is that he feels your son is best off with his father."

Rowena shook her head violently, taking a step closer to the child as she did. "Nay! I would die before losing my son!"

"That won't happen." Clara gripped her friend's arm. "I won't let it. Now, you need to eat so your milk will be stronger."

With a smile, Rowena hugged Clara. "I'm so happy to have you as a friend. I don't know what would have happened if I hadn't come into Colchester that day."

Clara set the food on the makeshift table she'd created and watched Rowena smear honey on a hunk of bread and bite hungrily into the cheese. 'Twas damp and cool in there. On a prior visit, Rowena had said she was afraid to start a fire for fear it would attract attention. She was, after all, living in the king's forest, something King William had forbidden. Soldiers could easily smell a fire and investigate. But hot water was needed, so Clara kindled a fire and set a pot to boil. "You did the right thing, leaving Lord Taurin, if he threatened to steal your babe. Now, let's have a look at him."

Clara examined the boy, and after talking with Rowena, confirmed that she needed more food to keep nursing. Clara encouraged the woman to eat and drink more, leaving also some strengthening herbs to steep in hot water. Clara also suggested the woman carry her child in a pouch, to take advantage of her body's heat and relax both her and the child for nursing. They spent the rest of the afternoon fashioning Clara's wimple and shawl to act as a tightly slung pouch for the babe. He awoke, and after Clara had prepared another, smaller meal for Rowena and was satisfied that the boy was nursing well, she departed.

'Twas nearly dark when she reached Little Dunmow. Her first stop was the smithy's house, where she collected Brindi. Yesterday, during her rounds to see the new mothers, Clara had asked the smithy's wife to take the girl when Clara was out and about.

"I did just as you said, Clara," Brindi announced as they exited the smithy's house. "When Kenneth tried to bring me back to the hut, I ran down here."

"Good. I hope you helped Gwynth, too."

"I did! I played with the babes and helped knead bread, and swept and changed the threshing. Why don't we have threshing on our floors, Clara?"

"In Colchester, 'tis not as easy to acquire. So I merely swept every day. Remember, we had a plank floor, not a dirt one. 'Twas easier to keep clean."

Skipping, Brindi began a tale of the game she played with the little boys in her care. Clara barely listened. Her mind lay on Rowena and the cold hut in which she stayed. The spring weather might be mild, but the fens and peat bog held the damp cold all summer long.

They returned home just as the sun shot one final, reddish ray across the sky. But, being already deep in the keep's shadow, the hut did not enjoy its warmth.

Kenneth sat in the hut's main room. A fire crackled in the hearth, and a pottage of roots and lentils simmered slowly above it. The scents of supper filled the room, offering the only hint of cheerfulness.

"I bid you good evening, mistress," Kenneth announced with marked sarcasm. "Did you have a good day visiting?"

"Good evening to you, too, sir. I had a satisfactory day. You've made supper, I see. What a fine wife you will make someday."

"Do not jest, woman. I could have reported you to Lord Adrien for your behavior."

"What behavior is that?"

"The ruse you created with Brindi and stealing away to visit Rowena."

"'Tis your own fault for not seeing through it at the time. I would have thought a seasoned soldier like yourself would not be so gullible."

Kenneth stiffened, and immediately Clara set her sister behind her. "You would be in far more trouble had I reported you," he said.

Clara lifted her jaw. "And you would be, also, would you not, for falling for such a ruse?"

"I won't make that mistake again."

They glared at each other for a long moment. Clara wanted so badly to order the man from her home. But she was glad he hadn't said anything about her absence, even though she was certain his discretion was in part not wanting to report his own failure. She had no desire to incur more of the wrath she'd already earned.

Who knew what would happen then? Brindi could get hurt, or the two of them could be sent to the dungeon together. If both of them could not visit Rowena, who would protect her? The woman had refused to start a fire, and living in such cool dampness for too long would only cause both mother and son to sicken.

Clara swallowed hard. Keeping Rowena hidden there was only a temporary measure; they hoped Lord Tau-

rin would give up his search for the child. But how long
would that take? Without protection, Rowena wasn't safe
living deep in the woods by herself. She would certainly
not survive the winter there.

Clara bit her lip. If only she could trust Kenneth. He
could do so much for Rowena. On the way home, Brindi
had told her of his concern that she'd been hurt when
she'd fallen in the hollow.

*Lord, give me someone like that who can protect Ro-
wena.*

Abruptly, Clara's stomach growled, reminding her
that she'd not eaten all day. And before her stood a Norman soldier whose culinary skills surprised her. The
steamy warm scent of his pottage wrapped itself around
her like a warm cloak.

She'd been so nasty. She cleared her throat. "Thank
you for preparing this meal. You did not have to."

He shot her a fast sideways glance as he bent to stir
the food. "'Twould seem I need to prove my abilities to
be a good wife."

Clara cringed. "Forgive my sharp tongue. It has
caused me more trouble than I care to think of. I
shouldn't have said anything. Your meal smells wonderful, and I am grateful for it. I haven't eaten all day."

"Not at Rowena's?"

"Nay. I made her a meal and checked on the babe.
He's been fussy lately."

"What was wrong with him?"

"Rowena has not been eating enough, I suspect. He
was hungry himself. That's why I prepared *her* a meal."
She shut her mouth firmly. She'd said too much already.

"The boy would not go hungry if he was with his
father."

With Brindi helping, she hastily set the table. "I disagree, and you know that. Lord Taurin had no right to treat Rowena so poorly and no right to threaten to rip a babe from her arms."

Kenneth straightened. "But at least the babe would not go hungry."

"He won't now. I've left foodstuffs for her."

"Aah, that's where the quarter of cheese went. I guess we didn't need it."

Pursing her lips, she smacked down the last bowl onto the table. Brindi shot another look up at her sister, no doubt waiting with bated breath for another argument. "Are you so starving that you could not live without it? Look at me! I'm no more starving than you. Indeed, I have far more roundness that most women."

Brindi snickered as she held out her bowl for some of the pottage. Kenneth took it and winked at the little girl. "I would never be so bold as to assess your roundness, Clara." He served up the supper. "You have rosy cheeks, thick strong hair that refuses to be tamed, no doubt following your personality, and you seem to be in the best of health. Neither of us needed the cheese. I just noticed its absence, that's all."

"Are you saying I have an untamed personality? Next you'll be telling me I am a raving madwoman!"

"Well, you have the hair for it." He handed her a bowl of steaming pottage while eyeing her unruly curls, made all the more so without her wimple to tame them.

She dropped to her seat with a huff. Brindi smiled into her bowl. Only after grace was said did Clara listen to her stomach's request for food and dig in.

It was delicious. He'd added herbs to flavor the stew.

And 'twas welcome after the coolness of the evening and spending the day in a damp peat cutter's hovel.

With that thought, the meal turned heavy in her stomach. Rowena was correct to be wary of starting a fire and attracting attention. In the king's woods there were those who hid from the Normans, rebels who would take one look at the delicate Rowena and her dark, Norman-looking child and—

Clara shoved away the rest of her meal. She couldn't eat while Rowena struggled to hide from Lord Taurin. But Clara didn't dare bring her here. Lord Taurin had already scared the townsfolk in Colchester and he'd not yet visited there. Should he come here…

"Is there something wrong with the meal? I assure you, 'tis good food."

She shook her head. "Nay, 'tis not your meal at all. 'Tis my worry for Rowena and her babe." She lifted her hand. "Please, I don't want to hear your thoughts on it. 'Twill not change my mind. But I am concerned, and sitting here, eating hearty food, enjoying the warmth of a fire while she cannot, does not sit well in my belly." She rose to tidy up her hut.

Brindi leaned over the table and dragged Clara's bowl closer to her, not willing to waste a spoonful of the meal. Clara let her. It *was* good. A fine meal indeed, but she'd lost her appetite.

As Kenneth rose to help her, she began to rearrange the pots and jars of herbs on the shelf above the fire, with no direction but the need to keep her hands busy. She flicked up a section of coarse cloth that lay beside the hearth. It should be folded and tucked away.

Behind her, Brindi gasped and her spoon clattered into her bowl.

Chapter Seven

Kenneth spun in time to see Brindi scramble off the bench to kneel at the base of the hearth where he'd found the apple.

"It's gone!" she cried.

Clara frowned. "What's gone?"

"My apple! Someone stole my apple!" Brindi's wail increased through her words, finally ending with a blatant cry of anguish.

"What apple? I don't have any apples here."

"Nay!" she wailed further. "Lord Eudo gave me it and now 'tis gone!"

Kenneth stilled. "That was *your* apple?"

Brindi sniffled. "Aye. Lord Eudo gave it to me when the soldiers took me to him after finding me living alone. The guild masters were called and they said I should come here. I was crying and one of the guild masters yelled at me, but I couldn't stop crying. So Lord Eudo gave me an apple to eat on the way here."

Clara frowned and tipped her head. "But you saved it and hid it here? I didn't see it."

She nodded. "I moved it around so you wouldn't find

it. 'Twas my treat, but we've had good food and I have not been hungry yet." Her wail increased. "But it's gone now!"

Clara shot an incredulous look at Kenneth. "Did you eat it?"

He shook his head. "Nay. Well, I ate the skin, but the rest is out on the roof now." He didn't want to say his plan, but it had to be said. "I carved it into a head."

Brindi howled louder.

"Shush, Brindi, or we'll never get to the bottom of this!" Clara frowned at Kenneth. "You carved it? What on earth for?"

He blew out a sigh. "'Twas to make a doll's head. For Brindi. She has no toys. I thought a doll would be fun for her. I had nothing else to carve. I'd used up all the wood I could find on your door. So when I found the apple yesterday, I thought 'twould do fine as a doll's head."

A curious look passed over Clara's features before she turned to her sister. "Why didn't you tell me you had an apple? We wouldn't have eaten it had we known you were saving it."

Trying to control her sniffling, Brindi managed to get out, "I was afraid you'd give it to Rowena." Her wailing started anew. "I know 'twas selfish, Clara. I know the chaplain says I am to give up worldly things, but it was so perfect and I was afraid I would be hungry again! But now 'tis gone and no one can eat it!"

Clara drew her sister into her arms, her raised brows and dumbfounded expression almost comical on her face. She looked at Kenneth. "Where is the apple now?"

"Tucked into the thatch of the roof to dry. I didn't want to hang it in here because I wanted it to be a surprise."

A cold silence fell on the room. Even Brindi stopped her crying. She didn't look happy, considering he'd just said he was trying to make her a doll. In fact, she looked so incredibly sad that regret washed over him like the icy waves of the channel when he'd landed at Peven's Eye. That landing before the battle at Hastings had been met with choppy waves and the chill that came with the expectation of war.

Right now, the same expectation lingered, not with Brindi, as she looked absolutely crushed, but with Clara.

"And what of the rest of the apple? The peelings? Boiled, they make a tasty juice, and the leavings are good for the hens."

He swallowed. "I ate them on the way up to the keep."

The chill remained. He threw out his arm. "I've brought pastries from the keep's kitchen to finish off the meal!"

"Why did you return to the keep?"

"After you two left, I returned my mail, and the cook offered the pastries to me. It bothered her that Brindi had slipped away the day of her arrival, as if she thought Cook was an ogre." He didn't bother to add that he had also asked Margaret about making a body for the head. Maybe that part could be the surprise.

"I didn't think she was an ogre. I just wanted to see my sister," Brindi finally said, her tone calmer now. She was also eyeing the cloth-covered platter, knowing that pastries lay within.

Kenneth took it down from the mantel and lifted the cloth. The pastries were shiny and golden, their crusts sprinkled with honeyed nuts. Even his mouth watered at their sight.

He looked up at Clara, anxious to change the subject.

"You mentioned being concerned for Rowena. How long have you known her? Did she really just wander into town looking for a midwife?"

Clara handed a pastry to Brindi. Her apple temporarily forgotten, the girl bit heartily into the treat. "Rowena was brought to me," Clara said, watching her sister. "She'd been traveling with a family, and the mother was anxious to be rid of her, probably having guessed her circumstances. I promised I would help her."

"What did she say had happened to her? Did she simply admit to you that her child belonged to a Norman lord and that she needed help to keep it away from him?"

"She said nothing at first, though I knew she was in trouble." Clara sat down and took the smallest pastry on the platter. Oddly, she returned it a moment later.

Brindi snatched it immediately, making Kenneth smile as he took the last one on the plate. They ate in silence, until he began again.

"Did you hide her before or after the babe was born? Lord Eudo thinks after."

Clara didn't answer right away, and when she looked up into his questioning gaze, he knew she was assessing him.

Aye, she knew he wanted to know where Rowena was, and he held his breath, hoping beyond hope that she would blurt out the answer.

"Why ask me that? It won't help you locate her."

Kenneth sat back. He wasn't used to women who were as forthright as Clara. She was so far from the Norman women he knew. His mother had taught by example the importance of being demure and reserved. Clara was plainly bold, strong in personality and blunt in her questions.

Yet, while not a delicate expression of womanhood, she was *all* woman. Strangely, he could understand her suspicions. After all, she'd been forced out of her home for standing up for what she believed was right. Could he fault her for being cautious and reluctant to trust?

He shrugged. "If I am to protect you from Lord Taurin, for we at Dunmow Keep take our oath to protect our people seriously, then I should learn a bit about you. It must have been hard to hide away a woman so close to giving birth."

"I hid her after the birth. I didn't dare risk not being available at her time. Had she been hidden away, I would not have known when she had need of me."

"So the townsfolk knew of her?"

"Of course. 'Tis a small town, and a woman heavy with child is easily noticed. But Colchester is also a busy town. Many ships come up the Colne to trade, and people from the surrounding villages are often there. She was noticed, but no one questioned who she was."

"How did you find out she was a runaway slave?"

Clara folded the cloth that had covered the pastries. "When the babe was born, 'twas obvious that the child's father was Norman. Rowena is a fair Saxon, and the babe was dark-haired with strong Norman features. She was always afraid, and when she first came to me, I saw yellowed bruises healing on her. I knew she needed protection, so I finally asked for her story, with the promise that I would protect her with my life if necessary!"

Her final words were filled with warning and Kenneth read them with immediate clarity. Clara had pledged to protect with her life, so even if Kenneth learned the truth of Rowena's location, he would have to battle Clara first before turning the information over to Taurin.

That challenge issued, it could not be ignored. What was he to say? His pastry now sat heavily in his stomach. He had pledged to discover where Rowena was and hand her and the babe over to Lord Taurin. 'Twould save potential bloodshed for the village he had sworn to protect. But Clara would stop that with her life, and he was to protect *her,* too.

A saying he'd heard in London once returned to him. *Only time will clear muddied waters.*

But would they have enough time?

His gaze strayed to Brindi. The girl's eyelids had grown heavy since she'd polished off the second pastry. Noticing it also, Clara stood. "'Tis time for bed, Brindi. You've had a busy day today." With that, she bustled the sleepy girl into the other room.

Kenneth remained at the table, idly listening as Clara helped her sister settle for the night in the other room. Their voices rolled over the crackling fire that was yet to be banked. Clara said prayers with Brindi, thanking God for the blessings of the day and praying for Rowena and the babe, and for the cook who'd so kindly sent the sweets.

The whole prayer was punctuated in various spots by Brindi asking God for a kitten, and Clara trying to get the girl's attention back on her prayer. Kenneth smiled.

Shortly after, Clara lifted the cloth that hung between the rooms and went to stand near the fire. Kenneth noticed that she, too, bore heavy eyelids. For all the answers he wanted from her, compassion held him back.

Still, her exhaustion raised questions. Did that mean that she'd traveled far to reach Rowena? Wherever the mother was, 'twas within half a day's travel. But Clara had stayed long enough to prepare two meals, so the mother and baby must be closer.

As Clara stoked the fire, Kenneth considered the countryside. To the west, villages dotted what was left of this county, while meandering streams fed the Colne River. But between the fields, there were many tiny woolsheds that could easily be fashioned to hide a woman and her child.

Or were they to the east, where fens and bogs made travel nearly impossible? To the south, where rebels and Saxon curs filled the king's forest? 'Twas closest to Colchester, but a dangerous choice.

"Come, sit, Clara. You're dead on your feet. Let me make you some tea."

Following her instructions on what herbs to use, Kenneth brewed a tea for her. Years ago, as a squire, he'd hated having to learn to cook for Lord Adrien, who could barely boil water, but it had been part of Kenneth's duty when they'd camped before battles. Now he was glad for it. At least he could manage to create a decent meal.

Kenneth pulled a short, wry smile. Should they go to battle again, young Harry would have to learn that duty quickly. Or Adrien might have to learn to boil water after all.

When he'd finished preparing the tea, he sat down in Brindi's seat across from Clara. He watched as she sipped and nodded to himself when she visibly relaxed.

"Tell me about yourself. I know you lived near the shore, a league from Colchester."

"And you promised to teach me more letters," she reminded him.

"Aye, I will, but not tonight. You're too tired. Now, where were you born?"

"There, by the shore, but not directly on the sea. I grew up at Wiunhou. 'Tis a village at the mouth of the Colne." She smiled suddenly, a small but wondering smile. "'Tis odd that the river behind the keep is the same one. Ours is filled with brackish water, reeds, greens and all kinds of fish life. At high tide, my father would take out a boat and fish as close to the sea as possible. At low tide, he would gather oysters while my mother would scoop winkles to sell in Colchester."

"They would go into Colchester?"

She shook her head. "My uncle did, and when he married, my aunt stayed in Colchester. She was a midwife there."

"That's how you became a midwife. But that doesn't explain your ability to ride a horse."

"When I was young, I would travel with my uncle on horseback. My mother was not well and had a houseful of children. Getting one out for the day eased her burden." Her smile grew. "And I was one of the bigger burdens. So I would ride with him. Beside their home in Colchester stood a blacksmith's shop. The smithy would let me ride the horses that were brought there. The blacksmith taught me the correct way of riding."

"A smithy wouldn't have the best riding skills."

"True," Clara answered. "But he told me to watch the nobility ride. My aunt agreed and encouraged me to learn to ride properly. Poor riding posture leads to aches and pains later."

"You learned to be observant."

"And I also learned to deal with all kinds of horses at the smithy's. Gentle ponies all the way up to difficult coursers."

Kenneth lifted one brow. "It doesn't explain why,

when we first met, you felt the need to correct my riding skills."

"They were terrible." She shrugged. "'Tis said that those who live by the sea are critical of anything bigger than a mosquito. My mother said my outspokenness was because of my red hair. My brains were too hot, she told me. But to me, our disposition comes from having the stench of fish and seaweed always in our lungs."

Laughing, Kenneth leaned back and watched Clara as she wrapped her small, chapped hands around the earthenware mug that still steamed slightly. Relaxation seeped into him, and he could think of nothing better than to listen to Clara talk about her life.

"So you eventually moved to Colchester to learn midwifery from your aunt."

"Aye. And to be a decent healer. 'Twas needed, not only in Wiunhou, but also in Colchester. Yet, despite all that, 'tis still scorned by the guild members."

"Are there a lot of them there?"

"Too many!" she scoffed. "You can't swing a wet nappy without hitting one of them! Those high-and-mighty so-and-sos." Suddenly, she leaned forward, her eyes flashing. "But mark my words, healers like me will have their own guild someday. One as powerful as the goldsmiths or the weavers."

"Women with their own guild? What did I put in that tea, woman, for you to talk so foolishly?"

She straightened. "'Twill be true. Healers will become very important. Everyone gets sick sooner or later. Women will always have babes that need care."

He knitted his brows together. "Is Rowena's babe sick?"

"Nay, but Rowena was when she came to Colchester. And full of bruises." Clara wet her lips and swallowed. "She'd been traveling for days. When she reached me, Rowena was almost dead on her feet. Her babe had sapped her strength and had taken all nourishment from her."

"You said she had bruises."

"Aye. Bruises on her body and her soul. She was terrified of Taurin, and yet, she could not return to her family! They'd sold her into slavery."

Kenneth shook his head at her exaggeration. "Slavery has been abolished, Clara."

"It has?"

"Aye. 'Twas one of the first laws King William signed. The girl would be protected from being sold."

"Protected? He would have taken her anyway, and then she'd get beaten for running away, or returned to her family, who care so little for her that they sold her in the first place."

Her gaze pleaded as it roamed up his frame to meet his eyes. "I could no more ignore her need than I could refuse my next breath. I had to help her. Then when the babe was barely a week old, we could see it was not thriving. At first, she stayed with me. My aunt and uncle have passed away, and I had their home. But when I heard that Lord Taurin's men were there, I feared that they would take her away, so I hid her. 'Twas when the babe sickened further."

"That's why the guild masters demanded you tell Lord Eudo where she was?"

"Nay, you have it wrong! They wanted me to tell them where I'd hidden Rowena, for Lord Taurin's men had come looking for her. I refused. I couldn't turn her over to Lord Taurin. He would kill her!"

"Kill her? I doubt he'd go that far."

"We've been through that. The punishment for running away is a beating, but she would never survive one."

Kenneth said nothing for a moment, then redirected the conversation. "Sold into slavery by her own parents," he murmured.

"Aye. Rowena's mother had many girls, and Rowena the last child. Her sisters all have strong male babes, so her father promised Lord Taurin that Rowena could provide him one, as well. Aye, she was sold as a slave, plain and simple, for her family could no longer afford to keep her." She shook her head. "I could not allow the guild masters of Colchester to begin events that would strip Rowena of her babe and return her to a man who would surely beat her to death. I couldn't!"

Clara furtively wiped her eyes, as if hoping he would not notice. For a woman so stubborn and sly, her heart was quite soft.

Abruptly, she stood. Her voice broke slightly when she spoke again. "I will take my leave for a moment." She threw open the door and disappeared into the night.

"She's like that, you know."

Following the sound of the voice, Kenneth bent down to peer through the hearth. On the other side, Brindi lay prone on her bed, but far too wide-eyed and interested. "You should be asleep," he said.

The girl shrugged.

"You said that she was softhearted. When did that start?"

"When King Harold was crowned. We had a celebration service at the church, and after that service, Clara decided 'twas time she put her life in God's care."

"'Twas two years ago that Harold stole the crown. You remember?"

"Aye." Her expression saddened. "M'maw always says 'twas a double-blessing day, for we got a new king, and she got a new daughter who could care for me instead of M'maw doing it herself. Since then, Clara has helped the poor and cried a lot for them. I hope I don't cry like that when I get older." With that, she turned and put her back to the fire.

Kenneth straightened. Almost two years since Clara had declared her love for the Lord.

He'd always had faith. His family was devoted to God, and he couldn't imagine living any other way. He'd grown up with the belief that his family was always right with God and always in His will. When he'd taken on this task of watching Clara, in the hopes of discovering where she'd hidden Rowena, he'd known he was doing what was right.

He hadn't had all the facts, though.

Kenneth pulled in a sharp breath. Nay, now that he did, it didn't change his mind, despite the turmoil within him and the challenge she'd slyly offered him. The babe still would be better off with his Norman father. And as for Rowena, if she was truly in danger from Lord Taurin, then 'twas not unheard of to buy a slave's freedom. Benevolent souls, or even a wise priest, had done so. Mayhap he could ask Lord Adrien.

Couldn't Clara see that? Taurin would be reasonable, despite his supposed reputation. To Saxons, all Normans had dangerous reputations.

Slowly, Kenneth walked to the door and opened it. Bathed in moonlight as she stood in the middle of her herb garden, Clara stiffened her shoulders. She'd heard him step into the night.

He closed the door quietly. The breeze had died, easing the chill in the air.

"Don't tell me again how much better off the child will be with his father," she said, her voice as cool as the evening.

Kenneth stopped. How did she know what he was thinking? She turned to face him. Surprisingly, the moon's glow hit her eyes and he could see tears still glistening.

He wasn't sure how to convince her. The boy would never starve if given to his father. Rowena had no resources to care for him on her own, especially with her need to stay hidden. How could he make Clara see that?

Mayhap 'twas best to say nothing at all.

He stepped forward. She held up her hand. "Please, Kenneth, can I not have a moment of peace to pray and weep for my friend? You want her to hand over her only child, mayhap the only one she will ever have, and 'twould break her heart. Can't I have this moment to ask God for a blessing?"

"We can find someone to buy her freedom. Rowena is young and has obviously caught the eye of Lord Taurin. She will catch another man's eye, as well."

Clara shook her head in disbelief. "Who? A drunkard at an inn, mayhap the only place she can find work and a roof over her head? She was little more than a child when her father rid himself of her, and it twists in me like a knife to think she was sold off like a bale of hay. And what of her son? Would he stay with her?" She spun to set her back to him, her shoulders stiff.

His heart went cold and his gut tightened. He had no

desire to see Clara suffer, and even now, as she prayed and wept for her friend's troubles, he hated to see her steeled spine and hear her smothered sobs.

What could he do? Even as he asked that question, he found his hand circling hers and his feet leading her to the bench where he'd repaired his mail this morning.

He ran a hand along the bench's seat, discovering the dew had already fallen and dampened it. He pulled off his outer tunic and laid it across the wood. Wordlessly, she sat beside him. He then set his cloak to cover her shoulders.

His eyes roamed upward to where the apple was tucked into the thatch. With this dew, 'twould take a while for the head to dry and turn into something that looked like a shriveled old woman's head. He should bring it inside to dry more quickly. But for now, his attention was needed by the woman beside him.

He sat down, took her hand and held it. They said nothing for a long time.

"Brindi says you have become softer since putting your life in God's care."

"Brindi is repeating our mother's comment. She can hardly remember a time before I decided to trust God."

"She also hopes she doesn't cry like you do when she gets older."

Clara laughed. "Our priest says 'tis the Lord working in me, but she need not worry. 'Twill not be the same for her. I was the one with the temper to match my hair, so naturally, any change would be noticeable. But not all redheads are like me! Father had red hair but was far more mild in manner."

"How did he die?"

She nodded. "One day, as the tide rose, he went out

to fish. When the tide receded, only the boat remained. 'Twas found by some men on the far shore of Mersea Island. The wind was high that day, so I expect he was knocked overboard. He could not swim."

"I'm sorry. They didn't find him?"

"Nay." She sighed. "'Twas a long time ago, and one of the reasons I went to work with my aunt and ended up staying in Colchester." She looked up and studied him in the dim light of the nearly full moon, but said nothing as she dipped her head again.

Compassion had fueled his apology, compassion for a difficult situation. Back in Normandy, he had both a mother and father. They'd been given a portion of good land and lived well, free landholders whose children had all survived childhood. He, their youngest son, had been strong enough to be sent as squire to Lord Adrien when Kenneth was barely fourteen and Adrien just given his knighthood.

Yet, war and soldiering had not taught him compassion. No, his Lord had, as He had taught it to Clara. Could He also teach her wisdom in this difficult situation?

Kenneth reached up and touched her hair. She turned to look up at him again. "You have compassion, Clara. Something the Lord gave you. Now trust that He will protect Rowena. We don't always know the wisest things to do. Sometimes it's our own stubbornness that masquerades as God's decisions."

She slapped his hand away. "'Tis not stubbornness! 'Tis knowing the right thing to do!" Her eyes suddenly narrowed. "You're as silver-tongued as the keep's chaplain with his smooth words about trusting God and obeying those over us. I do trust the Good Lord, and He has given me the strength to help!" She jumped to her feet. "You are the one being stubborn. Nay, you're being a fool thinking that I will simply hand over Rowena to you because *you* say that God will think it wise to do so. Are you in such good stead with the Lord that He will tell you that and not me?"

His own temper flared. "Aye, I do believe that! 'Tis as obvious as the nose on my face that Taurin can provide for the child far better than a slave with not even two coins to rub together!"

She strode away, and he jumped to his feet to cut off her path to the door.

He felt something furry dash between his legs and started quickly. Already slickened by the dew, the wet stones on the path offered no resistance to the smooth soles of his shoes. In his next breath, which was knocked from his lungs, his back met the hard flagstones of her path through the garden and his head smacked them with the force of a galloping courser.

Chapter Eight

Clara gasped. She could see the moon reflected in Kenneth's eyes, wide between his swift blinks of stunned shock. She hurried over to him. "Are you all right?"

He groaned as he tested each limb and found them all working. "Aye. I'm not badly hurt. What was that thing?"

"A cat, I think. At night, they slip into the village from the keep to prowl." Then, ensuring that he could see her intense expression as clearly as possible in the moonlight, she leaned close and planted her hands on either side of his shoulders. "Since you are unhurt, allow me to continue our conversation. You may believe you have the wisdom of God at your disposal, sir, but rest assured, I believe the same. Only time will tell whose wisdom prevails, but I have the advantage. Only I know where Rowena is and I plan to keep it that way."

When she realized her proximity, she pushed away from him and watched, ready to help as he stood. "I also have the advantage of being able to awaken on the morrow without any aches and pains. But do not worry. I have an excellent tea should you require something to ease your soreness. And I'd be happy to make it for you."

With that, she spun and marched into the hut, going straight through the small main room and into the tiny bedchamber.

Brindi bounced back onto the pallet and under the covers. "You should be asleep," she told the girl sharply.

"You and Kenneth made a lot of noise. And I can't sleep without you. You usually come to bed at the same time I do."

"You were on your own for a month, Brindi." But what she said was true when they were together. In Colchester, the days were busy, but the nights were quiet, each person still too concerned with staying out of the Norman soldiers' ways. Sometimes, though, after Brindi had fallen asleep, Clara would slip out and visit Rowena. The trip into the woods was dangerous, but not too far. All she'd had to do was follow a small stream upward to its bend and step into the thicket a few feet. A small, man-made warren, probably used to hide a thief at one time, had been Rowena's temporary home after the baby was born.

When Clara had discovered that she was to come to Little Dunmow, she'd moved Rowena to a hut she'd discovered, deep in the woods, that skirted a small, nearly depleted peat bog. 'Twas why Rowena was so reluctant to have a fire there, for sometimes a Saxon would pilfer the scraps of peat for fuel.

After that moment of silent thought, Brindi spoke. "Shouldn't you pray for forgiveness for tripping Kenneth?"

"I did not trip him! A stray cat darted out of our garden and he slipped on the flagstones."

"He could have died."

Clara groaned. "No, he couldn't have. People don't die from falling, unless they are very old."

"He could have hit his head and then died. You should have prayed for God to forgive you."

"He didn't die. He's fine and 'twas his slippery shoes on the wet stones that caused his fall, not me."

"You made him jump up. You were arguing with him."

"Like you are arguing with me?" Clara sighed. "I will pray, but sometimes we have to fight for what we believe in. And you shouldn't have been listening at the door. Now go to sleep."

Brindi didn't answer. Shortly after, Kenneth entered and prepared the table to be his bed. Clara refused to surrender to her curiosity and peer through the hearth to see if he was limping. She'd find out in the morning if his fall had left any ill effects.

Still, Brindi was right about one thing. She should pray for forgiveness. For she surely had lost her temper with the man and hadn't really felt sorry for his fall.

Lord, forgive me. Keep Rowena safe. Help me find the best place for her and the babe.

She huddled deeper into the bedclothes. But Kenneth's occasional groans were too much for her curiosity. She twisted about and peered over the dying fire.

He *was* limping. And rubbing his head. Clara bit her lip. She should check him out. Her aunt had told her of one old man who'd fallen and cracked his head open, only to die in his sleep.

She should check his head and see if he had any broken bones.

She sat up, and Brindi opened her eyes.

"Get to sleep, Brindi."

"Are you going to see if his brains are falling out?" the girl whispered.

"I'm sure his brains are fine. I will check him for broken bones. But if you don't get to sleep right now, I will have you doing all the chores tomorrow."

With that threat, Brindi flopped over onto her side and fell silent. Clara pulled on her cyrtel and hastily tied up the belt and neck. Kenneth had already seen her hair, so her spare wimple wasn't necessary. She shoved back the curtain and stepped into the light of the main room. "Let me see your head."

"I'm fine," he grumbled back.

"Not according to those groans I hear. Be sensible, sir, lest you get ill from the rap on your head."

Kenneth wisely sat on the bench as she turned up the lamp's wick. She also lit a rush soaked in tallow and set it on its brace for extra light. "Turn around, with your back to the light. I want to see where you hit your head."

Kenneth turned, though with reluctance, Clara noted. She gingerly felt his head, avoiding touching it with her sore hand. Unfortunately, he'd long discarded that absurd Norman fashion of shaving the back of his head. Right now it would have helped her see his wound better. When she pulled back her fingers, they were dry. 'Twas good. "There's no blood, but let me bathe it. Cool water will soothe it."

She wet a cloth and pressed it to his head, cringing when he sucked in his breath. Then she dabbed it with soured wine and lavender to stop a bruise. "There. Do you feel better? Is there any other place that aches?"

Without waiting for an answer, she began to squeeze his shoulders and arms gently. "I don't feel any broken bones," she said.

He shrugged and shifted slightly. "Just some bruises on my elbows and shoulders."

"Let me dab them with the wine and lavender." Twisting, she reached for where she'd set it. The pot felt heavy on her sore palm, but she was thankful that her wound was healing. Easing the lid off, she prepared to dip the linen into its contents.

His hand shot out to capture her wrist. "Nay, Clara."

She looked into his dark eyes and fell still. *Those eyes.* She'd never seen any so warm, so intense. They pierced into her the way a hot coal melted through winter snow.

As a midwife, she knew well the ways of men and women. But never, never, had a man given her such a heated look as Kenneth gave her now. Suddenly she was very aware of her proximity to him.

'Twas this the way men looked at women to have them turn soft and compliant? Too many wives shrugged their shoulders when Clara told them they were pregnant, most saying 'twas bound to happen.

"Nay, mistress," Kenneth repeated softly into her thoughts. "I will apply it myself."

Heat blossomed into her face. Suddenly she saw him as he really was, and the shock of that realization flooded through her.

He was a man, fully and overwhelmingly so tonight. And the urge to flee back to her chamber where Brindi lay, probably listening in, rushed through her.

Clara stepped back, pulling in a breath that should have restored her courage and her will, but did nothing save make a ragged, shaky noise. "I…I… Of course, sir. 'Tis only proper."

Her words, as stuttering and foolish as they sounded,

proved to restore her good sense. She may look like a fool, or worse, a woman of whom good maids only whispered, but she was no such person. Nay, he would dab on his own lotion, as 'twas proper.

"I will bid you good-night, then, sir. I hope the lavender helps and you sleep well. I will check your head on the morrow."

With a spin, she fled back to where Brindi lay. She wiped her damp hands on her cyrtel as she went, out of sight of Kenneth, though his presence lingered.

Kenneth was up before her the next morn. Clara hid deep within the warm bedclothes, close to her sister, trying to gather the courage to rise and break her fast with him. Surely, he would see that 'twas pointless for him to stay here? She would never reveal Rowena's location, and beyond all that, the awkwardness last night would surely grow to burst out of this tiny hut.

She sighed. Well, awkwardness or not, she had work to do, and she would not allow any regret, nor any attraction, to stop her. She slipped free of the covers, leaving Brindi to sleep in, and quickly prepared for her day.

Kenneth had gathered the eggs successfully this time and was cracking three of them into a well-seasoned pan he'd set on the coals. Pierced on a stick was a large slice of yesterday's bread. Its angle over the fire would allow a gentle toasting. Higher up, also pierced, was half a quarter of cheese. Any drippings from it would fall into the pan of eggs. The locals here called the dish poor man's rabbit, and now the smells of such a breakfast filled her, reminding her of how hungry she was. Nearly always, her first meal was cold broth, while the noon meal was more bountiful. Clara liked it the other way around, but too often did her day start at a gallop, allowing little time for a hot meal.

"My thanks for preparing the breakfast, sir," she told him. "I assume you're feeling better?"

"Aye. That lotion eased my aches, and I think the lump on my head has gone down." He sniffed the air. "Though I am not sure I care to smell like flowers."

She laughed, then abruptly cleared her throat. "Good," she answered briskly, glad the tone of the conversation didn't reflect the sudden awareness of last night. Brindi, obviously smelling food, appeared at the curtain and quickly dropped down onto the bench, her expression saying she fully expected to be fed.

Kenneth grinned. "The true sign of a good meal is when it rouses a child from a comfortable bed." He set before her a piece of the toasted bread smeared with part of the melted cheese and dropped an egg on top. Brindi dug in immediately. He leaned forward and lowered his voice. "I am truly sorry about your apple. But 'twill make a good doll for you."

She looked up. "If it's ugly, can I eat it?"

"Brindi!" Clara sighed. "'Twill not be ugly. Don't speak of a gift like that!"

Kenneth smiled at her, his sidelong glance warm enough to hint at the heat it had carried last night. "Nay, mistress. 'Twill be quite ugly. Like an old woman." He faced Brindi. "But such are the people that need our love the most. So promise me you won't eat her just because she's ugly. 'Twould set a dangerous precedence."

She frowned. "What's that?"

"What if you get old and ugly, and someone younger decides to eat you?"

Brindi laughed, her gaze fixed on Kenneth, so forgiving for accidentally taking her apple. She was captivated by him, and it snagged in Clara's throat. Oh, dear, 'twould do no good for the child to be taken by Kenneth's charm. He was here only to wait for her to reveal Rowena's location, despite all that talk of guarding her should Lord Taurin arrive. He must soon return to his duties at the keep.

Clara cleared her throat. "Let's break our fast. We have much to do today."

'Twas the day before the Sabbath, and Clara, with Brindi and Kenneth in tow, went to the keep to check on Lady Ediva and her new son. Kenneth was a bit stiff, she noted, but said nothing when she loaded him and Brindi with supplies. If she could, she'd like to slip away and visit Rowena, and returning to the hut for more supplies would arouse suspicion.

"Why do we need to take all of this?" Brindi asked with a petulant note in her voice.

"I may need them. So 'twill save you a trip if we simply bring them with us."

"We've never needed as many things before when we visited a new babe. Why so much?"

Clara directed a fast glance at Kenneth, whose eyebrows shot up in curiosity. Flushing, she hurried them both out of the hut. "I won't take a chance that Lady Ediva needs more. She had a difficult delivery."

Before long, Clara, with Brindi, who never tired of looking at babes, was examining the keep's first son. Kenneth stayed out in the corridor, and Clara was glad. His mere presence kept recalling in her the closeness of last night. And she needed her concentration. It didn't help that the room was very warm.

"Is he well?" Lady Ediva asked from her bed. It had

been several days since the heir arrived, and Clara had ordered bed rest for her for at least until the Sabbath.

Clara smiled up at her from the cradle, where she'd unswaddled the boy to examine him. "He's very well. Look how round and rosy he is," she said as she scooped up the infant. Then, after reswaddling him, she brought him to his mother. At the foot of the bed, both Brindi and Lady Ediva's maid, Margaret, beamed like proud aunts.

"I want to check how you're nursing," Clara said as she set the boy down in his mother's arms. The rest of the examination went smoothly. Her ladyship had birthed a fine young boy, and mother and son had slipped into their new routines with ease. So unlike Rowena and her son, who'd had difficulty nursing and seemed stressed and colicky. But then, everything was arranged to be easy for the keep's mistress and her son.

Lady Ediva had no cause to worry about where her next meal came from. Her solar could be made as toasty as she wanted it, without fear she'd be discovered. Her babe slept in a cradle of the best quality, while Rowena needed to keep her child close for warmth.

Tears sprang unbidden to Clara's eyes. As much as she had encouraged Rowena to eat and have a fire to keep her and her babe warm and their strength up, Clara knew 'twas fear that had slowed Rowena's nursing abilities and prevented her from taking comfort in luxuries such as a fire. That and the damp, moss-covered hut in the middle of nowhere.

"He looks so much like his father, don't you think?" Lady Ediva said with pride in her voice.

Clara swallowed and drew her thoughts back to her lady. "Aye."

A maid chose that moment to arrive with hot broth

and sweet biscuits and good strong cheese, as per Clara's orders. There were even two extra cups for both Clara and Brindi to share in the light meal. Clara spied Kenneth standing in the corridor and quickly looked away.

Beside her, Brindi sniffed the air long and appreciatively. Lady Ediva laughed as she gingerly climbed out of bed and set her babe in his cradle. "If I may sit at my own table, I want you both to join me in this meal. Brindi, I hear you have only just arrived. Are you glad to be with your sister?"

"Aye, milady. I came when Lord Eudo found out I was there by myself. M'maw had sent me back to Colchester, but I arrived after the guild masters ordered Clara to leave because she was causing trouble."

Clara groaned inwardly. Children had no compunction for stating what was on their minds. "'Twas not quite like that, milady. Aye, I was ordered here. I sent Brindi home to our mother, but M'maw is too old, so she sent her back. When Brindi was discovered living alone in my former cottage, Lord Eudo had her brought here."

Lady Ediva eased into her chair at the table, her expression chiding. "Nay, I heard the whole story. Last night, Lord Adrien told me about the letter his brother sent. The townsfolk were worried that Lord Taurin would cause trouble, not you."

"'Tis one and the same, I fear." Clara stared at the fine food before her. She was unaccustomed to such a fine repast midmorning, and the world around her suddenly began to swim in unshed tears.

A small warm hand reached over and covered hers and she looked up through unshed tears to see Lady Ediva's sympathetic expression. "Lord Adrien will keep you safe. And he would do the same for the woman you hide."

Clara shot up her head. "Nay! Lord Adrien believes the child would be better off in his father's house!" She shook her head vigorously. "But I cannot agree, milady. I'm so sorry, but 'tis wrong to snatch a babe from its mother's arms."

Ediva frowned. Clara watched her lady's gaze dance between her and Brindi, whose own eyes were more focused on the meal in front of them.

"I don't know what to say," Ediva began haltingly. "I understand your feelings, but Adrien says your friend's babe will not survive for long hidden in the woods." Abruptly, Lady Ediva's hand shot across the table away from Clara. She plunked a sweet biscuit and a piece of cheese in front of Brindi and bundled the rest of the food up in the large napkin Margaret had spread out. The only thing she kept out was the small tureen of broth.

"A flask, Margaret, one that seals," she ordered. Margaret quickly retrieved one from a small chest behind the table. Understanding her mistress's wishes, she filled the flask with steaming broth and sealed it tight.

Ediva shoved the bundle at Brindi, and the flask to Clara. "Loosen your belt and hide this on your person to keep prying eyes away. Your body heat will keep the broth warm. No doubt you will visit the woman soon, so take these things to her. If you hide them well, none will suspect that you carry them. I know Lord Adrien would not begrudge the woman nourishment, but I fear that Lord Taurin's influence might reach into our keep."

"Nay! Your soldiers are loyal, are they not?"

Ediva shook her head. "We've just received several new soldiers from London, as the king is concerned that

Hereward the Wake has settled in just north of here in Ely. 'Tis possible that one of them has been placed here by Taurin himself, for I hear he is as deceptive as he is calculating."

Clara's blood ran cold. Taurin's men, here in Dunmow? She swallowed hard. And with Kenneth outside, waiting for her to finish her examination, she would find it very difficult to slip out of the village. But she may be able...

Lady Ediva carried on. "I will speak with my husband. I cannot promise anything more, but I understand your plight. 'Tis all I will say."

The sound of Brindi biting into a sweet biscuit drew Clara away from her planning. She stood and bowed to Lady Ediva before shoving the flask under her chemise. Margaret, always the good lady's maid, helped her secure the warm bottle so 'twouldn't slip out. The bundle of food went into her deep basket of herbs. "Brindi, you carry this basket," Clara said softly, "but keep eating a biscuit in case one of the soldiers smells the others you have and believes you're stealing them."

She turned to Lady Ediva. "I know 'tis wrong to set you against your husband on this matter, but my heart twists to think of Rowena's suffering."

Ediva shook her head. "You won't be setting me against my husband. I can open my heart to him anytime and he understands it. He also allows me the right to run my keep as I have for years. It often included alms and foodstuffs for the poor. Adrien understands and encourages that."

Clara bit her lip and she listened to Ediva's voice soften and her expression ease into love at the mention of her husband's name. Oh, to have such love and intimacy in a marriage! She knew so few people whose marriages were not to align families and what small plots of land King William allowed the Saxons to own. Even the poorest of the poor had to obtain the lord's permission to marry, and the unions were oft to secure some form of property.

She looked at Ediva. The lady of the keep was blessed, indeed, to have found such love and have it returned. The mere thought caught in Clara's throat.

"I will return after the Sabbath to check on you. Keep drinking all the broth you can, and get your rest. Remember, milady, never lift anything more than your babe." Clara curtsied again and hurriedly took her leave, throwing open the door and thrusting into Kenneth's arms the bundle of cloths that held jars of salve she'd known she wouldn't need. "We have other babes to visit, and the landowner's wife at the north edge of the village has a rash. Come, we have lots of work to do." With that, she strode past him and down the corridor.

All the way through the bailey to the gate, with Brindi close on her heels eating the pastry and Kenneth striding at her side, Clara fought back tears. Seeing Lady Ediva healthy and strong, her babe eating well and as robust as a newborn could be, was all too much for her. Rowena's babe suffered, where Ediva's did not.

Her throat hurt. Was it right for her to risk the lives of Rowena and her child because of her pledge to keep them from Lord Taurin? Wasn't she supposed to help people get better?

Was it possible to do both?

She slipped a sidelong glance at Kenneth as he strode so very close to her. Was it possible for her to slip past him and deliver this food before the biscuits turned to crumbs and the cheese molded?

Mayhap not possible at all.

She bit back a sob.

Chapter Nine

In front of Brindi, Clara pressed her forefinger to her lips, then eased the girl backward through the thatched roof to the outside.

When she'd first arrived here, she'd discovered that the thatch on the front of the hut was not secured to the lowest rafter, and several bundles could be lifted together, revealing a hole two hand lengths high.

Listening carefully to her sister's soft step onto the bench outside, Clara then hiked up her cyrtel and swung herself up and slid through. She soon found the bench with her feet.

'Twas after evening services and she had told Kenneth that both she and Brindi were exhausted from the day of checking out all the babes in the village. Only after she'd heard Kenneth retire for the night did Clara make her move. Feeling again to make sure the flask of broth was still secure at her side, she took up the bundle of foodstuffs in one hand, Brindi's small palm in the other, and began to hurry around the back of her hut.

Thankfully, all was quiet, and once they had skirted the village, they hurried down the road to Colchester.

Partway into the forest the road split. To the left, the road disappeared into the forest, down a new path. She had to be careful, as this was her route.

Where the path ended, she'd already created a narrow trail, marked with the occasional bow of wool to jog her memory. They hurried into the bushes and trees, following the tied-wool trail until it opened into a small peat bog and the moss-covered hut that must have once belonged to a long-dead peat cutter.

The cold scent of moist earth filled her as she gave the secret tap on the low door and then entered. No sound came in reply. Clara hurriedly struck a spark and lit the lamp she'd brought with her to find her friend curled up on the floor like an animal. Rowena opened her eyes and looked up at her. She was huddled in her cloak, her babe tight to her body to help conserve the babe's body heat, for the night was cold. The child let out a weak whimper.

Clara's heart sank. This situation could not go on much longer. Summer was still growing. 'Twould warm up the hut, but also dry the peat bog, thereby making it more accessible for harvesters hoping to further deplete it. The danger of being discovered increased.

When the danger lessened with colder weather, winter would come and surely mother and child would die. Tears sprang unbidden into Clara's eyes. How had this situation become so dire?

Without a word, she hurried to the small hearth and lit a fire with some dry kindling she'd stacked earlier. Heat began to seep into the hut.

"Is it safe to light the fire?" Rowena whispered, standing and brushing off her dark cyrtel.

"'Tis night. No one will be harvesting peat now." Clara bit her lip as she took the babe from the girl.

Rowena was so young. Too young to have delivered a babe, and though lacking in some things, she seemed to understand so well other things, like what men might do. But she'd been the youngest of her family, probably ignored a lot, barely thirteen when her uncaring father sold her to Lord Taurin. Even now, as a mother, she seemed too fearful to have a fire in the night.

How could she be expected to raise her child alone? She was a babe with a babe. *Heavenly Father, give her some sense.*

Brindi began to lay out the foodstuffs they'd brought, thankfully not asking Clara for a taste herself. Immediately, Rowena dived into the meal, eating so swiftly that Clara feared she'd choke.

"Slow down, Rowena, or you'll be sick. You will need to drink something. I've brought a good broth to wash it all down."

"'Tis a wonderful pastry, Clara. Did you make it yourself?" she asked, slowing down.

"Nay. 'Tis a gift from Lady Ediva, who worries for your health."

Rowena sagged. "How kind! Mayhap I can thank her someday. She bakes a wonderful meal."

With Brindi's knowing eyes on her, Clara pressed her lips into a thin line at the girl's innocence. "Nay, Lady Ediva did not bake these. She has a cook."

"Oh, how foolish of me." Rowena's eyes were wide and apologetic. "I feel like I know nothing."

"You're young, that's all. Nor have you ever known a mistress of a keep and her ways." Clara had asked once where Lord Taurin had kept the girl after he'd bought her, discovering that he'd kept her at his smaller estate, a manor house that knew no mistress save a surly old chatelaine brought from Normandy who treated Rowena like the dirt beneath her feet.

Recalling that difficult conversation, Clara quickly changed the subject, insisting on examining Rowena and the babe to see if the feeding was being done correctly. The cut on Clara's hand was fully sealed now and 'twas easy to manage all her tasks.

Satisfied all was as well as possible, and thankful that Brindi had had the sense to put the broth into a pot and heat it further, Clara finished her task and insisted Rowena drink all of the warm liquid.

They stayed awhile longer, talking about babes and nappies and rashes. Clara offered advice on all she thought that Rowena could handle and saw that Rowena was managing to feed her babe well enough, despite her stick-thin appearance.

But soon, they could stay no longer. On their way back, Brindi spoke. "Is Rowena addled?"

"Nay! She's just innocent."

"She didn't know that Lady Ediva was too important to cook her own meals."

"True, but she was just a farm girl. How many baronesses do you think she's met?"

Brindi shrugged. "I'm smarter than she is."

"Don't talk that way, Brindi. 'Tis rude and boasting, which is shameful."

"I am, though." There was a pout in her tone. Clara trudged on in front of her. Aye, Rowena was remarkably innocent. Mayhap the loneliness was attacking any good sense she'd had. Clara pushed further along the trail, hating that Brindi was correct. She did have more sense than Rowena. But only because Clara had seen to her sister's education.

Was it safe, then, to keep the girl so thoroughly hidden away when she didn't have a dram of good sense to see to her own care? And the babe? What of him? Was it healthy to keep him there with his mother, who could not fend for herself? Mayhap she could train the young woman. But when? How?

Tears sprang anew in her eyes and she slashed her hand across both of them so her vision would not blur in the darkness.

Keeping Rowena hidden wasn't safe, but what else could Clara do? She couldn't bring the girl home, certainly not with Kenneth there. Nor could she ask another family to take her, not when there were new soldiers from London who might be spies for Taurin. That would put the generous family at terrible risk.

All was quiet when she approached her home. With as much care as they'd used escaping, Clara eased Brindi back under the thatch first so she could guide Clara in as quietly as possible. She sighed when her feet hit the hardpan floor. Safe back home they were, though Clara knew that this night, sleep would elude her and guilt would keep her eyes wide open.

As Kenneth, Clara and Brindi left the chapel and walked slowly down toward the bailey gate, Kenneth followed the sisters, only half listening to Clara.

Something was amiss, he was sure of it. Just what it was, however, he wasn't sure. He'd slept soundly last night on the table, as was his custom, but this morning, Clara looked as though she'd barely shut her eyes. And she'd allowed Brindi to sleep later than usual. Though it was Sunday, Clara didn't seem the type to let Brindi avoid chores, especially the less strenuous chores left for the Sabbath.

He pulled in the sharp morning air. It carried with it the scent of moss and damp, although the days were growing warmer and they'd not had rain recently. He sniffed again. The scent came from Clara's cloak, he was sure of it.

They couldn't have slipped out to visit Rowena. As soundly as he'd slept, he still would have awakened if they'd tried to leave the hut. He'd shoved the table against the door, and neither of them would have been able to move it with his weight on it. So why the odd scent?

At the corner of his eye, Kenneth spied Margaret stepping out of the chapel. Lady Ediva was still confined to her bed, but had allowed the maid to attend services. The woman drew in a deep breath, as if pleased to be outside after many hours tending her mistress and the new babe.

Kenneth touched Clara's arm. "Excuse me for a moment." Then he hurried back toward the chapel to cut off Margaret before she reached the keep.

"Mistress," he began politely, flattering her with a form of address not usually given to a lowly lady's maid, in thanks for the favor she was performing for him. "May I have a word with you?"

Margaret smiled at him and pulled the sides of her lightweight cloak closer. She was comely in a rather ordinary way, though given to fluster when disturbed, not unlike one of Clara's hens. She stepped up close to him, her gaze bright. "Aye?"

He cleared his throat, catching a glimpse of Clara frowning in his direction. He turned back to Margaret. "I had spoken to you about making a doll. Do you remember?"

Margaret nodded. "Aye. Is the head ready?"

"Nay, not yet. But I was wondering if you could have the body done without the head, so that as soon as the head has dried I can attach it to the body." He explained what he'd used and how he planned to attach the head to the body.

She nodded. "If milady rests all afternoon, I shall have time. We have some scraps of material and some wool to stuff it."

"I was hoping for it to be an old-lady doll." He smiled crookedly, feeling a bit foolish suddenly. "'Tis the only thing I can carve."

Margaret's own smile broadened. Unlike Clara's simple clothing, Margaret's was of good quality, probably cast off by her mistress. Scraps from her clothes would make for a fine doll indeed. The soft pink she wore today matched her cheeks. "Lady Ediva gave me an old shift of hers, in a pale blue."

"I know you can make something pretty for young Brindi."

Margaret beamed. "Aye, that I can. I'll start on it today, sir, while milady rests. 'Twill be quiet in the solar then." Her smile lingered on him a little too long, so clearing his throat, Kenneth bowed to her and took his leave.

Curiosity burned in Clara, and 'twas hard to rein it in as Kenneth stood speaking with Margaret. What were they discussing? Kenneth should have no need to speak with Lady Ediva's maid.

She drew in a sharp breath. Did he suspect she'd mentioned Rowena in the solar? Kenneth would have no right to question milady, but he could easily ask Margaret, who, by the flush on the girl's face, was thrilled with the attention.

Well, let him ask away! Margaret knew nothing.

"Ow! Clara, why are you squeezing my hand so hard? I wasn't going anywhere!"

Clara snapped her attention to her sister. "I'm sorry!" She immediately released her grip. Pulling a face, Brindi rubbed her hand.

Pah, the girl was fine. Clara turned back to where Kenneth and Margaret spoke. The maid beamed like the sun, but with his back to Clara, Kenneth's expression was hidden. Was he smiling, as well? What if it had nothing to do with her or Rowena?

What if Kenneth was courting Margaret?

Clara swallowed, trying to push away the accusations that danced in her head. Kenneth had the right to woo the maid. And she had no right to stop it. But he'd been ordered to protect her and, aye, find out where Rowena was. The longer that took, the longer Kenneth was away from the keep. Was he explaining that to the maid?

The urge to put an end to this duty of his surged through Clara. 'Twould save his relationship with Margaret, and mayhap Clara could sneak out more.

But Kenneth took his duty too seriously to abandon his post for a woman. Did he want to? she wondered. Did it sadden him to think of the hours wasted in Clara's cottage that could have been spent with Margaret?

Tears sprang into Clara's eyes as Kenneth turned. In the blurriness of the moment, she didn't catch his expression, and with a wash of vulnerability, she turned and quickly swiped her eyes free of the tears.

Kenneth reached her. "My thanks, Clara, for waiting for me. 'Twas not necessary."

"But," she answered brusquely, "had I left, you'd have found me in short order."

His answer was a short laugh. "Aye. Little Dunmow is too small to hide anyone, let alone a fiery redhead."

As they walked, Clara considered his words. Aye, Little Dunmow lived up to its name, and should she have considered bringing Rowena here, everyone would have known soon enough. Nay, 'twas too dangerous.

After they stepped out of the bailey, Clara watched her sister run up ahead after a small butterfly. "Kenneth," she began with a deep breath, "do you really believe that Lord Taurin would spare Rowena's life should he find her?"

Kenneth looked at her somberly. "Are you considering revealing her location?"

She stiffened. "Nay. 'Twould end in her murder. Of that I am very sure."

"Then why ask me?"

"Why won't you answer my question?"

He said nothing as she watched him closely. Her strong reaction to seeing him speak with Margaret still lingered in her, leaving distaste on her tongue. Finally, he spoke. "The king abolished slavery of Christians."

"You didn't answer my question. What do *you* think Lord Taurin would do if he caught Rowena?"

"We've had this discussion. Aye, she would probably be beaten. But Lord Taurin must know he would need her to feed the child, and since neither of us know him, how can we say that he is cruel?"

"Rowena arrived with bruises from a beating—a harsh one, for the marks to linger so long."

"She could be lying."

Clara shook her head. "Nay. I believe 'tis not in her nature to lie. She is really quite innocent."

"Then she shouldn't be alone with a child, if only for the child's sake."

Clara swallowed. Kenneth didn't know how close he was to the truth with that statement. She lifted her chin. "But if slavery is against the law, where would your duty lie? With Lord Taurin, who searches for the slave he shouldn't have, or with the king, who has abolished it?"

Kenneth stopped and his gaze grew distant. The moment stretched between them with Clara barely breathing as she awaited his answer.

Then he tipped his head, his eyes softening. "I don't have an answer for you, Clara. I serve the king, but the king is not here. And should Lord Taurin arrive with a writ from the king allowing him to take the slave, I would be bound by my oath of obedience to King William to help Lord Taurin."

Clara felt new tears spring into her eyes. She'd posed an unanswerable question. It made her stomach ache. "What about your faith? What does it tell you?"

"The priests say we must obey the laws."

"The law is clear about slavery."

He sagged. "I pledged my life to King William, Clara. He makes the laws. These are laws of man, not of God."

She looked away. Aye, what Kenneth said was true, and she knew in her heart that God wanted her to obey England's laws. But they were made by a Norman who came as a conqueror with other Normans who bore far too much power. The power to murder.

"'Tis hard, isn't it?" he whispered suddenly. "Sometimes there is no clear answer."

She pulled herself to her full height, hoping that it was

enough for him to see that such a dilemma wasn't hard for her. Her faith was sound, she told herself sternly. So was her pledge.

"Nay. I know what is right to do. You may serve King William, but I am to help the sick and the women and children. I stand by my decision."

She searched around for Brindi, who had stopped some distance off and was staring intently into her cupped hands. Obviously, she'd caught the butterfly. Around them, the people were dispersing, ignoring Clara and Kenneth as they returned to their homes for the noon meal. The villagers were so used to Norman soldiers now that the sight of one talking to a woman meant nothing to them. And the turmoil within Clara's heart was lost on them, for they all had troubles of their own.

No one would have an answer for Clara's impossible situation. Even as she glanced skyward, hoping for some whisper of an answer from the Lord Himself, nothing came.

Except the doubt that trickled into her.

Chapter Ten

Brindi spent the Sabbath after services playing with the other village children. She returned at suppertime grubby and sweaty and smelling of sheep and their distasteful manure.

"We played with the new lambs, Clara," she announced brightly when she arrived home. "They are so pretty and soft, but their mothers don't like us. They stamp their feet to scare us away."

"It didn't work, I see," Clara said, her hands on her hips.

Behind her at the table, Kenneth chuckled. She turned to him, dark circles under her eyes as she snapped out, "You'd best leave so I can give this girl a good and proper scrubbing down."

Smiling at the distress growing on the girl's face, he took his leave. Outside, he sat on the bench, only half listening to what was going on inside. Since yesterday when Clara and Brindi had visited Lady Ediva, Clara had been far more quiet and pensive than usual. What had happened? He leaned back against the daub of the house. Should he use his influence with Margaret to discover what had been said? He frowned in distaste at the idea.

A small amount of daub crumbled around him. This house was old, in bad need of repair, and the daub on this side had seen many decades. He looked down to inspect the damage, wondering if there was anyone in the village able to redaub the wall.

There certainly *was* a lot of the plaster about. He looked up at the wall.

Then he stood and stepped back. Faint footprints and scuff marks painted a broad line from the low edge of the thatched roof to the dirt below. From inside the house, Brindi's tired complaints told him Clara was scrubbing her sister hard. A moment later, the girl complained that the water was too cold. Kenneth stepped back farther to view the entire wall. Now Brindi could be heard complaining that the herbed paste was too smelly.

He focused back on the wall. It had been climbed, as evidenced by the muddied prints on it. It had happened recently, too, for they'd had no rain in the past week to wash the dirt away.

He reached out and fingered the larger of the prints. Both the dried mud and the wall crumbled as if they'd been given a scrubbing like Brindi was now receiving.

Footprints? Two sets. One slightly larger than the other, but both smaller than a man's. His mouth pressed into a thin line.

He peered at the ground, then followed the line of prints up to the thatch that he could now see had been broken and bent, and showed a disturbance in one small area. The rest of the thatch remained cut and clean, the only oddity being the carved apple he'd shoved in there. Idly, he turned the apple to allow the other side to dry.

Then he looked again and saw more disturbances in the roof thatch. The pieces of the puzzle all came together. Clara had slipped out of her hut in the night to visit Rowena. 'Twould explain Clara's obvious fatigue today, if she'd been out all night.

Silently berating himself for not waking up when this was happening, Kenneth turned. Above, on the battlement that trimmed the top of the keep's bailey wall, was a lookout. 'Twas rarely used, for it looked down on the center of the village. The other sentry points watched over the road to Colchester and the road that headed north. There was no need to guard the middle.

Tonight, however, he would see that a sentry was placed there to watch this side of the village. Nay, better that he be here lying in wait for her himself! He pulled the bench on which he'd been sitting into the shade of a large tree at the far edge of Clara's garden. He'd sit there tonight and watch as she slipped through the thatch.

A thought came to him. He'd noticed a mackerel sky when he'd spoken to Margaret today. The small scaly clouds marked the beginning of days of rain, and wind had already shifted to come from the north. Bad weather was imminent.

A short time later, when Kenneth was pacing the garden path deep in thought, Brindi poked her freshly scrubbed head out of the door. Her hair was still damp but tightly braided, and her face shone with rosy, clean cheeks. "Clara and I are so clean, we squeak like new leather!" she announced with her usual cheer. Her plight inside was forgotten.

Despite knowing Clara's subterfuge, he laughed. "Good!" he said as he entered to find Clara tidying up as the remains of his pottage warmed over the fire. "I was noticing the sky earlier and I fear rain is due," he said mildly. "We will have days of it, I'm sure."

Clara looked up at him, alarm blossoming on her face. She hastily covered it with a calmer expression. "'Tis true. I also saw the sky. I hope 'twill not be heavy rain. It makes everything damp."

"True. We may be stuck in your home for days." He shot her a sideways glance but she did nothing to warrant concern. Would she risk another visit to Rowena? With the possibility of days of rain hanging over them, could she even dare leave the girl alone?

The sky clouded fast that evening, Kenneth noticed as he volunteered to close up the chicken coop. Dusk threatened to be a gray, dismal affair. 'Twas an evening to stay by the fire, and he hoped that Clara would relent to the fatigue she must now feel, having been awake the night before. As they ate the small meal in silence and Kenneth watched Brindi's eyelids droop, he hoped that Clara would do what he suspected she would—sleep now and rise in the middle of the night to visit Rowena before the rains began.

'Twas a risk, assuming that Clara might retire early and sleep a bit before sneaking out. But 'twas a risk he would take. There were plenty of people who napped in the evening, only to rise later to stoke fires, attend midnight services at the chapel or even take in a small meal. 'Twas more a custom in Normandy than here, but was not unheard of, even in small villages such as Little Dunmow.

Clara smothered a yawn, as did Brindi, prompting Kenneth to comment, "You're both tired tonight."

"Thank you for noticing. Aye, Brindi and I will be off to bed shortly."

"Go now. I'll tend the fire and tidy up." He set the basket of bread down close to the curtain that separated the rooms and busied himself with the remaining chores. If she did as he suspected, she would wait for him to fall asleep and then take this bread to Rowena. He may as well make it easy for her.

Although Brindi complained about the early bedtime, the pair disappeared into the bedchamber. Kenneth banked the fire, deftly leaning a large log across the hearth to block Clara's view through the fire to the main room of the hut. He then pulled out the blanket he used for sleeping. Quietly, he peeled off his outer tunic and rolled it and his cloak into a long form on the table where he slept. He covered the entire roll with a blanket. Then, satisfied that it resembled his sleeping form, he silently escaped the hut.

The wind had died, but the sky was low, and with no moon or stars to light the village, Kenneth had to wait quietly in the dark for the sentry on the battlement to light torches at the corners. He stood near the trees that separated Clara's yard from the next one and rubbed his arms. Without his cloak, he felt the evening chill seep quickly into his bones.

In due time, he heard what he'd hoped to hear—soft scraping. When he stood and walked to the corner of the hut, he watched, eyes widening, as Clara stuck her foot out the section of thatched roof that he'd noticed had been disturbed. His gaze dropped to where the bench normally sat. What if she gave up when she couldn't find her foothold? Hastily and quietly, he returned the bench, but a mischievous impulse had him set it so she wouldn't immediately drop to it.

Then he stepped back into the trees and stayed stock-still.

Her leather-clad foot searched around to find the solid purchase of the seat, around and around, until Kenneth struggled to contain his mirth.

Clara was a capable horsewoman. She had grace and strength and dignity, but tonight, in the light of the sentry torches high above, she was quite the opposite as she swung her foot wildly around. Finally, after catching the edge with her toe, she shoved out her other foot and slid not so quietly down the daub wall to the ground, her cyrtel riding upward until she was secure on the earth and could pull it down.

She immediately looked around for the bench he'd moved. Finding it slightly to one side, she muttered something he didn't catch. He shouldn't have moved it, for anything that discouraged her trip to see Rowena lessened his chance to find the girl. But he'd given in to the whim of the moment and allowed a wide grin to split his face.

Ahead, Clara reached in through the thatch to help her sister climb out.

"Where's the bench?" Brindi asked far too loudly as she, too, tried to step onto it.

"Shh!"

"But we'll need it to climb back in!"

"Be quiet! It's here, and we'll move it back in a moment."

Kenneth swallowed hard to stop a snicker from rising. This was far too serious a situation to give in to humor. 'Twas just amusing to watch them. They hadn't a clue he was standing so close.

The pair stepped out into the lane that divided the village from the keep. Kenneth watched them while putting a decent amount of space between them. They hurried toward the road to Colchester before he began to follow at a safe distance, keeping close to the homes so he could duck behind one should the need arise.

Clara stopped at the edge of the forest, and Kenneth could see her peering down the tree-darkened road. He closed some of the distance, stopping at the blacksmith's house, for it was the last one before the forest. Somewhere behind him, in the village, a dog barked out a warning. Normally 'twas nothing but scents on the wind that excited dogs, but tonight, something had triggered a nervous reaction from the animal.

Kenneth tilted his head as he peered at Clara and Brindi, several feet ahead. Then distant flickers of light dancing through the trees snagged his attention. He cocked his head, hearing a low thunder of hooves increase.

Increase quickly, he noted.

He had but a heartbeat of time to react. Whatever group was charging through the forest toward them would not see Clara and Brindi until it was too late. Dread filled him at who might be blazing through the night toward Dunmow.

He rushed forward, grabbing Brindi at the waist as he ploughed an alarmed Clara into the trees and bushes that encroached on the village. They all fell with a thud and even though Kenneth hoped that the force knocked the wind and words from both sisters, he still ordered a harsh, "Quiet! Not a word nor movement!"

For once, Clara and Brindi obeyed. Still and silent, they lay in one heap. Clara and Kenneth turned their heads around just as the charge of horses came to a swift halt nearby.

A man's voice rang out in the damp night air as one horse, larger than the others, stamped and kicked up one foot. "What is it? Why have you stopped?"

"Something dashed across the road in front of us, Lord Baron," another rider answered.

The baron turned his horse around, and in the torch-light 'twas easy to see foam on the bridle from the hard ride. Again, the horse kicked out his foot and danced. The baron tore off his helmet and spat out a nasty word at the edgy animal. The torches that several of the men carried showed a hard expression on his sharply featured face.

"'Twas probably just a deer," he finally snapped. "Listen. It has set a dog barking. Dunmow Keep is ahead. Ride forward and demand they open the gate for me immediately! I have no wish to run my courser anymore. There is something wrong with its shoe."

The Norman soldier in the lead turned his horse. "Aye, Lord Taurin," he said before he galloped away.

Chapter Eleven

Clara gasped. Immediately, Kenneth's hand pressed firmly against her mouth. She could hear Brindi hiccup, but thankfully, the girl remained still, and the men heard nothing over the panting of the horses and the chink of chain mail.

Through the bushes, Clara watched the men ride away. About ten of them, two of whom carried torches, galloped up the road that led to the bailey gate. Shouts followed, and within a few breaths, torches lit up the parapet and the gate creaked opened.

She felt, rather than heard, Kenneth sag with relief. He'd startled her when he'd come from nowhere and plowed her into the brush. His one command had come with such urgency that she and Brindi had swiftly obeyed. She was glad for her sudden obedience. Now he eased away from her. After standing, he pulled her up and out of the low growth of ivy and shrubs that skirted the taller trees and had hid them from view. She turned and helped Brindi out. Kenneth stepped beside the overgrowth, but kept back enough to appear part of the shadows. Clara did the same with Brindi in tow behind her.

"'Twas Lord Taurin!" she hissed. "How did you know? How did you get here so quickly?"

Kenneth pulled her farther into the shadows of the forest. "Shh! I *didn't* know who was coming, I just heard the sound of horses. In fact, due to the king's curfew that many of your fellow Saxons feel they need to break, I expected 'twould be thieves coming to raid the village." Beside her, he stared at the keep. The bailey gate shut tight behind the travelers, and the extra torches on the parapet were extinguished. "I wasn't expecting Lord Taurin this time of night any more than you were."

"What should we do? He's here because Lord Eudo has told him where he sent me! He's here for us!"

"We don't know that."

She huffed out her disbelief. "Oh, so he's traveling at night because he prefers to, and thought he'd come to pay his respects to Lord and Lady Dunmow? Next, you'll tell me he's on his way to Ely to talk some sense into that Hareward the Wake because the man plans to fight King William!"

She waited for Kenneth's response to her sarcasm, but when it came, it brought what she feared most. "Nay, Clara. I expect he *is* here for you. But I read Lord Eudo's missive to his brother. I cannot see how he would simply give away the truth of your whereabouts. Lord Eudo doesn't trust Lord Taurin, nor would he want his brother put into the danger Lord Taurin brings with him."

"Then who else would tell?"

Kenneth turned, and though the night was deep, she could easily recognize the scorn in his dark eyes. "Your fellow Saxons, I expect. Those guild masters didn't want you to remain in Colchester for fear Lord Taurin and

King William would discipline the entire town for your actions. What would they do if they felt threatened?"

Clara bit her lip at the question. She had to agree with him. Lord Eudo and his brother were very close. One would certainly not endanger the other. But the guild masters were more worried about their town than about a pair of Normans. If Taurin had come with writ from the king for her arrest and Rowena's capture, many of them would reveal where she'd been sent in a heartbeat.

Tears stung her eyes. Her own people, those guild members who'd accused her of risking their safety to save a fool girl who'd been sold into slavery. They cared naught for a young woman. And they cared naught for Clara.

Nay, she'd done the right thing helping Rowena and would stand by her decision. When they'd first met, Rowena was scared and needed a friend. She'd been terrified of Taurin, and after viewing the man's face just now, Clara found herself shivering with fear. He was thin and dark, and an ugly scar divided the edge of his right brow and cheekbone. His dark hair glistened with grease and sweat, and his lips had curled when he spoke.

Last night, she'd questioned the wisdom of hiding Rowena, for the damp hut was hardly good for her or her babe. But now, seeing Taurin for herself, she'd never felt more confident in her decisions.

She reached into the bushes to retrieve the bundle of food she'd planned to take to Rowena. "How did you know I was here?" she asked Kenneth.

"I was following you."

Clara straightened. "I checked on you. You were sleeping. I wasn't loud enough to awaken you."

"Nay, my outer tunic and cloak were sleeping, but not me. I waited for you in the shade of a tree. I was the one who moved the bench."

Heat splashed into her cheeks. He'd been watching her sneak out in the most graceless fashion possible, hose and under tunic bared to his view. "How did you know the way I'd sneak out?"

"While you two bathed, I noticed that someone had scuffed up the daub wall and realized 'twas a way you could slip out."

She pulled a face as she stared him down. He wore braes, and a belt cinched at his trim waist pulled in his plain, lightweight shirt. Only then did she notice he'd folded his arms. 'Twas not only because he was defiant. He was probably cold.

She drew her sister closer. "What should we do now?"

"Take me to Rowena. You were headed there, anyway."

"Nay! The fewer people who know where she is, the better and safer 'tis for her."

"Safer? We're expecting rain soon. So unless she's snug in a warm house with a fire and furs, she will be safe from assault but she won't be healthy. She's in a damp place, isn't she?"

"How would you know that?"

He kept his arms folded. "I smelled moss and damp on you early this morning on the way to the chapel. It confused me at first, but then I realized that while there is no moss here in Dunmow, there is in the forest, and the farther east you go, the damper it gets. We are three leagues from Colchester, about ten miles, and the distance has many damp spots along the way."

She held up her hand, hoping it would not shake. "I

will say nothing more on the matter. No one, not you, nor Lord Taurin, will be able to force the location from me, even if you threaten to kill me!"

"Fool woman! Your death would only bring on Rowena's death!"

Brindi gasped beside her but Clara stood firm. She would not be intimidated, though the threat was real. If she died, what would happen to Rowena? Brindi may try to help, but she was a child herself.

Your death would cause the deaths of both Rowena and her babe. You promised to God and your aunt never to willfully do that.

Her head hurt and she fought back the growing headache.

Lord, give me a way to save Rowena and her babe.

Kenneth took the hand she still held up. "Come, we'll return to your house."

"Nay!" She stepped back. "What if Lord Taurin comes?"

"Lord Taurin will do little tonight. He expects the village to be fast asleep. Besides, Lord Adrien will protect you."

She opened her mouth to protest, but he held up his hand. "Do not argue. I will see that you are protected. But I can't guarantee that you won't be called into the keep to answer questions. And if you aren't in the village on the morrow when they look for you, 'twill only go poorly for you when you're found. *And you will be found.*"

He paused, then, abruptly, he took her shoulders to emphasize his point. She could feel his hands on her, full of warmth that belied his lightweight clothing and the cool night air. She could hear the worry in his voice when he spoke to her. She shut her eyes. All she wanted in that moment was to have him tell her all would be well.

He tipped his head close, and as she opened her eyes, she fully expected him to brush his lips against hers, even in Brindi's presence. Instead, he chose to speak. "Trust me, Clara. Just this once."

Oh, she wanted to! Yet could she? "How? You can't stop Lord Taurin, especially if he comes with orders from King William. You can't make him stop this search for Rowena!"

"Nay, by myself, I cannot. But I trust God, and I know He loves all, even Rowena. He will protect her."

She wanted to share his confidence, but what if God believed as Kenneth did? "You didn't give your word never to harm anyone. You didn't promise a young mother and son that they would be safe. My aunt made me promise God I would never allow harm to come to the people in my care. What am I worth if my promises are so easily discarded when things became difficult?"

Tears burned again in her eyes, and she fought them back. "Have you never had your pledges tested? Do you know what that's like?"

Kenneth felt his lips thin.

Have you never had your pledges tested?

She had no idea how much his pledge to Lord Adrien was being tested. He'd promised he would find Rowena and the babe to turn them over to Lord Taurin. He still believed the babe was better off with his father, but his pledge to use Clara to find mother and son was being so sorely tested it hurt his belly. Surely the Good Lord didn't like how Kenneth considered scheming and bullying to discover Rowena's location.

Clara had pledged to God she would keep all under her care as safe as possible. To her, that meant keeping Rowena and her babe hidden. Was it right for him to force her to revoke *her* promise to God so he could fulfill his?

Nay. The chaplain at the keep had said 'twas a sin to cause your fellow Christian to stumble.

He had to convince Clara that 'twould be better for the child to go with its father. The child would grow strong and healthy, as he'd heard Lord and Lady Dunmow's babe was now doing.

Clara gripped his arm and whispered, "Don't make me break my promises. They are all I have. Please, Kenneth. I gave my life to God's care and direction, and now you want me to follow yours instead?"

She was so close to him. She was warm, and her riotous hair had escaped her kerchief to brush along his hands as he gripped her shoulders. Her pleading whisper stole his focus. If the moon was out, he would see clear skin that resembled polished marble and lips as soft as summer evenings. Aye, he'd noticed her beauty before, but suddenly, the very truth of it ripped all good sense from him. He should be taking her back to her house, barring the door and preparing for an order from the keep—

But he could do nothing but hold her face and battle the desire to lower his lips to hers.

Brindi shifted beside them, and the moment of addled intimacy burst apart like a spark from a pithy log tossed onto a fire. He jerked back and let Clara go.

"We should return to your home. 'Twould be best if

you followed me. I don't want us walking down the road past the keep in case someone sees us. The sentries are all awake now."

They all turned to peer up the hill at the keep. Only the guard points on the battlement were lit by torches, but a low hum of activity reached through the night air to them.

"Aye," Clara whispered. "We should travel close to the forest, behind the smithy's home first, then the other buildings. But be careful. We don't want to trip over fences or wrench an ankle in holes or furrows."

They picked their way behind the blacksmith's house and workshop, Clara leading Brindi by the hand. Kenneth took her free hand. At the third home, a dog somewhere ahead of them heard their slinking and began to bark. The forest seemed to encroach upon them, forcing them to slip back along the road. A few people were still awake in their homes, judging by thin beams of light that escaped from under closed doors or through shuttered windows. 'Twould be easy for those awake to come out to investigate why the dog barked so.

A raindrop hit Kenneth's arm, and he felt another on his shoulder. The rain had begun, a soft spitting that confirmed what the clouds had told him earlier that day. He heard a woman's voice inside the closest house warn of the rain, and he knew immediately the weather would keep many villagers from attending midnight services. At that moment, the rain increased, turning quickly into a steady downpour.

With the sentries preoccupied by the visitors to the keep, and the rain making it more difficult for soldiers to spot them, they were able to slip close to the graveyard and the keep. Kenneth stole a look up at the top of the tower. Lord Adrien and Lady Ediva's bedchamber was up there, and through the parchment shutter, a light grew in intensity. Aye, the whole keep would be awake now. But with that, fewer sentries would be as vigilant, choosing instead to peer into the bailey to see why Taurin had arrived. The trio made it to Clara's home undetected.

Despite being soaked, Kenneth breathed a sigh of relief as he bolted the door. Of course, should Lord Taurin's men want in, 'twould not be hard to kick it in, as Kenneth himself had done a few days ago with the old door. But Lord Taurin would not overstep his authority. 'Twas not the king's standard one of his men carried, but the baron's own. Lord Eudo had traveled often with the king's flag to ease his passage and represent the king, but it would seem that Taurin did not have that luxury. At least, not tonight.

Light bled into the hut's main room and Kenneth immediately noticed Clara's worried expression.

Outside, the rain increased, though the thatch muted the steady thrum. "We're safe for the night, Clara. No one will come out in this rain."

"True." She pursed her lips. She took Brindi's cloak and her own and hung them near the fire to dry. Then she faced Kenneth. He could sense a sudden awkwardness within her. "You should retire, Clara. I suspect 'twill be a long day tomorrow and you didn't get much sleep last night."

"Aye." Clara shooed her sister into the other room. She then turned. "Kenneth, thank you for tonight. If you had not followed us, we'd have been trampled by Taurin's men, or worse, recognized by them, for surely they have a description of me from the townsfolk in Colchester who told him of my whereabouts."

"I do suspect 'twas the townsfolk, and not Lord Eudo who told him. I can't imagine that he would simply reveal where he'd sent you. That letter Lord Eudo wrote implied that he didn't trust Taurin at all."

She bit her lip. "Did you really read that letter? I mean, read it like the chaplain reads from the Bible?" she asked softly, almost in awe.

"Aye. Before I became Lord Adrien's squire, I had learned my numbers and letters. 'Tis rare to be taught, I know, but our parish priest had offered the lessons to the boys in our village. I suspect he wanted to see who was capable of doing his job, for he was an old man and was also our village chronicler. He needed someone to replace him."

"You weren't chosen?" A small smile lifted the corners of her mouth. "You weren't the most capable of learning to read?"

He thought a moment, then laughed abruptly. "Nay. In fact," he said with a chuckle, "the most apt pupil was a girl. Adela was her name, and she dressed in her brother's clothes and slipped into the chapel that first day with hopes of learning her letters and numbers."

Clara's eyes widened. "Was she caught?"

"Aye. Her brother denounced her immediately. But our old priest agreed to teach her and she learned well. I, however, only wanted to squire a knight and not bother with foolish lessons. It reflected in my studies, I'm ashamed to say."

"You must have learned enough if you could read that missive."

"It worked out well. Lord Adrien took me as his squire when he was barely an adult himself. He continued my lessons, for his family has ties to the royal court and could afford to school their boys. I've learned consistently since."

Silence dropped between them. Kenneth found himself staring at her in the dim light from the fire and the lamp. Clara was lovely, with her pale skin and with hair so unique a color that it competed with the flames for boldness and with the world for words. He felt like a fool struggling to define its beauty, for he knew no words to describe her effectively.

Then she smiled softly, and at once, his attention to her hair broke and he found himself drawn to her lips again.

The need to touch her lips with his flared within him. Immediately, he pulled himself back emotionally. "Clara, I need to go to the keep and find out Lord Taurin's plans."

She swallowed and nodded. Then, looking away, she moved toward the curtain.

"Clara?"

She pivoted when Kenneth spoke. "Aye?"

"I know Rowena needs you, but 'tis a hard rain and the night is as black as pitch. Promise me you won't slip away again tonight."

She paused. "I promise."

For the first time, Kenneth saw resignation in her eyes. She'd shown worry, confusion and pensiveness as she worked out plans in her mind, but tonight, she was exhausted and resigned to stay inside.

Also for the first time, Kenneth actually believed her words. And with that realization came a wash of compassion.

"Good night, then. I shall be asleep should you return," she whispered, drawing back the curtain to step behind it.

"Good night. But, Clara, I will not sleep."

She sighed. "I just told you I won't leave."

"'Tis not why I'm going into the keep. We need to know what Taurin wants. Someone will still be awake who'll know what his plans are."

"He plans to find me and force me to tell him where Rowena is!"

"But how and when? He has to find you first. And I need to know what Lord Adrien intends to do with him." He stepped closer. "Trust me, Clara. I won't reveal where you are, and I will tell the men to say nothing, as well. Do you trust me with that?"

Clara blinked, swallowed and finally nodded. "Aye. You saved my life tonight. And Brindi's, too. The least I can do is trust you this one time."

He smiled, albeit briefly, at her. A part of him too big for its own good flared up, wanting to stay here with Clara. So rarely had he seen the softer, more feminine side of her. 'Twould be nice to explore it.

To kiss her.

Nay. Such would only distract him. After freeing his cloak from the bed he'd made and tossing it around his shoulders, he disappeared into the wet night.

Chapter Twelve

The gatekeeper was still awake and ordered the guard to open the small door. Kenneth slipped inside. The rain continued on, soaking his cloak and hitting the guard's helmet in a steady rhythm that surely caused a headache. The torch the guard held sizzled and threatened to snuff out.

"Here, Sergeant," the gatekeeper said, handing Kenneth a storm lamp. In the unceasing rain, it did very little to light his path, but the gesture was appreciated.

Kenneth made his way toward the keep's main door. The stables to the right were lit and he could hear several men settling the newly arrived horses down for the night. Taurin's courser neighed loudly, fretting and stamping its foot. Kenneth hurried on. Within the keep, little stirred, but what did felt fraught with tension, humming like the air before a lightning storm.

He spied Harry slipping into Lord Adrien's private office. As he hurried toward the boy, he stopped to peer into the Great Hall. As was the custom of soldiers, the trestle tables had been set up around the fire, and each had someone sleeping on it. All except one, the one closest to the fire. 'Twas empty and obviously set aside for Taurin. Already, several men were snoring, various rhythms rolling around the room.

Taurin had not been given Lord Adrien's office to sleep in? It had room for a good brazier to drive away the damp chill.

Did that mean that Lord Adrien distrusted the man as much as his brother did?

Kenneth looked to Harry. "What has happened?"

The boy glanced over his shoulder as he opened the door to the office. "An important baron has arrived," he whispered, looking up as Kenneth followed him in. When he shut the door, the boy peered up at the sergeant with earnest, worried eyes. "He took my sleeping bench."

"Never mind that. And I know all about Lord Taurin. What else has happened?"

Harry swallowed. "He demanded an audience with Lord Adrien. Milord rose, but said nothing would be decided tonight and he would talk to him on the morrow."

"Lord Adrien retired again?"

"Aye, he did." Harry cocked his head and listened. "Lord Taurin is awake and somewhere in the keep. I heard him walking about when I went to sleep behind the kitchen with Cook and the maids, before she kicked me out. She said I was too old to sleep with the women."

Kenneth suppressed a smile. The boy's pout suggested he had little idea what the cook meant, and indeed, for all of Harry's precociousness, he was still naive of the ways of men and women. "You have this room, though 'tis unheated. Is Lord Taurin searching the keep?"

Harry shrugged. "I don't know. Cook asked one of the guards to stay outside the door, though." Again, Harry cocked his head. "Listen! That Lord Taurin is coming back!"

The boy hurried to the door and pressed his ear against it. "He is a terrible man, sir. He ordered us all off the tables so his men could sleep, and he smacked Rypan when he didn't answer him."

Kenneth tightened his jaw. Cook's nephew, Rypan, was a simple boy who didn't speak. But he was a good worker and a slap was unwarranted. "What did Lord Taurin say to him?"

"He ordered him to curry his horses and bed them down for the night. Rypan was terrified, and when he didn't answer, Lord Taurin backhanded him." Harry held up his hand and listened. "He's speaking to his men."

Kenneth cared not for eavesdropping, nor could he hear anything, anyway. But Harry had the ears of youth, and when his eyes widened, Kenneth gave in to his curiosity and worry. "What do you hear?" he whispered.

"Lord Taurin has ordered a search of the village at daybreak."

"What kind of a search?"

"For a woman with red hair. He says they must rouse all the villagers before they dress for the day, so as to catch them unawares." Harry peered at Kenneth. "Red hair? Is he after the midwife, sir? Why?"

"Never mind. Just remember that you haven't seen her in days."

"Aye, 'tis true, anyway. But what if Lord Taurin asks where she lives?"

"He can't ask you if he can't find you. Make yourself scarce. I know you've done it before when there's been work to be done. And take Rypan with you. The boy doesn't deserve to be pummeled."

"What are you going to do, sir? They will surely find Clara at daybreak."

"Nay, they won't." Kenneth paused. "Has Lord Taurin gone into the Great Hall?"

Harry pressed his ear against the door again. "Aye, I think so. That man is as evil as they come! You can hear it in his voice. He even got mad at his horse for something about its shoe."

Kenneth eased open the door. He had to get back to Clara. What he would do, he wasn't sure, but he knew one thing. Clara had not been lying when she said how dangerous Lord Taurin was.

The corridor was empty, but he would not slip past the entrance to the Great Hall, not while there was a good chance Taurin was still awake. He moved to the right, through the kitchen and out the side door that led to the small garden.

A plan formed jot by jot in his mind as he pulled his soaking cloak closer around him. The rain beat down steadily as he made his way around the keep toward the stables. As Harry had said, Taurin had ordered that his horses be sheltered, which meant the keep's old mares were shoved outside and tethered to a post to stand in the rain. Lord Adrien's courser and Lady Ediva's fine mare, a wedding gift she had yet to ride, were safe inside, but the pair of old ponies here hung their heads.

Rypan was busy inside, tossing straw into the stalls, occasionally wiping his tears away. The boy was practically a man, but in his mind, he still lingered in childhood, and Kenneth's heart wrenched at the sight of him crying.

When the boy spied him at the door, he froze, his eyes wide with fear and his body tensed to take flight.

"Nay, Rypan," Kenneth said softly, "I am not here to discipline you. I will take two of the mares tonight and give them shelter elsewhere."

'Twas of little use to ask Rypan to explain, should anyone ask where the mares had gone, for the boy would probably not speak. Kenneth lifted his finger to his lips to indicate quiet and secretiveness, and the boy gave the briefest of nods in return.

Tethered together, the mares followed obediently as Kenneth made his way to Clara's house. He would hide them behind the house, where the encroaching forest would give them some shelter and their body heat would offer each other some warmth.

On the morrow, he would rouse Clara and Brindi before daybreak and take them away from the village. The details of his plan would fill themselves in as the night progressed, for he knew he wouldn't be able to sleep anyway. He'd be worried he'd awaken too late, to the sounds of Taurin's men breaking down the door in their search for Clara.

The horses settled for the night, Kenneth crept inside. No sounds came from the bedchamber, save the pair softly breathing in tandem. He was glad Clara had finally been able to sleep. He banked the fire, set his cloak close to it to dry and then tidied up the foodstuffs Clara had planned for Rowena.

Lord, keep her dry tonight.

The suddenness of the prayer jolted him. He had not yet considered Rowena's lodging in the form of a prayer. He shivered from the dampness. At least the night wasn't cold.

Needing to do something to pass the time, Kenneth pulled from his pocket the one thing he kept with him constantly, a few verses of Scripture he'd handwritten many years ago. The priest who'd taught him to read had made them all rewrite passages, and though his script was messy and blotted by unsteady attempts to control the ink, the words were readable. And had long since been committed to memory.

He turned up the lamp, sat down at the table and began to read, forcing himself to fight fatigue with every word and hoping the verses would give him strength.

"Clara?"

A harsh whisper pulled Clara from her sleep, and she fought it away. Her dream was pleasant and she wanted to stay in it.

"Clara!"

Something shook her, and she bolted up. Her first thought was that someone was sick, but in the semi-dark of the room, she could make out only Kenneth's long form leaning over her. Automatically, she drew up the bedclothes. "What is wrong? Why are you in here?"

"We need to leave. Now! Get dressed, and get Brindi ready. The rain has let up, but dress warmly, for there is still a drizzle. We'll break our fast later."

He disappeared back into the outer room. Still in the fog of sleep, she blinked. What was going on? 'Twas still dark out, but she could hear him moving around in the other room. Hastily, she roused Brindi and dressed her warmly. When ready, they both slipped past the curtain.

Kenneth had rearranged much of the main room and bundled a large parcel together. She looked around. Her pots and herbs and all that she needed as a healer were tucked away out of sight.

No one would know she even lived here. "What happened to my things?"

"'Tis of no importance, Clara. We must leave now." He took Brindi's hand and led them both from the hut. Clara turned left and stalled when she saw the two mares standing obediently on the flagstone path. "Where are we going? Kenneth, if you think—"

"No time for words. And nay, I do not expect you to lead me to Rowena. We're headed north." He scooped up Brindi and set her on the withers of the larger horse. When he turned, he held out his hand. "Come, Clara, show me how much better you ride. You and Brindi take the bigger one. I will ride the smaller mare."

He set his interwoven hands down at the mare's belly, and without hesitation, Clara stepped into them to mount. Neither animal had a saddle, but both were bridled and 'twas all she needed. She accepted the reins as she looped one arm around her little sister. Brindi was quiet and half asleep, and with the sense of urgency racing around Kenneth, Clara was glad that the girl was too sleepy to complain.

Indeed, feeling the tension in the drizzly predawn morning, she could not bring herself to remind Kenneth that she didn't need to show him how well she rode.

"Follow me," he said, kicking his heels into the horse's sides to urge the beast forward. They trotted onto the road and away from the village, quickly covering the distance of open field to the north of the keep.

Clara had traveled this way before a few times, for there were several landowners and a miller less than a mile north, and they'd dealt with a fever a few weeks ago. There was also an old watchtower. Was Kenneth taking them there?

Nay. Before the forest began again, Kenneth stopped. He dismounted as he spoke. "I dare not go to the watchtower, for 'tis common knowledge that people hide in it. I don't want to go as far as the gristmill, either. There is no point in putting the miller and his family at risk."

"At risk? What has happened? Has Lord Taurin hurt someone? I should be at the keep, then."

"Nay, Clara. The keep is the last place you should be. Taurin has not hurt— Nay, 'tis not true, for he smacked Rypan last night. The boy is fine. I brought us here because Taurin plans to search the homes in the village at daybreak. To search for you."

"Search? Kenneth, you promised me that Lord Adrien would not allow anything—"

"Lord Adrien knows nothing of this, I am sure," he interrupted her. "He'd already retired for the night when Harry overheard Taurin give the order to his men."

Clara dismounted and helped Brindi down. The girl's eyes widened now that she was awake and listening. Clara led the mare closer to Kenneth. They tied the reins to a large apple tree at the edge of the woods, moving to tuck the animals in behind. "Have you been awake all night?"

"Aye. There was much to do and I wanted us out of the village before the sky lightened."

Clara scanned the vista in front of them. The land rose slightly, offering them an expansive view of the village to the left and the keep ahead. Beyond, behind the village and forest, a pinkish sky reached through the light rain, barely enough to be seen yet. The day was still far off. She turned her attention to the keep. At the back end, the keep's tall tower rose high, and she noticed that below, on the bailey wall, several torches were lit. Her heart stalled. 'Twas true, what Kenneth said? Taurin would defy Adrien's authority and search the village for her?

She bit her lip and drew her cloak in closer. It had dried overnight, and she was glad for its warmth. Brindi stepped close to her and she drew her sister into her arms, throwing one section of her cloak over Brindi's thin shoulders.

"Come, Clara. Sit by this tree. 'Tis dry here."

Clara and Brindi both obeyed and found the whole section between the tree and the ponies dry. 'Twas sheltered from the north wind that had driven last night's rain, and the ground was littered with blossom petals. She leaned against the tree and shut her eyes. Kenneth eased his frame against the trunk on the opposite side and they all said nothing for a long moment.

"I'm hungry," Brindi announced.

Clara was about to soothe her, for she had no desire to break open whatever foodstuffs Kenneth had brought with him. Before she could speak, Kenneth rose and tossed off his cloak.

"Brindi, I promised you an apple. And here is an apple tree."

Clara looked up at him. "You're addled from lack of sleep. 'Tis too early for apples. The tree has just lost its petals."

"Aye, but the apples have already formed." He smiled at Brindi. "I will find the biggest and most perfect young apple and tie it with a leather thong so we can come back in the fall and know exactly where it is."

Pushing up and away from the trunk, Clara gaped at him as he grabbed a lower limb and swung his legs up like an acrobat. After hauling himself onto the branch, he began the difficult climb. The tree was old and in terrible need of pruning. It sat tall and 'twas thick with branches growing in every direction. 'Twas likely hard to squeeze between most of them. And the morning was barely light enough to see.

"Let's see here," he began as he searched the small fruit. "Where's the best one?"

Dumbfounded, with her mouth sagging open, Clara watched Kenneth agilely move through the tree. 'Twas as if he were a young boy like Harry, acting foolish for a friend. All she could do was shake her head. He was only distracting Brindi from her hunger....

Nay, Clara amended to herself as she watched him closely. He peered around, not for potentially perfect apples, but rather through the branches at the village down the slope.

She turned and followed his gaze. And swallowed hard.

The sky was considerably lighter now and 'twas easy to make out several soldiers moving about. Automatically, she confirmed that she and Brindi were safe and out of sight behind the trunk and that the ponies were also well hidden. One man on horseback waited on the road. Another carried a torch, but as the day grew, 'twould be less useful. Clara squinted, then gasped. The soldiers had dragged out the family beside her home and lined them up on the road. In the dreary morning, they'd not yet bothered to rise, and the woman's blonde hair was easily seen even through the light rain. The family huddled together, the small children tucked in between the parents.

One man indicated a height from the ground with the flat of his hand. Brindi's height. They were describing Brindi! The Saxon threw up his arms as if arguing and—

Clara gasped as one of the soldiers drew back and punched the man in the midriff. The Saxon fell forward. His wife rushed to his side, only to be shoved away.

Above, Kenneth also startled at the harsh action and Clara stole a look up at him. Their gazes locked, but with Brindi now dozing at the base of the tree, she dared not say a word.

Kenneth tore his gaze free first and returned to watching the scene unfolding below. Clara also watched as another horseman galloped out of the keep at the far end and up to the group of soldiers.

"Who is that?" she dared to whisper.

"'Tis Lord Adrien."

She bit her lip, daring not to ask if he'd joined the search.

The men on horseback spoke, but at this distance, only the broadest of movements could be seen. Finally, Lord Adrien rode away, followed by Taurin. The foot soldiers gave up their search and followed.

Clara could hear Kenneth's sigh of relief. She craned her neck upward. "Come down. Never mind the apple. Something has happened."

He looked down at her. "Lord Adrien has ordered a stop to the search. And just at the right moment. One more house…" He didn't finish his sentence.

"We're here, Kenneth. We're safe."

"Still, I am glad I brought you up here."

Clara was more than glad. But…but what had just happened here? She watched him make his way down. Her heart pounded in her throat as she realized the truth of their situation.

"You hid us."

"Aye. For your own good," he answered as he dusted himself off and picked up his cloak again.

"For *my* own good. To protect *me* from Taurin."

Fixing the brooches of his cloak, he frowned. She added, "As I have hidden Rowena."

His hands stalled. He swallowed. She could see his throat bob.

She held his gaze, refusing to let it go. "You did exactly as I did. Can you still claim 'tis best to hand Rowena and her son over to Lord Taurin? Can you just simply say that we must trust that God will work this out and that we shouldn't do anything when you did as you saw fit? Where is your faith now, Kenneth d'Entremont?"

Chapter Thirteen

Clara's words stabbed into Kenneth, their truth cutting like a double-edged sword.

He was no better than Clara. Nay, he was worse, for he'd boasted that he would trust God with this terrible situation and then had simply done what *he* thought best. He slowly fastened his cloak, but 'twas as though it choked him. He couldn't even argue with her that this was different, for 'twasn't so. He'd made a decision without prayer or petition, not even warning those in Dunmow Keep about what Taurin planned. Of course, 'twas obvious Lord Adrien had learned of it in short order, no doubt from Harry, and had corrected Taurin's assumption that he could blaze through the village as he saw fit.

But still, Kenneth had found a solution and done only what he felt was right. How could he demand now that she tell him where Rowena was?

And how could you not at least pray about this?

The internal reproach squeezed his heart. Nay, he hadn't even prayed for wisdom. He'd simply assumed he knew what was right.

He grabbed the bundle he'd brought and led Clara's mare out from its hiding place. "Let's go," he growled out.

"Where?" Clara asked him.

"Back to the hut. I'm tired and 'tis obvious that Lord Taurin will not be back searching the homes." Refusing to listen to any argument she may have, Kenneth called sharply to Brindi before scooping her up to deposit her on the larger horse. "Get on, Clara," he told her gruffly.

Wordlessly, Clara accepted his help. After he mounted the smaller mare, they both began the trot back into Little Dunmow.

At her home, Kenneth lifted Brindi off and ordered her inside. He turned to help Clara dismount, but she held the reins tightly. "What you did, 'twas not a bad thing, Kenneth." Her voice softened, gently turning into the smallest reproach. "You protected us. Do not be so hard on yourself for not knowing sooner that Lord Taurin is truly evil. Learn from your mistakes."

"It is not Lord Taurin's actions that upset me, but rather my own. I should have prayed about this. I have been telling you that you must trust God, and look at me. I'm no better than a hypocrite."

She reached out her hand and covered his as he stretched to help her down. "Kenneth, no, don't think that way. 'Tis only hypocrisy if you do it again and again, and never see the truth. Don't rebuke yourself for a lesson learned. *Please* don't. 'Twill do no good to your soul or your stomach. I know. I have rebuked myself often for speaking when I should have been silent, and it has caused many ailments inside of me."

Her hand settled on his, forcing it down to the mare's withers. He found it surprisingly warm. Aye, she'd been one to speak out of turn, far too often, but had she actually regretted such folly? Her words settled into him and, like her hand, they warmed him. And oddly, they comforted him.

His heart stumbled a bit, for no reason but a foolish one of a beautiful woman touching him.

He pulled back his hand. 'Twas just the moment of reproach that caused him to feel this way. Aye, just the moment and nothing more. He reached out to grab her, somewhat roughly, and brought her to the ground. Averting his eyes, he ordered her into the hut.

"What about the mares?"

Kenneth smacked both on their rumps and they trotted off toward the bailey gate, no doubt with warmth and food on their minds. Then, ignoring Clara's questioning look, he grabbed her hand and pulled her into the hut.

Inside, Kenneth hung up the cloaks and stoked the fire. He was dead tired, but with all that raced through his mind, he knew sleep would elude him.

"We had begun those reading lessons," Clara said softly. "Mayhap we can do them again? It's not good to sleep the day away."

He jerked back. That offer to teach her to read had been a ploy to earn her trust and discover where Rowena was. His motives of a few days ago suddenly felt shameful.

But along with being a hypocrite, would he also go back on his word? What about his promise to Lord Adrien to find the mother and child? Was he so dishonorable that he could discard that, as well?

His stomach tightened. 'Twas not fair to Clara, but how could he rescind his offer? Or tell Lord Adrien he'd been unsuccessful in discovering where Rowena was?

"You don't really want to read, do you? 'Tis not necessary for midwifery. Besides, Brindi bested you during the last lesson."

"The previous midwife could write, and so should I also learn. And I am not intimidated by Brindi."

He narrowed his eyes. "'Tis the only reason?"

Looking back at him, she shook her head too quickly. "Nay, though Brindi would be good at it. She is bright and learns quickly." After a pause, her voice dropped. "'Tis for Rowena that I want to learn. She will need to know something, anything, if she is to be more than a slave. She can farm a bit, but she was sold into slavery too young to have learned much. As the last child, and a girl, she was discarded as nothing more than a waste of time and food. It tears me apart to think her parents believed that. 'Tis hardly a Christian way. But she will need something or she'll die, for I cannot keep her hidden forever."

"You want to teach her to read?"

"Aye, and do numbers. I can do some in my head, but to write them down would be wonderful. She's so innocent now, almost foolish, but I know I can teach her many things."

He didn't answer. He was dead tired and not nearly strong enough to deal with having Clara close.

Abruptly, Clara said, "You're tired. We should nap."

"Aye." He turned away from her, lest she see more than just that. 'Twasn't just the fatigue that weakened his self-control. He also did not like that neither of their solutions with Rowena was ideal. His would see Rowena handed to a brutal master, and hers would see a life of the girl looking over her shoulder.

* * *

A sharp pounding jolted Clara awake. She jumped and rose quickly, throwing open the curtain and finding Kenneth also rising from his bed. Before she could reach the door, he was there, his sword in his hand.

"Who is it?" Kenneth barked out.

"Me, Sergeant. Harry!" A pause followed. "And two of your men."

Kenneth opened the door. Daylight spilled into the room. Squinting, Clara could see 'twas late morning. Harry stood in front of two of the soldiers under Kenneth's command. When she realized that all she wore was her under tunic, Clara stepped back behind the curtain. 'Twas likely that the men were there to see Kenneth and had no immediate need of her. Brindi turned in their bed, and as Clara threw on her cyrtel, she motioned to her sister to stay quiet.

"What is it?" Kenneth demanded.

"A message from Lord Adrien, sir," the young boy said as Clara stepped back into the main room. She was decently dressed, but her hair was still loosely braided, and while she didn't mind going bareheaded, she felt exposed as the young Norman soldiers behind Harry stared at her.

"What's the message?" Kenneth asked, stepping to the left to hide her from view. Suddenly, Clara felt her cheeks warm. She had only allowed Kenneth into her home because the small house had two rooms and he was ordered here to guard her.

Now, though, the fact he was here felt far too personal.

But necessary. Lord Taurin had prowled through the

village before daybreak, and no doubt the message Harry conveyed had something to do with that.

"Sir, Lord Adrien has ordered both of you to the Great Hall immediately."

Clara stepped forward. "Nay, I won't go! Lord Taurin is there!"

Harry frowned. "'Tis an order from Lord Adrien!"

"Never mind," Kenneth answered briskly. "Did Lord Adrien say anything else?"

"Only that Clara is to wear this." He held several pieces of material and chose one of them. "And not to say a single word from the moment she enters the bailey. All the women are to stay silent."

Clara reached past Kenneth to grab the light-colored garment. 'Twas a wimple, and judging by the quality, one of Lady Ediva's older ones, faded by the sun and basic in shape. And tailored to fit close to the head.

Kenneth peered at the wimple, then back over to young Harry's frowning face. "Just us?"

"Brindi is to report to the kitchen to help the cook," Harry answered. Then he shrugged. "Milord has ordered all the villagers into the Great Hall. All the women, even those with babes, must come. And also those from the road to Cogshale."

Cogshale? Wasn't that the road they'd taken this morning?

If he hadn't been stopped, Taurin and his men would have ridden right up to them.

Harry's blank look at Clara's realization showed that he had no idea why Lord Adrien had given such an odd command, but she knew. If Adrien was sending Harry out that far with these orders, 'twas likely that Taurin had planned to check the homes out there, also—the miller's and the landowners'. She peeked up at the guards. They either did not understand Harry's English or were as confused as Harry was. But in their hands were several other wimples and veils. Quite a few, Clara thought.

"And," Harry added, "the women are to dress modestly and the men are not to introduce any of them." With that, the boy turned, split the two soldiers behind him and left.

Kenneth closed the door. "An odd instruction indeed."

"Nay." Her hand smoothed her hair as Brindi, now dressed, appeared from the bedchamber. "Since Lord Taurin is here to find me, what better way to hide me than in a hall full of women? And Lord Adrien suspects Lord Taurin would have visited all the homes, near and far, so he plans to present the same number of women."

Kenneth frowned. Then, as if a light dawned in his brain, he nodded and smiled. "And the wimple will hide your red hair. But you are the only redhead here, so why the other wimples?"

"I suspect 'tis Lady Ediva's idea. She will no doubt say she insists on modesty for all women, and to ensure it, extra wimples are being distributed, for some of the poorer folk may only have a kerchief."

"And when Lord Taurin looks out to a sea of beautiful young women, each modestly dressed, each wearing a similar wimple, 'twould not be good form for him to insist each woman remove her headdress."

She couldn't stop her brows from shooting up. "A sea of beautiful women?"

"Aye. This village is like none I have seen before. They breed lovely women here."

"Oh." She looked down at her wimple. She sniffed, feeling oddly miffed. "I suppose so. I hadn't noticed."

"You'd best get yourself and Brindi ready. I suspect the instructions are for her protection, as well. Lord Taurin would consider it beneath him to stride into Lord Adrien's kitchens with a demand to see all the girls."

"'Tis a clever plan. I can only pray it works."

"It will, but only if you and the other women stay silent. For some it may be easy." He looked at her, one eyebrow lifted. "For others, not so."

"By others, you mean me?" Unreasonably hurt by his comments, Clara steeled her spine and lifted her chin. "All those *beautiful women* bred here will no doubt help me." With a sniff, she tossed aside the curtain and disappeared into the bedchamber.

Shortly after, Kenneth led Clara into the bailey. She wore the wimple provided her, and the traditional veil over it, with a wrought diadem, her only one, for they were very expensive. She rarely wore it and 'twas hardly as fine as others she'd seen, but 'twas needed to keep the veil from lifting away in the wind, despite the rain that had decided to revisit Dunmow.

Clara's heart stalled as she entered the keep. She had not seen so many people since the guild meeting in Colchester that resulted in her departure. There were families from far down the road, plus older women who worked under the cook's direction. So many people, several of whom seemed to press around her. 'Twas as if they had timed their arrival to coincide with hers.

Kenneth ordered Brindi to accompany the other young girls heading into the kitchens. They did not climb the main steps up the motte but went to the left, where the kitchen met the gardens. And, thankfully, probably due to the steady rain that fell, they were all ignored by the drenched guards.

Kenneth led Clara into the Great Hall, though the crowd pressing around her would have carried her forth like a spring tide racing up the Colne River. Already, soldiers lined the walls, watching the villagers with suspicion.

Each woman wore a wimple. Clara hated the smothering feeling it caused, and this one fit far too snugly over her thick hair. But she was glad for it and the veil she draped over it. 'Twas loose enough to drape into her face, its upper fringe low enough to reach her eyes.

The hall wasn't silent, but neither was it noisy. A low, anxious murmur filled the air, mixing with the scents of meals from the kitchen and the unwashed bodies of the soldiers. Clara pulled the veil over her nose to filter the pungent odors. There was no room for anyone to sit, except for the raised dais at the front that bore several comfortable chairs.

The crowd by the door parted and in walked Lord Adrien, holding his wife's hand. Margaret followed them with the babe, and a soft, appreciative murmur flowed around the room at the sight of the young heir to Dunmow.

With the keep's chaplain in tow, the ensemble headed for the dais.

'Twas like a celebration of presenting the babe, but when Lord Taurin strode into the hall, the mood snapped back like a new leather thong.

Taurin waited for the lord and lady of the manor to be seated before he addressed them.

After his greeting, he snarled, "'Tis not a festival, Lord Adrien. Why are all these people here?"

Adrien looked blandly around the room. "I caught you rummaging through Little Dunmow before the sun even rose, without the king's standard or warrant. I thought mayhap you should first meet those poor villagers you wish to search. *My people.*"

Clara held her breath. They were deep in the crowd, she and Kenneth, and she could no longer see Taurin's face as he had his back to the crowd. But she heard his growl clearly.

"Lord Adrien has subtly reminded Taurin that his brother often carries the king's standard and therefore is more likely to have the king's ear than Taurin," Kenneth leaned back and whispered into her ear.

She nodded, daring not to speak. Was it wise to raise Taurin's ire?

"Lord Adrien," Taurin called out, his voice turning smoother, "I am not here to take lives, but to save them."

"You rode into my keep late last night and demanded an audience. This morning you terrorized my village until I put a stop to it." Adrien spread out his hands. "I promised you last night you would be heard. What is it that you need?"

"I need my son!"

Clara peeked through the crowd to see Adrien lift his palms heavenward. "I don't have your son. Neither does anyone here, that I know of."

"My slave has my son!"

"Slavery has been outlawed, Lord Taurin. You cannot have a slave."

Taurin's spine stiffened. But not in defense, Clara was sure. Not with the way his head tipped knowingly to one side. It seemed he was prepared for that and had an answer at the ready. A chill raced down her spine as she wondered what he would say.

"Nay, 'tis against the law to have a *Christian* slave.

The girl and her family don't follow our faith. They are pagan."

Clara gasped. Kenneth turned slightly. "Is this true?"

"I don't know," she stammered softly. "I didn't ask Rowena. Is it that important?"

"Aye, or else Taurin would not remind Lord Adrien. It could change everything."

Her throat hurt and she swallowed to soothe it. Was it possible? Clara had not dared to take her to the church for services, nor had the girl asked to go. Holding her breath, she snaked out her hand to grip Kenneth's arm. If what Taurin said was true, 'twould be dangerous for Rowena. The law didn't protect her.

But Rowena was young and naive, having lived all her life in an isolated farm. Mayhap she'd not even heard the Good News, for there were many who still chose to follow the old pagan ways.

A wash of worry poured down Clara's frame. Next time she saw her, she would ask Rowena. Yet, as she decided this, fresh worry rinsed like cold water through her. What if Taurin was right?

Taurin spoke again, and the hairs on Clara's arms prickled. "The girl is my mistress. I only want to see that she's safe."

"Then go get her."

"I have yet to find her!" With that remark, Taurin's voice thinned, his patience obviously stretching to the limit. "If I knew where my mistress was, Lord Adrien, I wouldn't have ridden in late last night. But you have a woman here who knows where she is!"

"And who is this woman?"

"Her name is Clara. She's your midwife. She has a sister named Brindi."

Bands of steel wrapped around Clara's chest. She could barely breathe, and what little breaths she took caused spots to dance through her vision. Kenneth's hand found hers and squeezed it tightly. The pressure ached the healing cut in her palm, but Clara made no move to pull away. Indeed, she stood stock-still, afraid the crowd around her would part and leave her open to Taurin. Somewhere to the left, a babe cried, followed by a toddler's howl. A soft voice tried to soothe both children.

Again, she was thankful for the wimple and veil, which she'd drawn modestly over her cheeks and nose. The crowd around her, people whom she'd met only briefly, did not even glance her way. All were mesmerized by the confrontation in front of them.

She squeezed Kenneth's hand in return, all the while sending up a prayer of thanks that God had given him to her, if only for a few days.

Aye, Kenneth was a comfort, she thought, biting her lip. He'd been a disturbance in her home, and yet his very presence comforted her. He was here, protecting her.

Ahead of them, Lord Adrien rose. "I will not hand over anyone to you simply because you demand it. These people look to me for protection. I pledged to God, to my wife and to them I would keep them safe. What do you plan to do with this woman? Does she not have the right to certain protections?"

"She will tell me where my mistress is!"

"No God-fearing man should have a mistress!" the chaplain interrupted. Clara wet her lips. So true were those words, but they were often ignored.

After a glance to the chaplain, Lord Adrien turned to Taurin. "Even our king obeys that commandment, for he loves his queen very much." His stern expression deepened. "How will you extract your information from this midwife? Your reputation is not one of gentleness."

"The way I get answers is of no concern to you, Lord Adrien. The woman has wronged a Norman, and she should be punished."

"I have no proof she has wronged you or any other Norman, Lord Taurin." Adrien's voice remained cold and calm. "I cannot see how any Saxon woman here *could* wrong a Norman. You should already have realized by now that my village is filled with modest women who don't speak to strange men. It took me a year before some would even look me in the eye, so I doubt any of them could have wronged you or any Norman here. And because I vowed to protect them, I certainly cannot allow any one of these good women to enter into *your* care."

Lord Adrien then sighed. "But, anticipating your request and in all fairness to you, I have assembled all the women of the village, and you may question any of them, here and now, with all of us as chaperones."

Taurin spun and several ladies in the front row shrank back. Clara had to admire Lady Ediva's ingenuity. Her idea to have each woman wear a wimple and modest dress was perfectly in keeping with Lord Adrien's words. Aye, even the weather today favored the modest clothing.

Taurin's glare raked through the crowd, with women looking away or pressing closer to their menfolk. Clara fought her instinct to glare back at him. But she, like others, kept her gaze averted and downcast.

He spun back to face Lord Adrien. "These women are all wearing wimples! I cannot tell their hair color! How am I supposed to find the right woman?"

"Why would you want to know their hair colors?"

"You know why! Order them to remove their wimples, de Ries!"

Calling Lord Adrien by his last name did not amuse the man. Clara swallowed and crept closer to Kenneth. He held her hand tightly in encouragement.

Abruptly, the chaplain pushed to his feet. "Lord Taurin! 'Tis an inappropriate order and ill-mannered of you to demand it!"

Aah, so that was the reason for the chaplain's presence on the dais.

Taurin growled out something Clara didn't catch. Then he drew in a breath and stood tall. "My apologies, Lord Adrien. 'Twas indeed an unnecessary demand. I am only beside myself with worry for my child. But know this. I will keep searching until my last breath for the babe, for all of *my* people are precious to me, as yours are to you." He dipped his head in a show of respect.

"But if it pleases you, my Lord Adrien," Taurin went on, "I would like to stay for a short time. Last night, my courser threw a shoe, and 'twill need to be shod again. Have you a farrier here?"

"Aye, our smithy shoes horses. My squire will take care of your horse."

"Nay. My mount is willful and strong. I have seen your squire and he is too small to handle him. I would prefer that my courser be put into—" Taurin waved his hand carelessly about "—your sergeant at arms' hands. The horse is valuable to me."

"Valuable?" she whispered so very low that only Kenneth could hear. "He cursed the animal last night and ran it with a shoe missing!"

Adrien stared at Taurin. Clara could not believe the strength of willpower within the man. He, nor his wife, nor the chaplain, even glanced her way. Nor did any others. Lord Adrien must have great control over the people here and over his men, for not once did any of them look her way.

Of course! 'Twas no doubt part of the plan to keep her anonymous.

"As you wish, Lord Taurin. Where is my sergeant?"

"Sir!" Kenneth released Clara's hand and stepped forward through the crowd, sideways slightly so that the parting of people would not reveal Clara. Her heart leaped briefly at his forethought.

Kenneth stood beside Lord Taurin, and Clara could see that he was slightly taller. "See to Lord Taurin's mount," Lord Adrien said. "Ensure it is properly shod."

"Aye, my lord."

"So, Lord Taurin," Adrien said, rising. "I see that the rumor of you devastating villages and scaring women is only that. You *are* a reasonable man. And my people can return to their homes safe in the knowledge you will not harm them." He smiled. "I knew 'twas so. No Norman who has pledged himself to King William would be so cruel. And I can see that you are faithful in your pledges. The next time I am in London, I will be sure to mention your *honorable nature* to King William."

The veiled threat lingered above all in the Great Hall like a heavy smoke, and Clara allowed herself to ease out the breath she'd been holding.

She dared one last glance at Kenneth as he stood beside Taurin. Taurin nodded curtly toward the dais before striding out. Kenneth, without looking her way, exited with him.

The crowd filed out after them, and Clara was careful to position herself in the center. She peeked out from under the veil and tight wimple to meet Lady Ediva's eyes. The woman looked at her, but 'twas the shortest of looks.

As she exited the keep on swift feet, Clara spied Kenneth leading a big stallion through the bailey gates with several of Taurin's men in tow. She glanced swiftly around, all the while being bumped by the crowd of villagers as they hurried down the steps. She didn't blame them one jot. Taurin had a way of scaring the most stalwart person, with the exception of a few Normans like Kenneth and Adrien. She was glad Brindi wasn't there.

Clara turned. Only one woman trotting down the steps met her gaze and 'twas only briefly. Clara looked away, moving sideways toward the kitchen garden. There, in the shelter of where the keep nearly touched the outer bailey wall, the cook sat preparing some roots for supper. She looked up, her face a mask of disapproval.

"I'm looking for Brindi," Clara said.

"I sent her to help the smithy's wife. Those were her two babes you heard crying in the Great Hall. Brindi knows the boys, so I sent her to help the family."

Clara gasped. Brindi had walked straight to where Taurin's men would be! And the smith's wife, Gwynth— or worse, the older babe, a toddler whose speech was strong—could easily call out her unusual name!

Chapter Fourteen

Clara hurried as quickly as she could through the bailey gate without drawing attention to herself. To her left was the path to the village. It divided, with one branch leading to the smithy's house. Clara glanced feverishly about, but Brindi was nowhere in sight. She speeded her steps.

Behind the small house was the smithy's forge, and there she spied the back end of a large horse, its tail swishing. Clara stopped at the door to the house and rapped quietly, hoping that Gwynth and not Brindi would open it.

Her knocking wasn't quiet enough, and out of the corner of her eye, she spied two men peering around the corner of the smithy.

Kenneth and another Norman soldier, the one who'd spoken to Taurin last night, frowned at her. Immediately, Clara stilled and drew her veil up modestly. Kenneth turned, ignoring her completely.

The soldier looked to Kenneth. Her basic French caught the question "Who is she?"

Kenneth glanced again across the short distance of hard-packed ground to meet her eyes. And for that moment, Clara had no idea what Kenneth might say. Nor could she read his expression, it seemed so bland and uninterested.

He shrugged and answered in a mix of French and English. *"Une aimee. A godsibb."*

A gossipy friend? Clara flushed and kept her face averted. Immediately, Gwynth opened the door. Clara hurried inside. "Is Brindi here?" she whispered after she shut the door firmly.

"Nay. I sent her home." Gwynth took Clara's hands in hers. "'Tis obvious that Lord Taurin will do everything he can to find you. You should leave."

"They know I'm here. Now I must trust in Kenneth d'Entremont to protect me."

"The man out there with the horse? My husband likes him, but he isn't a baron like Lord Taurin. What power does he have?"

The voices from the shop rose, and Clara moved toward the door. "I should get back home. I don't want Brindi to be alone."

She slipped out, pausing after a few steps. Kenneth was explaining to the smithy in English what needed to be done.

"Will you finish the shoeing today?" the Norman soldier asked the smithy, also in English.

"Nay." The smithy set down the big stallion's leg after inspecting it. "This courser has large hooves. I'll need most of morning on the morrow to get the fire hot enough to make the new shoe."

"The morning? Start it now, Saxon. 'Tis only just after noon."

The smithy shook his head. "Wood alone cannot get my forge hot enough. I'll need dried peat."

"Then get some."

"I need to find some first." He glared at the soldier. "I know of one place, but I cannot get it this afternoon."

"Why not?"

Clara swallowed as the smithy frowned and answered, "'Tis too far for me to go and return. I will not leave when the sun is dropping. The peat bog is not safe after dark."

"'Tis only a bog. Why would it not be safe?"

The beefy Saxon paused. Then, looking uncomfortable, he finally said, "Last week, I went to dig peat and set it up to dry. I heard someone in the bog. I couldn't see him, but he was there."

"Just another Saxon digging peat. Ignore him. None of you are allowed in the forests anyway, though we know you hide your thieves in there. Mayhap we should go with you."

The smithy bristled. "Whoever it is has scared off others, too. There are rumors of whispers in the wind and things tossed at visitors. I heard a fearful cry once that would freeze your bones. I can't say what or who was there, but it followed me last week and stole my lunch."

Immediately, Clara pressed her back against the smith's house and drew her hand to her mouth to stem a gasp. She hadn't seen any evidence that the peat bog was still used. That was why she'd chosen it. But the smithy used it, and apparently others, as well. She leaned her head against the rough daub of the wall as she tried to order her heart to stop pounding.

This was the moment she had long dreaded. Could she flee now and get Rowena away before the smithy returned for peat?

Please, Lord in Heaven, keep Rowena safe.

The Norman laughed. "I was about to say you were a superstitious fool, blacksmith, but 'tis obvious that some of your fellow Saxon curs have followed you and stolen from you."

Clara dared another glance around the corner. But all she could see was the smithy level his stare at the Norman. "I won't be able to shoe this horse if I am attacked by one of those *Saxon curs* who is forced to hide from your fool Norman laws."

The horse snorted between the smithy and the Norman. The blacksmith lifted his hand to soothe the nervous beast. Aye, Clara thought. The horse smelled the tension between the men.

The soldier waved his hand. "So your fellow Saxons like to dig peat between attacks against innocent Normans? Are you a man or a timid boy afraid he'll lose his next meal?"

The smithy lifted his chin and folded his arms. "Say what you like, Norman, but I will not dig peat after the noon hour. Someone evil lives in the bog, and 'twould do you no good should I be injured. I care not that my lunch was stolen, but whilst I dig peat, who knows who could come up to me and crack me on the head? Where would your master's horse be then?"

Despite wishing the smithy would stop talking, Clara had to smile. He stood up to Taurin's soldier well.

"Enough!" Kenneth ordered. "Even if he did have the peat, he couldn't work into the night. Do you see any lanterns to light this shop? Let it go, soldier."

The Norman stepped forward to close the distance between him and the blacksmith. "Very well, but be warned. People around here may say that Lord Adrien has the king's ear, but so does Lord Taurin. Should the king learn you delayed his knight due to fear of some old hermit, it will not bode well for you or this village."

Peeking around the corner, Clara bit her lip. Would this argument come to blows? From the corner of her eye, she spied another of the new soldiers closing in and hurried onto the path toward the center of the village, praying all the while that Kenneth would not be caught in any fray that might start.

Her concern was for naught. As she tried to walk casually away, she could hear Kenneth end the argument. "Soldier, return to the keep. 'Tis a pointless argument and the rain is not making your temper any better." He spoke to the smith. "Keep this horse in your stable. And be up at dawn to harvest your peat. You have the afternoon free of work, so I suggest you use it wisely. Mayhap you should prepare for the task ahead."

Neither the soldier nor the smithy answered. Clara kept up her steady pace, hoping that the two soldiers, the one who argued and the one who seemed to have appeared out of nowhere, would pay her no mind. To them, she was nothing, and she was glad for it.

A few paces along, she noticed the soldiers had headed back to the bailey, and she eased out the breath she'd been holding.

Until someone grabbed her elbow.

She started and grabbed it back. But Kenneth took it again and led her through the rain toward her house, saying nothing. As they made their way out of sight of the bailey gate, Clara judged his mood. By the way he gripped her elbow, she would say his temper had been thinned by the argumentative pair he'd just left.

He said nothing until they reached her house. He closed the door behind him. "You shouldn't have followed me down to the smith's. You were being ignored up to that point."

She felt her cheek warm and busied herself removing the soaked veil and choking wimple. Her cloak weighed heavily, too, and as she peeled it off she peeked into the small bedroom to see that Brindi had decided to lie down on the pallet. Her eyes were closed. Poor thing was tuckered out. "I'm sorry. I went there to look for Brindi. The cook in the keep sent her to Gwynth to help her with her boys. I didn't want one of them to call out her name. Taurin had already mentioned it." She eyed Kenneth carefully. "'Twas a tense situation at the smithy."

Abruptly, he looked up from his task of removing his cloak. Their eyes met squarely, his drilling into her soul until Clara was sure he could see every secret she was keeping.

"Nothing unusual," he said, still studying her closely. "I have handled worse. I think that Lord Adrien did well today. We will see Lord Taurin depart on the morrow, empty-handed."

"Aye, Lord Adrien and Lady Ediva are quite clever. You did well, also."

Slowly, a smile eased onto Kenneth's lips. "As I live and breathe, I never thought I would hear a compliment from your mouth. I shall die a happy man."

She sniffed. "Just not in my home, please. I merely meant that you did well with the smithy and that soldier. It could have come to blows."

"Aye. Two stubborn men arguing over a horse's shoe of all things. 'Tis foolish."

'Twas foolish indeed, but the smithy had been adamant about not going into the bog late in the day. Was it Rowena he felt watching him? Clara wouldn't have thought it possible that the girl would try to scare the man away. But a free lunch sitting there by the bog would be too much temptation for a hungry, nursing mother.

Most likely, Rowena was caught outside and took advantage of the available food. The smithy probably heard the babe and thought him an animal.

Kenneth pulled off his cloak. "Let's hope that the soldier doesn't go to the bog this afternoon to harvest the peat for himself."

Clara's gaze shot up, as did her eyebrows, as she gasped. "Would he? Does he suspect—" She clamped shut her mouth. Then, realizing that silence would only add to any suspicion, she continued, "I mean, would he do it to prove he was braver than the smith? To curry favor with Lord Taurin?"

Kenneth stepped closer, his focus honing in on Clara as he draped his wet cloak over the end of the table near the embers of the morning's fire. She tensed.

"Mayhap he might go there to prove his bravery," Kenneth answered smoothly.

She turned her head to watch him remove his surcoat, that outer tunic of a simple design. He tipped his head and studied her until she was forced to wrench free her gaze and sit there on the bench, feeling his presence as close as the dampness of the day. She could smell the faint odor of mint and mallow around him, the herbs he'd washed with earlier.

"Clara?"

She shot him another look. He was even closer now as he spoke. "Or mayhap he has put together the clues and knows where Rowena is."

Chapter Fifteen

An icy hand gripped Clara's heart. She heard her own gasp before she realized she'd given herself away.

"I'm right, aren't I?"

Tears threatened, and she hated that they chose that moment to arrive. She reached forward and grabbed his tunic. Automatically, he snagged her arms to capture her movement. Like her, he was wet from the persistent rain. Everything they wore was damp and cold. Her heart twisted in her chest to think that, out there in the bog, Rowena lay huddled in a peat cutter's hut, a hut that probably leaked rain like a tree in spring. But she was still safer there than in Lord Taurin's grasp.

"Please, Kenneth, leave Rowena alone. Don't say a word to anyone! If you tell Lord Adrien, he may tell Lord Taurin! And if you go to her yourself, surely you'll be noticed, and one of those soldiers will follow you and discover her!"

He pulled her closer. "Clara, what have you done?"

She looked away. "I had no idea that the smithy used that peat in his fires! The bog is old and very small. I thought it had not been used since the Romans were here."

"You must have known the peat would be used, especially by the smith!"

"Nay, the smithy in Colchester used coal brought in from the west."

He leaned forward, disbelief hanging so heavily on his features, it almost changed his whole appearance. He shook his head slowly. "You left Rowena and her babe in a *bog?* You say you have sworn to never hurt anyone, but you abandoned a new mother and child in a bog?"

"Nay, not abandoned! There's a hut there. The smithy must not have noticed it or else paid it no mind. 'Tis mossy and low and almost completely hidden. The bog is nearly gone, for the nearby channels dug years ago have drained the land. I heard of it just before I was ordered to come here, from visitors to Colchester who said even those Saxons who defy King William's curfew were afraid to go there. I hid Rowena in it because 'twas closer to Dunmow than where I kept her before. You know I have been going there most nights, delivering food and checking on them. Only since this rain have I not been."

"It can't be healthy for her to stay there." He lifted his brows and eased his grip. "Well, at least there is peat to burn for warmth."

"Nay. Rowena is afraid to light a fire in the hut for fear of drawing notice. I don't even know if she has the sense to know she *can* burn peat." Clara caught him with a fresh grip. "Oh, Kenneth, tell me you won't say a word about her location! You've met Lord Taurin. You've seen him now! Would you trust a child to his care? Why, he hasn't even brought a cart in which to carry the babe, should he even find him!"

The tears swelled, and she felt them roll down her cheeks. Kenneth blurred in front of her and her throat hurt. When she pulled in a breath, it wobbled and wheezed like a set of broken bellows.

"Taurin would take Rowena with him."

"So the girl is to ride with a babe, when she probably can't ride at all? And ride to her death?"

If Kenneth had an answer for her, he kept it to himself. Clara swallowed and peeked up at him. His brows were furrowed, his lips a tight, thin line, Kenneth was worried.

"Let's pray that she's still alive, for the day is cold and the girl can't be strong."

"Nay, she's not. She was too young to have motherhood forced on her." Her heart squeezed again, and grief crimped her throat.

Then, with a sigh, Kenneth moved his hands up to cup her face. With his thumbs, he wiped away the tears that wet her cheeks. Immediately, 'twas as if her fears drained away. It felt so good to have him hold her, and she pressed her eyes shut to savor the moment.

She must be addled to want his nearness when she knew she'd disappointed him so. But she couldn't help her feelings, even knowing he would most likely leave in the next minute to report Rowena's whereabouts to Lord Adrien.

Please don't leave, Kenneth. Please stay here with me.

Aye, she was indeed addled to think he would stay. Addled to want him here and not only because the alternative would result in Rowena's capture. She'd never felt such a desire for a man's presence as she felt for

Kenneth's. He was everything that was wrong for her. He was a soldier, a Norman in a land where Normans weren't wanted. And while she'd pledged never to do harm, always to help the sick and injured, he was a soldier who'd battled his way from Hastings to London with his soldier king. He would kill, while she must heal and help.

What a fool she was! She must be, for here, now, with Kenneth holding her face and wiping her tears, all she knew was how much she wanted Kenneth to hold her.

"Kenneth, forgive me. Hold me."

"Aye." His word brushed over her like a breeze at the beach. His eyes drifted shut, urging hers to follow. She could feel him shorten the scant distance between them. She knew his head tipped to the left, and she knew she did the same.

She hadn't ever kissed a man before, but she knew immediately that the first time was going to happen and there was nothing she could do about it.

And nothing she wanted to do about it.

Kenneth pulled her closer, dipping his head just as his lips touched hers. The kiss wasn't what she expected. Weren't kisses supposed to be passionate, out-of-control things that were so full of emotion that they swept a woman away? 'Twas what the minstrels sang of and poets crooned of, wasn't it?

Yet Kenneth merely brushed her lips with his, so lightly she could scarcely feel it. She didn't feel as though she was being swept away. Instead, with breath held, she felt as though she was clinging to a rock as the tide surged in, threatening to swallow her whole.

Suddenly, Kenneth's kiss deepened, growing more forceful and demanding. Her reply came from that passionate sea, where she was being tossed by the wind and swept along like a piece of flotsam upon the water.

Still, she opened herself to him, kissing him back and clinging to him with the ferocity of a life afraid to die.

'Twas wonderful. Clara had never considered a kiss would be so wonderful, but 'twas so.

But was it only a ploy to divert her attention from Rowena?

He released her face and wrapped his arms around her, moving his mouth to her cheek, her ear, the hair that was finally free of that terribly constrictive wimple. His whole frame pressed against her, and she reveled in the feel of his warmth and strength.

Then she recalled Rowena.

She stepped out of his arms. A maid's first kiss should be exciting, born from love for her man, carrying with it a promise of a life together. It should be a kiss shared at the altar, not one built on shame and subterfuge.

Kenneth stiffened. "On the morrow, we will decide what needs to be done with Rowena."

Her traitorous tears welled up again. Nay, she was sure Kenneth had kissed her to distract her from trying to convince him to stay quiet about Rowena.

Nothing had changed.

Except that she was in danger of caring too much for Kenneth. And of Rowena being returned to a man who would surely kill her.

Kenneth knew his words had frightened Clara, and he wished with all his pounding heart that he could pluck them from the air between them and toss them into the fire.

But what had been said *was* true. They would deal

with Rowena on the morrow, for he couldn't decide to-night. Their kiss seemed to smother his good sense and he dared not do something he might later regret.

In front of him, Clara spun and began to stir the embers to rekindle the fire. Her movements were jagged and harsh, born of shaking hands.

Kenneth didn't need a fire, for her kiss had warmed him to his very core. But performing other tasks gave them both something to focus on other than the passion that had arced between them like lightning from the clouds to the earth.

The steady beat of rain outside increased. Muted by the thatch, its sound was almost a hum. What he could see of the day was fast dwindling. Brindi slept on soundly, as only a child could sleep.

"I should return to the keep to ensure Lord Taurin hasn't turned his anger on someone else, like Rypan, again."

Clara's attention shot up with alarm. "To the keep?"

He swallowed. "Aye. Clara, I have promised you that we will decide what to do with Rowena on the morrow. Too much has happened today, and I fear our emotions will tamper with our good judgment. And Taurin must be watched, even though he doesn't know where to find you."

Throwing on his damp cloak, Kenneth stepped outside into the rain. The weather had worsened, and he spied his carved apple set out to dry. 'Twould never do so in this weather. He pulled his hood up and pushed through the rain toward the keep.

Where the road met the path to the bailey gate, Kenneth turned, half expecting to see Clara hurrying down the lane after him. But the road was wet and empty.

All remained quiet. Feeling unexpectedly disappointed, he moved along the path. The gateman let him in, and he hurried up the motte and into the keep through the kitchen. He found the cook and two maids preparing vegetables for the morrow's meal. Hovering at the edge of the glow of lanterns was Rypan, obviously too fearful to return to the stables and mayhap hoping for a bite to eat. The cook was his aunt, and Kenneth knew she would often slip him extra food when she thought no one was looking.

"Next time, keep Brindi with you," Kenneth told the cook. "'Twas dangerous to send her out among those soldiers."

The cook frowned. "The smith's wife was struggling with her children and needed someone to help. But aye, sir, I won't allow her out again."

Kenneth nodded. "What is happening in the hall tonight?"

"Lord Adrien and Lord Taurin are discussing battle foolishness there. Milady has retired for the evening. I can't say I'll be sad when that Lord Taurin puts Dunmow Keep at his back and is gone for good. The castle has been in an uproar since he arrived and that was only last night. Word is that he'll be gone on the morrow."

Rypan jerked, catching Kenneth's attention. He shook his head so quickly, the sergeant wondered if 'twere just a twitch due to his condition.

Kenneth bade the cook goodbye and walked out into the corridor. The Great Hall was noisy with the sounds of men, but this stretch of space was empty. Sensing someone behind him, he turned.

Rypan stood there, nearly as tall as Kenneth, but far lankier, all elbows and knees. "What is it, Rypan?"

The boy rarely spoke and now he bit his lip.

The cook appeared behind the boy. "Is something wrong?"

Kenneth nodded. "Rypan wants to say something."

The cook took her nephew's arm gently. "Rypan, you can tell us. What do you need to say?"

Rypan peered down at his shifting feet. His body shook. Kenneth felt sorry for both aunt and nephew. Rypan was addled most of the time, and for as long as Kenneth had been here, he'd only heard Rypan mutter a few words.

"I have a sweetmeat saved for you, Rypan," the cook coaxed. "Tell us what you need to say. Slowly."

"Taurin won't leave…m-morrow. P-plans," he stuttered.

"What would you know of his plans?" the cook asked, her voice still calm. She'd had years of experience with him and obviously cared for the boy.

Still, darting his gaze to Kenneth, Rypan began to back up. Knowing that the boy would soon flee, Kenneth smiled at him, telling the cook calmly, "'Tis very good. He deserves that sweetmeat, doesn't he, Cook?"

The woman looked doubtful but went off to retrieve the pastry as Kenneth led Rypan back into the far corner of the kitchen.

Alone with Rypan for just a moment, Kenneth asked quietly, "Did you overhear Lord Taurin speak?"

"He p-plans to find C-Clara," Rypan whispered.

Amazed that Rypan sounded so lucid, Kenneth stepped back. He wanted to ask more, but the cook had returned, and Rypan snatched the sweetmeat and bolted away. Kenneth looked to the cook. "Rypan says Taurin plans to find our midwife."

"He said all that?" the cook asked. With a sigh, she shook her head. "I suppose he could. He's been growing up fast, and he likes Clara. She refuses to give him that horrid root the old midwife dosed him with. Mayhap his head is finally clearing. But how would we know what Rypan says is true? What if he's confused?"

"I saw his expression change when you mentioned Lord Taurin leaving." Just as he'd seen Clara's expression before he left her hut. At the mention of the bog, she'd looked worried. "Nay, I believe him."

Kenneth bade the cook good-night and stepped back into the corridor. Guards in front of Adrien's office chamber told him the two barons were inside talking. A shame for Kenneth, as he would have liked to consult the maps stored there.

Far to the right behind the keep stood the stables. With Taurin's courser at the smith's, only one horse was relegated to the outdoors. Ahead of Kenneth, the chapel door was shut tight. Above, two torches burned on the battlement, though should this heavy rain continue, they would not last much longer. Kenneth let himself out of the gate and hurried along the road that divided the village from the keep.

If Rypan was right, Taurin was planning something. But what? With his courser still unshod, 'twould be difficult for him to leave. Regardless, Kenneth decided, he needed to be with Clara. When he entered her home, he turned and bolted the door.

Clara had built up the fire and heated some leftover stew for both of them. After checking on her sister, she stepped back into the main room, looking tired herself. He rose to serve her some stew, which she gratefully received.

Sitting beside him, Clara shut her eyes as she said grace. When it was completed, he noticed, she stayed still for a moment, quietly inhaling the aroma of the hot food. Finally, she opened her eyes and began to eat.

"You regret my knowing Rowena's location, don't you?"

"Aye," she answered quietly.

He grimaced at the mistrust and the sudden change it provoked in her. She was not a quiet, reserved type of woman, but rather strong, willful and bold. Tonight, 'twas as if fear and nerves had trapped her character and bound her mouth.

Regret rushed through him. Now that he knew Rowena's location, his duty here was finished. He should return to the keep and inform Lord Adrien.

Nay, he'd promised Clara that they would wait until the morn, when the sun put right all the fears of the night before.

He had the luxury of this one last evening with her. But 'twas hardly a luxury, with her so worried and both of them knowing Rowena was out in the bog. Too soon, they would have to make a decision.

He gritted his teeth. He certainly didn't want Lord Taurin to ride off with a babe after beating Rowena. And since Rowena might not be a Christian, there would be nothing to stop Taurin from taking her with him, as well—back into the brutal life she had fled before.

Kenneth found his eyes narrowing. "You didn't ask Rowena about her faith? 'Tis hard to believe England is not fully Christian by now."

She looked at him. "Sometimes, Christianity is just a veil. And an isolated community could continue believing what they always had." She sighed. "Taurin is crafty.

If Rowena is a pagan, he has the right to keep her. But he will punish her for running away."

His mouth thinning, Kenneth set down his spoon and pondered Clara's words. Intrigue was rife in royal circles, and while Lord Eudo and Lord Adrien were honest, faithful men, not all barons were that dedicated to justice. Such subterfuge was usually reserved for people seeking to gain power. Kenneth could well believe that Taurin was as ambitious as he was ruthless, but what role did the slave play in his schemes? Rowena could hardly assist in Taurin's bid for power.

But could her child? Taurin was just a baron, and the title was not hereditary. But he might have family or influence back in Normandy that would require a son to carry on the family wealth.

Still, any inheritance would come only after Taurin's death, so what would he care? It made no sense.

Kenneth rubbed his light beard as he shoved away his bowl. Regardless, could he simply hand over the woman or child to a man as cruel as Taurin?

Mayhap, if he requested that Lord Adrien keep the woman safe. Nay, Lord Adrien may be able to save Rowena's life, but he still believed that the child was better off with his father, and that would end in Rowena and the child being separated. What would they feed it? The babe would surely die before they found a nursing mother. And he'd heard enough of Clara's midwifery advice to know that the boy would not nurse if terrified.

Even if the best answer was to drop into his lap, Kenneth wasn't sure he would recognize it. If Taurin left without his child, Rowena would struggle in poverty, free, aye, but free to die from sickness or starvation. If Taurin found the babe, he'd be separating them, most likely by death. If Lord Adrien discovered them, he would save the child and mother, but mayhap also separate them. Clara would be hurt by any of these possibilities. And the idea of hurting Clara sat heavily in his belly. So heavily, he couldn't eat.

Kenneth stole a look at her as Clara continued to pick at her meal beside him. His heart hitched at the sight of her lovely, perfect profile, and he knew that his time with Clara was ending, along with any chances of winning her love and respect.

They finished their meal in silence, then Clara rose to tidy up and barely nodded to him before disappearing into the bedchamber.

With a heavy heart, he banked the fire and set about making his bed. But tonight the hard table refused to make his rest comfortable, and Kenneth found himself lying awake and scowling at the fire, his hip aching where it pressed on the wood. Outside, the rain let up. Inside, the air remained cold and dismal. Still, Kenneth continued on, wide-awake.

Abruptly, a shout reached him through the walls. Pounding feet raced past the house and more shouts echoed in the distance. In the next breath, a cry of pain rent the night.

Chapter Sixteen

Clara threw back the curtain to find Kenneth already dressed and standing. "What's going on? Someone is hurt outside!"

She raced past him toward the door.

"Nay, stop!" He lunged for her, and in the next instant she was tight in Kenneth's arms, her back pressed to his firm chest. "Nay, Clara. Look at you. Your hair is loose!"

"But someone has been hurt! I'm needed out there!"

"Nay, you can't go. You have no veil or wimple on, and with the moon out, 'tis bright enough to see your hair. I'll go."

She twisted around in his arms and gripped his surcoat's front. "Bring the injured here, then."

He was close, and in the light from the low fire, Clara could see the sharp lines of concern in his expression. True and fearful concerns. She searched his face. "What's wrong? You look as if 'tis more than an accident! What more could it be?"

With his hand, he brushed back the red curls, and her heart fluttered in her chest in response. "Stay here, with the door bolted. 'Tis not unheard of to create a ruse to flush out an enemy. I won't discount that this could be such to flush *you* out."

Tears sprang *again*. Oh, how she hated them! And Kenneth drew them from her eyes so easily.

Lord, must I live from one tear to the next? I am not a foolish maid!

She blinked them back and leaned forward into Kenneth's gentle hand as it swept away the wild curls from her face. He tucked one strand over her ear, keeping his hand there, as if the fire in the color could warm his fingers. "I won't risk you until we know you won't be hurt. Let me go first. I won't be long. Stay here and open the door only for me."

"Let me come, too—I could put on a wimple!"

"Nay. Lord Taurin would know you immediately, for most women who come out would not take the time to do so, and your position as healer would be evident by your work on whoever may be pretending to be injured." He leaned toward her, and for a moment, her breath stalled, as if expecting a kiss. Instead, he spoke. "Remember when we were under the apple tree yesterday? Taurin had begun a search of each house, and the women who were forced out did not take the time for a wimple and veil. He chose that time, in the early hours of morn, for that exact reason. He may be trying it again."

"It didn't work then. Lord Adrien stopped him."

"One thing you must know about soldiers, Clara, is they use tactics that are familiar to them. Very few soldiers try new strategies until they have exhausted all else. Taurin will try what he's used before, believe me."

Beyond, more shouts. No more cries, but anger spilled down the lane. No anguished pain, but fury in the voices that reached into the hut.

Her throat tightened and she struggled to speak. "And you? What if something happens to you? Who will bring *you* back so I can mend you? What if I can't heal you?"

He tightened his grip. "Nothing will happen to me, Clara. I'll be careful." They stared into each other's eyes for a moment, then, as swiftly as a nighthawk dips in flight for prey, he dropped his mouth to her lips.

Firmly, powerfully, passionately.

She shut her eyes. Aye, this was a kiss like those of which they sang.

But too soon it ended, and Kenneth grabbed his sword and charged out the door.

Hastily, Clara shut it behind him and drew the bolt firmly across. She then dropped her forehead onto the new wood and shut her eyes. *Please keep him safe, Lord.*

"What's wrong?"

Clara turned. Brindi stood holding back the curtain. Her sleeping shirt was just her under tunic. Her hair was truly messy, evidence of Brindi's habit of thrashing in bed. She looked fearful and innocent, with eyes as wide and round as the bowls Clara kept for stew.

"I don't know. A commotion has started near the keep, and I thought I heard a cry of pain."

"Will you go out to help?"

Clara swallowed, hating that she must stay here. "Nay, Kenneth was afraid 'twould be a ruse to lure me out. Should Lord Taurin learn where I am, I fear he would force me to tell him where Rowena is."

Brindi gasped. "Would he torture you?"

Knowing she must not let her fear show, Clara straightened and shook her head. "Kenneth would not allow that. I hate this, but I must stay here in order to save Rowena."

"I heard Kenneth and you talking tonight. Will she be okay? Will she die in that hut? I wouldn't want to be there without a fire."

Clara didn't speak. She wasn't sure how long Rowena could survive if the rain should continue, for the peat cutter's hut was a dank and awful place to keep a mother and child. She quickly bustled Brindi back to bed, thankful that this hut had its warm thatch roof and good fireplace.

"Go back to sleep. I'll wait up for Kenneth. I'm sure 'tis nothing. Mayhap a soldier saw something in the woods and thought it a danger."

"Like a wolf?"

"Exactly. But we're safe here. Go to sleep."

Brindi returned to bed with reluctance to obey evident on her face. Clara sat on the bench close to the fire, poking it absently as she strained to listen to the sounds outside.

Kenneth spied the torches near the smithy's house. The lane leading to the keep was awash with more torches, and on the battlement above, numerous guards peered down, many with bows at the ready.

Odd. 'Twas not the scene he expected. Should the keep have come under attack, people would not have congregated at the smithy's home.

He charged into the fray of arguing Normans and Saxons. The whole scene threatened to break into full-out battle. Kenneth pried a pair apart, then headed for the smithy, who was arguing in broad, heavy English with the Norman who'd come with the courser earlier today. Those two again!

After he'd ordered the soldiers to stand down, he put his fingers into his mouth and drilled out a sharp whistle.

All stopped and turned to him. "'Tis better!" he growled out at the men. "All of you, what's going on? Are you all drunk to brawl like this?"

He focused on the Norman who'd helped bring Taurin's courser to the smithy. "Soldier, tell me what is going on here."

The Norman stood at attention. "I came down at the start of my guard shift to check on my lord's courser. When I discovered it missing, I awakened the blacksmith. The fool refuses to take responsibility for not latching the door to his stables."

"I did latch it! I know how to look after horses, Norman. I'm no fool, certainly not fool enough to allow Lord Taurin's mount to be stolen!"

"Steal it, nay, Saxon, but you were fool enough to let it wander away!"

"I latched the door!" Both men would have gone straight back at each other's throats had not Kenneth stopped them. Only then did he notice the Norman bore a gash on his forehead. It bled like an undammed river, too, as head injuries were apt to do.

The man touched his forehead and inspected his fingers. A quiet moment followed, and Kenneth wondered if the Norman was surprised that the smithy could inflict such an injury at all.

Then the Norman looked up at Kenneth, an odd, unusual look blossoming on his face. "'Twould seem that I am injured. Is the healer here? I will need to be stitched up, I expect."

Immediately, Kenneth's blood chilled. Was he correct when he spoke to Clara, saying this skirmish might be a ruse to lure her out? Yet, it didn't feel as though this was the original plan.

"You're lucky I didn't knock you out cold, Norman, for your accusations! 'Tis just a scratch and only because you stumbled in front of me!" the smithy snapped. He clenched meaty fists and looked as if he was prepared to do far more damage.

Nay, Kenneth thought. The smithy was the one who had inadvertently injured the man. He could not be part and parcel of some ruse to lure out Clara.

Kenneth looked around, actually thankful for the Saxons' mistrust of Normans and their refusal to cooperate with them. Surely some of Taurin's soldiers would have simply asked where Clara was. But obviously they had not been told a thing.

He glared at the injured soldier. "Are you a toddler who needs your mother every time you fall? Go back to the keep. I will tell the old cook to kiss your little cut better."

The soldier reddened. Kenneth prepared himself for a fight after his sarcasm, but several other soldiers hurried up. Kenneth knew them as Lord Adrien's personal guard.

Another thought hit him. Lord Adrien's soldiers, those who'd been here in Dunmow as long as he had, all knew where Clara lived. Some had been healed by her. Yet, they'd said nothing to Taurin's irksome band of men.

Encouraged, he pointed at the men who'd just argued. "Do nothing! Stand still until I tell you both otherwise!" He stepped through the mix of soldiers and Saxons until he spied his second in command of the armory. The young man, Pacey, straightened to attention. Kenneth led him farther away from the crowd.

"Before I decide what will happen, I need to ask you

something. Did Lord Adrien give you any orders as to what to say to Lord Taurin and his men?"

The man nodded. "Aye, after you left the keep with the midwife, we were told to say nothing about her. If we're asked, we are to say she's busy and often gone." The man looked grim but resolute. "'Tis true enough. The woman has traveled outside of the village and even as far as Cogshale. Milord also ordered us not to speak with any of Taurin's men. I know one thing—he cares not for Lord Taurin and will be glad to see him gone."

"Have you heard Taurin's men talking among themselves? Have they any suspicions of where to find the healer? Or have they questioned anyone about me?" Taurin's insistence that Kenneth take the horse to the smithy himself had had Kenneth wondering if the baron suspected Kenneth's connection to the healer.

"Nay," Pacey replied. "None seem to guess where the healer can be found. And they believe that you spend time in the village to be with your mistress."

Kenneth thought for a moment to protest the insinuation, but then subsided. While he hated that Clara would have this stigma, he knew, and his men knew, 'twas not the truth.

For Clara's and for Rowena's sakes, having a less-than-polished reputation was a risk worth taking.

Kenneth looked back at the men still standing beside the open stable. "I think that this was a plot to lure Clara out."

The soldier shook his head. "But the horse is missing. Lord Taurin wouldn't risk the animal, especially with a broken shoe, would he?"

Kenneth didn't know. But the look on that Norman's face as he'd asked for a healer was suspicious enough.

Disgusted at not knowing all the facts, Kenneth returned to the men now squaring off to fight again. "'Tis no time for fighting. Nor for placing blame." He turned to the soldiers. "Return to the keep. 'Tis too late and too dark to search for the horse. It's most likely grazing in some pasture to the west and will return on the morrow. They do that. But to make sure, rise at dawn and begin your search for him." To the smithy, he said, "I suggest you spend the rest of the night in your stable, keeping an eye out for the horse you lost, should he return to you."

The scuffle now broken up, people lost interest and returned to their homes, and the whole event died down fast.

Relief washed through Kenneth. This was just a little skirmish and thankfully settled quickly. Hot tempers were cooling fast, but this could have easily turned tragic. King William was heavy-handed when it came to punishment. Should he discover his soldiers had been threatened by Saxons…

Indeed, that eventuality still could happen, if the courser was not found before Lord Taurin awoke.

The smithy, muttering under his breath, obeyed, while the soldiers, some of whom were obvious malcontents, returned to the keep. Kenneth watched them all, wondering why neither Lord Adrien nor Lord Taurin had come to see what was happening. Suspicion nibbled at him all the way along the road through the village. Adrien, up high in his wife's solar for the evening, may not have heard. But Taurin, who slept in the Great Hall, would have noted this commotion.

Kenneth turned when he reached Clara's house. All was quiet and even the moon retired behind a bank of leftover clouds. The only light now in the village came from the smithy's stable. High on the parapet, the number of guards on the battlement was abruptly cut in half.

Suddenly chilled to the bone, he hurried to the house, his heart heavy with all that had occurred.

"What happened?" Clara asked as soon as he'd whispered through the door who he was and she'd opened it.

For the moment it took to bolt the door again, he wanted only to wrap his arms around her warm form and bury his face in her hair. He wanted to find comfort in her presence.

But what about Rowena? In her determination to keep the mother and child safe, Clara had chosen what could be a death trap for the pair. Her determination and that pride of hers. She would say 'twas her pledge to save lives, but it had been a poor choice. Yet, did she really have a choice? Finally, as he sat down, Kenneth told her everything, including Rypan's soft words that suggested Taurin was plotting something.

"'Twas not a ruse tonight?" she asked.

"I don't think so. Not a planned one, anyway." He added, "But Taurin and his soldiers will get increasingly frustrated with each day that they cannot find her." His next thought bit into his stomach like sour milk. "And we both know how King William deals with disobedience, Clara."

"Saxons will suffer," she said flatly. "I know that. 'Tis why I'm here."

Was the threat of death to many Saxons worth the life of one woman? Yet, if she gave the child to his father, her babe would be safe, wouldn't it? What more could a mother ask for?

"I know what you're thinking," Clara stated. "You

think that all of us Saxons here might be punished and you're wondering if it's worth it."

Kenneth scrubbed his hand down his face, feeling fatigue creeping into his body. "Aye."

She stepped up close to him. "And I have disappointed you. Mayhap 'twas my pride that made me hide Rowena in the bog. Or mayhap I didn't put enough faith in God. But would God protect Rowena? Taurin says she isn't a Christian. I didn't even think to ask. Indeed, 'twould have made no matter. I would have cared for her."

He blinked. Her faith was true. She would have helped Rowena regardless of the young woman's beliefs.

With a tight jaw, he reached for his bundle, where he'd put his small book of verses. "Sit down," he said. When they were both sitting on the bench, and the lamp was lit, Kenneth opened the book. "'Tis a book of prayers I had to write for my lessons." He read a few lines, his finger slowly tracing each word so she could see the sound each letter made. "'For God so loved the world, He gave His only begotten Son.' You did the right thing helping Rowena, regardless of her faith."

"But He still allows us to suffer. He still allows fighting and death," she said.

"Physical death, but not spiritual death." Kenneth sat back. "God loves us, and He wants us to love each other. But tension is so high between Saxons and Normans. Even though we both believe in the same God, this accident of losing Lord Taurin's horse will add fuel to the fire, I'm sure."

"What if it wasn't an accident?"

Chapter Seventeen

Clara watched Kenneth's mouth thin as he spoke. "The horse ran away. 'Twill return."

"What if it doesn't?"

"They do. Coursers are trained for battle and to return to their stables at day's end. He will know where the stable is, don't worry. And no one will approach him to try to steal him, either. Warhorses aren't pets to come running when is food offered. And they aren't like that old mare Lady Ediva learned to ride on," Kenneth said.

Clara nodded at his words. "Aye, but he's lost a shoe."

"True, horses don't like a shoe missing. It bothers them as much as 'twould bother you if you walked around with only one shoe. Coursers are very smart. He will return to be fed and sheltered, and to get his shoe replaced."

Clara sat back in thought before asking, "What if it wasn't an accident? What if the courser was hidden in the woods so it couldn't be found?"

Kenneth tipped his head, his frown deepening. "Do you *know* what you're saying?"

She swallowed. 'Twas an addled thought, but she'd

said it just the same. "What if Lord Taurin told his men to hide the horse?"

Cold washed through Clara, but she pushed on. "You spoke of a ruse to lure me out, but what if the ruse had a different goal? If Taurin's horse is missing, 'twould be a good excuse to stay in Dunmow and blame the Saxons for it. Seeing a few Saxons whipped in punishment may make one of them reveal where I am, just as the threat of it in Colchester made the guild masters conspire to be rid of me."

Taurin had been in Dunmow Keep for just over a day, and no one had revealed her location, right there in the battlement's shadow.

Not even the Norman soldiers who lived at the keep had revealed her location. Did she really deserve their loyalty? Nay, not when she thought of the awful place she'd hidden Rowena.

Kenneth stood and paced the short distance from wall to wall. "Why would Lord Taurin hide his horse in the forest? Wouldn't it be dangerous for it? There are wolves and bandits there. They would have to tie the horse up well to stop it from returning to the keep, then it may not be able to defend itself should a pack of wolves attack."

He went on, "'Tis hardly wise. The animal is valuable."

"True. And they're hard to approach, let alone ride. I know."

Kenneth lifted his brows. "You've ridden a courser before?"

"Just once. And it was no easy feat to mount it, either. They are big, brutish horses who like only one owner."

"Whose courser was it?"

"Lord Eudo's. He'd left it in the blacksmith's stables

to be shod, along with two others. The back end of the shop collapsed shortly after, pinning the blacksmith under some beams. All the horses needed to be led out quickly, but the stallion refused to obey the blacksmith's son. I climbed on it and forced it to obey. You need to be firm with them, not allow them a jot of their own way. I ended up leading him and several other horses from the stables, so we could reach the blacksmith."

Kenneth shook his head. "You never fail to amaze me. I knew you were confident on horseback when you criticized my riding the day I delivered you here, but I didn't realize you'd ridden a courser, as well."

She shrugged. "I had to correct you. Your technique was flawed. 'Twould become hard on your back as the years go on."

"Still, as you said, coursers are valuable animals. 'Tis hard to believe that Lord Taurin would risk his own mount. If the animal was injured, that could end its career on the battlefield and 'twould have to be put down, forcing Taurin to buy and train another. Only a fool would do that."

"Or someone desperate who is also wealthy and unscrupulous. Taurin would do anything to get back his heir."

"But why would Lord Taurin need this babe? Even if his wife can't give him a son, he can't give this child his title because it's not inherited."

Clara heard little of his words. She grabbed his arm as soon as he sat down again. "I must go to Rowena. 'Twas wrong of me to let my pride decide her fate. I need to move her someplace safer."

"With Taurin so close? He will stay here until his mount ret—" An idea dawned on his face. "Aye, you're right. He won't leave without his horse and he's a man who would cut off his own nose to spite his face."

Clara nodded. Her thoughts strayed to Brindi, who'd hidden that apple for fear Clara would give it to Rowena. In her childish mind, Brindi had known Clara would do anything to make sure she got her own way.

"In the morning, I should go into the keep to see if the horse has returned," Kenneth said. "But 'twill be unwise to leave the village, or even this house, Clara, for the forests and roads will likely be teeming with soldiers searching for the courser. I expect Lord Adrien will offer his men to help with the search, if nothing else but to hasten Lord Taurin's departure." He looked deeply at her. "We should retire. We don't know what the morrow brings."

They sat beside each other for a long moment, listening to the fire crackle and burn down. The sounds of late evening reached them through the wattle-and-daub walls and thickly thatched roof. Clara could hear Kenneth's quiet breaths, the rhythm a strange comfort to her. She blinked, thinking of poor Rowena.

Keep her safe, Lord, for I cannot. I have pledged never to hurt anyone, but I am hurting her and the babe in this awful way.

"Clara?"

She lifted her head to find him closer. His brown eyes and dark hair caught the flickering light from the hearth. "'Twill all work out. Trust God. And trust me."

"I will. But I find myself wanting to break my promise to her and take the babe from her. Rowena is too young to be a mother without help. I can teach her, but not right now. I wonder if I should just take the child, and I hate myself for thinking it."

"'Twould keep him safe."

She thought a moment, then shook her head. "Nay. A child needs its mother and cannot be separated from her for even a day. After Rowena gave birth, she had trouble nursing her babe. Fear and poor food can do that, and the babe was fussing so. I've just not been able to help her as much as I want to."

She sighed and wiped her wet eyes. "Oh, Kenneth, I have trapped myself! I cannot keep both the pledge to protect Rowena and my pledge not to do any harm! And if I cannot keep my word, what is it worth? What am *I* worth?"

Her lip quivered and she found herself being wrapped in Kenneth's strong arms. Oh, he felt so good, so warm and comforting when there was no answer for her.

They sat for a long while, clinging to each other. Then, finally, with reluctance she could almost taste, Clara broke the embrace and bade him good-night.

Kenneth nodded to the young soldier who opened the bailey gate to him the next morning. "Any word on the horse?"

"Nay, Sergeant. Lord Adrien has, however, ordered all available men to search for it."

Kenneth nodded. Aye, 'twas as he suspected. Adrien would not care to have Taurin around any longer than necessary. He hurried into the keep, but found few people there. Even the two barons were gone. He soon learned from Harry that they were out searching for the beast.

He walked slowly toward Lord Adrien's office, his feet heavy and tired. Last night, he'd wanted to reach down and kiss Clara again, but 'twould be a dangerous moment of weakness. Clara's contradictory pledges grieved her and 'twas not the time for passion.

She may have been upset last night, but Clara needed to sort out her life. He shouldn't confuse her, and he was the last person who should advise her.

Aye, they would be a poor match indeed. What kind of husband would he make if he didn't even know what to do?

A wail from above filtered down the stairs and despite his churning emotions, Kenneth smiled as he walked along the corridor. The new babe was demanding to be fed, no doubt. A healthy mother, a strong father and a warm home were all a child needed.

Was Lord Taurin so anxious to get his child because of desperation for an heir? What would happen should an heir not come? Most likely, the estates here would be passed on to his kin in Normandy, but only with the king's approval. Who was there that Taurin didn't want to inherit?

Kenneth stopped. What if he looked at this problem from a different side? Instead of asking what would happen if Taurin was without an heir, should he be asking what would happen if Taurin *had* an heir?

If he had estates in Normandy, they would also go to his son. Though the title of baron would be dissolved, it could easily be re-created and placed on the son. Mayhap baronies would be inherited someday, but William had other concerns right now.

Kenneth grimaced, feeling his head pound. This would all happen only *after* Taurin's death. What benefit would it be to him then? What benefit would a son be *now*?

The day wore on, and only when several soldiers returned without anything to report did Kenneth consider returning to Clara. She'd promised she would stay hidden, sending Brindi out to anyone who was in need and asking them to come to her hut. Lady Ediva stayed in her solar all day, with Margaret reporting that all was well there and that Clara need not come for another day.

The day was ending, with the scents of supper settling in around them. Beyond, the chaplain had opened the door to the chapel, preparing for evening services.

Out in the bailey, preparing to return to Clara, Kenneth stopped. Shouts from outside caused the gatekeeper to hurry to open the large gates. Several of Lord Adrien's soldiers rode inside hard and fast. Such was the commotion that Kenneth strode down to see what was happening.

"Did you find the horse?" he immediately asked the lead soldier when he reached him.

"Not me, Sergeant," the soldier said as Kenneth caught the foamy bridle. "But I can report that we met with several of Lord Taurin's men. They said that they had found his mount and that he had departed immediately for his estates to the west."

Kenneth straightened. "When was this?"

"A short time ago. I was commissioned to give his thanks to Lord Adrien for his hospitality and to say that the time had come for Lord Taurin to be on his way. He hopes to reach Broad Oak Forest by nightfall. The king has a manor there that will welcome him."

Kenneth tightened his jaw. 'Twas not only ill-mannered to depart on such short notice, without returning to the keep to deliver his thanks himself, but to leave this late in the day was very odd indeed, for Broad Oak Forest was some distance away. Kenneth ordered the soldiers to curry their mounts, then he returned to the keep.

Later, when Adrien returned, he glared as Kenneth delivered the news. Then, noticing Kenneth's curious look, he snapped, "Good riddance to him. He turned my keep upside down, and quite frankly, his ill-mannered departure is better than if he'd stayed another night. At least he found his horse and didn't demand to take mine. I almost expected he would."

Kenneth folded his arms. "Some suspect that Lord Taurin deliberately hid his mount."

"To what end?" Adrien asked, his eyebrows lifted. "To blame the smithy? That would be pointless. He knew I would support the only blacksmith in the village. The job is too important."

"Nay. I suspect to use it as an excuse to stay longer."

"Then why suddenly 'find' it?" Adrien sat down behind his desk. "Not a likely situation."

"I wonder if he felt you would order him gone when it became obvious that his search here was fruitless."

"I considered it. But I'd hoped that following Lady Ediva's advice to gather all the women, modestly dressed, would mean Taurin would take the suggestion that we'd done all we could and he may as well move on."

Kenneth lowered his arms. "Bringing the women here worked. I thank you both that you supported Clara in this."

Adrien tipped his head, his expression pensive. "Supported Clara? I protected my people. Regardless of what she believes is proper."

Kenneth shifted uneasily. Adrien straightened in his seat. "Sergeant? Is there something you should say?"

"Nay, milord."

Adrien rose and walked around the desk. "What is wrong?"

Kenneth looked up at the older man. He opened his mouth and then shut it again. "Nay, 'tis nothing."

Adrien laid a heavy hand on Kenneth's shoulder. "I have known you too long, my friend. You were my squire, now my sergeant at arms and my steward, but you should be far more for your loyalty to me. What is it about Clara?"

"I'm not so sure I can explain it. Clara was wrong to hide Rowena and her babe, but I did the same thing the day Lord Taurin searched the village homes. I hid her and Brindi."

"'Twas for a good reason."

"Aye, milord, but shouldn't I have trusted in you to keep Taurin at bay?"

"Is that your concern? That I would be disappointed in you?"

Disappointed. The word resonated within Kenneth. Clara had disappointed him with her choice for Rowena's hiding place. He hated that Clara didn't trust those around her. And he hated that he hadn't trusted Lord Adrien to protect the people of Little Dunmow.

And now he wasn't so sure that separating Rowena from her babe was the right thing to do. Not after having met Taurin. And realizing this now, he felt as though he was disappointing Adrien, for surely Adrien still believed that the babe should be taken from its mother, as wrong as it was.

He looked into his baron's face and knew he could never speak his thoughts. Adrien had earned Kenneth's respect a thousand times over. And the older man was now calling him a friend. For once, they were not lord and sergeant. Or even fellow soldiers, who'd fought together at Senlac. They were friends.

Kenneth felt his heart lift but he still could not state his opinion.

"'Tis as if a double-edged sword is pressed up to my chin. I move one way, I risk death. I move another way, I risk slicing my face off."

Adrien studied him. "I understand. More than you know."

Kenneth shook his head. "I refused to trust Lord Taurin. 'Twas Rypan who spoke against the man."

"Rypan? He has only ever said a handful of words to me." Adrien paused. "But they were important ones, in the stable when Ediva had gone on a quest to save my life. That herb the former healer often gave him stole his voice."

"Clara refused to dose him with it. 'Tis as if he has improved now."

"What did Rypan say?"

"That Lord Taurin had planned to stay. He must have overheard something."

Dropping his hand, Adrien walked back to his desk. "Then stay with Clara until I am satisfied that Taurin is gone for good. The village will be better off then, and mayhap 'twill be safe to draw out this young slave girl."

"My lord, does this mean you don't care where Rowena is? Or that she keeps the babe?"

Adrien stilled. "Kenneth, these past few days I have watched my own family, and I can no longer say 'tis a good thing to wrench a babe from its mother."

Kenneth's eyes widened. "But what about the child's health?"

Adrien looked grim. "Aye, I know what you are saying. 'Tis better to have a warm home and good food, but babes die in wealthy homes as well as in poor ones. And many a child has been unhappy in each."

"But less so in a wealthy one! Aye, babes can be taken from us, but at least in a warm home with good food, the child has a fighting chance!" Abruptly, Kenneth slammed shut his mouth on his arguments that weren't even his own. What was he saying?

Adrien shook his head. "I have no answer. All I know is that 'twould kill Ediva to be parted from our son, and I cannot allow that to happen to another mother just to please one of my fellow Normans. Aye, inside me, I also doubt myself."

'Twas good news to hear. Surprising, but good. But there were still other concerns. "And the fact that she is a runaway slave? We heard him say she isn't a Christian."

"Taurin is twisting the spirit of the law. All we have is his word on her religion, anyway. I saw Clara's expression when we were discussing it. She doesn't know Rowena's faith, either, and I won't condemn a person without at least asking them first, even a young slave girl."

Abruptly, Adrien smiled. "Go back to Clara. 'Twill help you sort out your feelings."

Kenneth nodded, but he doubted that being with Clara would help him sort out anything, least of all his feelings.

Chapter Eighteen

Clara had heard, Kenneth decided as he spied her hurrying into the bailey a short time later. With Brindi in tow, she practically galloped up to Kenneth as he descended the steps of the motte.

It had been an hour since he and Lord Adrien had spoken, and evening services were overdue. Kenneth suspected the chaplain had delayed the service until all the soldiers could return, and mayhap until all were certain that Taurin himself had left. Evening services could indeed help release the pall of Lord Taurin's visit from their community.

Clara reached him. "Is it true? Lord Taurin has left?"

"Aye." Kenneth led her toward the chapel, not pleased that she'd chosen only a veil for her head covering. He'd have preferred she err on the side of caution until they were sure Taurin was far away. "You should have remained in your hut."

"Why? You don't think he's gone?"

Because as night drifted in, 'twas obvious that the unwanted baron could have only traveled west a little way and might easily return. Kenneth stopped her far enough from the chapel door to speak without too many over-hearing them. "Lord Taurin can't ride too far this eve-ning. I doubt he'd even get as far as Broad Oak Forest, where he intends to stay. He would have to stay some-where in the marshland settlements along the way first."

"Let him, then. I want to attend services as I should." She squeezed his arm and smiled at him. "I want noth-ing more than to thank everyone for their kindness, Nor-man and Saxon, for none of them revealed who I was." She'd already begun to thank those around her, receiv-ing warm hugs and encouragement in return.

Ignoring the others, Kenneth turned to her. He didn't share her certainty that she was safe. Taurin wasn't to be trusted. Why had he given up and moved on? Kenneth felt as though this was a weak link in his chain mail. A hole that a properly aimed sword could puncture.

Despite his uneasiness, Clara stood before him, and his heart hitched at her penetrating look. Her eyes were wide, her lips parted with a smile of gratitude hover-ing there. And the memory of their kiss smacked him full in the face. He wanted, nay, ached with the desire to repeat it.

What a fool he was. He knew 'twould not be wise to fall for her. They thought far too differently, and what kind of husband would he be to her with all these foolish doubts dancing within him? A woman like Clara, one of strong opinions, deserved a strong man, faithful and wise and full of resolve. He was none of those things.

She tugged at his arm, as Brindi tugged at hers. Like a caravan, they entered the chapel, with Clara's steps ahead of him light and relieved, whilst his were heavy with anguish.

* * *

The sun had broken free of the clouds and now angled down on all who left the services. Though there was hardly any light left, 'twas as if the weather itself wanted to rejoice in Taurin's departure.

Kenneth felt only marginally uplifted. He stood and watched Clara speak with Lady Ediva, who had brought her babe to the evening services. After a few moments of quiet conversation, Clara left Ediva to rest and feed the child. She walked up to Kenneth where he stood near the chapel door with Brindi.

"I must go to Rowena," she told him softly. "I asked Lady Ediva if Brindi could stay with the maids tonight and she agreed. 'Tis not fair to drag the child out yet another night." She looked down at her sister. "Go to the cook, and don't be a nuisance. Help her in any way you can."

Brindi skipped off, excited by the prospect of an evening beyond their little home.

"And do you plan to go alone?" Kenneth asked.

Clara inhaled shakily. 'Twas only wise to ask Kenneth to accompany her to see Rowena. But even thinking that caused her nerves to dance and quiver. Aye, after all he'd done for her, she should be ready to trust him. And after giving grateful thanks in her prayers during the service, she *would* do the right thing and *show* her trust. "No, not alone," she answered.

Kenneth looked at her. "And you trust me enough to let me come?"

She shrugged. "Obviously, since Lord Taurin has left."

"Then there is little need to trust me, is there?" He paused. "Or allow me in your home anymore."

She frowned as they walked toward the village. 'Twas

getting dark here in the shadow of the keep, but the moon was waxing. "Don't be insulted, Kenneth. 'Tis not easy for me to ask for help. Take the offer of trust as it comes."

He didn't look impressed. Nor did his distant gaze light on her. "Is that what you're doing? Just asking for my help?"

"If you don't want to go, 'tis fine. I will go by myself. Mayhap you are afraid of the forest?"

"I'm not!" he growled out. Then stopped. "Do not think you can goad me, woman. I will go with you because 'tis safer for you. The woods are still dangerous and full of Saxon thieves and bandits. And I wish to see for myself if the boy is well."

"You still feel the child is better off with his father," she answered flatly. "Though his father appears to have lost interest."

She swallowed. And so did Kenneth, she noticed. She stepped closer to him. "Nay, Kenneth, we shouldn't fight so. We will always differ on this matter, but you should see why I have done what I have done, and to see it, you need to meet Rowena." She touched his arm. "Will you come with me?"

He stepped back, his expression like the steel of the blade that hung at his side. Disappointment squeezed her heart.

Nay! She would not feel hurt by this! Kenneth was probably glad to be rid of her, for they'd disagreed from the moment they'd first met. She had her pledges of healing and of keeping Rowena safe, while he had sworn fealty to a warrior king and would never understand her desire never to hurt a person, no matter what happened. He deserved a woman who was far more docile, like the Norman women that soldiers spoke of, who kept their peace, entering into profitable marriages with grace and dignity.

At her hut, Clara halted her thoughts. Saxon women had held more rights and power, but they also needed *morgangifts,* or dowries, to enter marriage.

She had none, for her mother was poor and her father gone. Her sisters had obtained small dowries from their uncle, but by the time Clara came of age, 'twas nothing left, not even an aunt and uncle. She and Brindi could offer nothing to a marriage.

Yet another reason she should not allow herself to fall in love with Kenneth. He would surely break her heart when he turned his affection to more profitable maids, like Margaret, who could be given a small dowry by Lady Ediva. Having a maid and steward married would be an ideal situation for a small keep.

Tipping up her head, she lifted her brows, determined to wear a mask of peace, though truthfully, peace seemed so elusive.

"The village is settling down," she said briskly. "Let me first gather a few things to take. 'Twill be cold tonight, so choose your cloak well."

"I'm not Brindi. I can deal with the cold well enough," he growled back.

She ignored him and bustled about, collecting all she needed. The night was as she said. Here, as in Colchester, when the moon waxed after a storm, the winds would turn to blow in from the sea and chill everything. Though summer was fast approaching and gardens were starting to produce, there could easily be a frost, one that would kill even the hardiest of vegetables and herbs. And tonight was as she'd warned.

She wrapped her cloak more snuggly around her

form, surreptitiously watching Kenneth do the same. They hurried from her hut, past the village and into the forest by way of the road to Colchester.

Before long, they'd reached the new road that was said to lead nowhere. Clara had heard from the villagers 'twas the place where Lord Adrien was attacked last summer. She could feel Kenneth's suspicion rise as they reached its beginning.

"This road is a dead end," he muttered.

She gathered the skirt of her cyrtel and started down the open path, slinging her bundle over her shoulder and carrying a lantern, for the forest was deep. "You sound as if I have planned a trap for you," she answered, feeling unreasonably testy. Indeed, 'twas a place that could make a person nervous, and her skin began to creep in reaction to Kenneth's growing tension.

At the bend, she turned left. The moon would brighten the way as soon as they left the dense forest. At ten long paces in, she stepped out of the trees, leaving the forest behind her. She waited until Kenneth caught up. The forest had thinned at the edge of the ancient bog. "To the left. Careful where you step. The bog still has holes and soft spots."

"Not to mention where the smithy has come to dig peat. We wouldn't see the trench until it was too late."

"There has been no digging at this corner. 'Twas why I did not realize the smithy came out here—I saw no signs of him on the route that I take. Follow me. The hut is just ahead."

The moon had risen enough to skirt the treetops, and their eyes adjusted well to the night as long as they didn't stare into the lantern.

"I can smell a hearth." He pointed ahead. "Aye, there it is. I see the smoke. At least she has a fire on."

Clara stalled and frowned. "Rowena never wanted to put a fire on and invite bandits and others to investigate." She bit her lip. "I hope the babe is well. I showed her how to strap it to her chest for warmth. I'd used my wimple."

"Well, that explains why you never seem to wear it. But you should have worn Lady Ediva's."

"My hair is too thick. That day we went into the Great Hall, my head ached. I need a bigger one." She stepped gingerly over several low spots before turning and shining the open side of the lantern onto them to ease Kenneth's passage.

They reached the hut without injury, something Clara was glad for. She tapped lightly on the only section of upright wood that wasn't covered in moss. The dull knock rang out in the clear air.

"Rowena, 'tis me," she whispered. No answer. Clara thrust the door open and stepped inside.

There had been a fire on, but 'twas dying and nothing but smoldering hunks of charcoal, now given a small breath of life from the night breeze that swung in ahead of them. Even what fire had been in here couldn't completely rid the hut of the smell of dampness and moss. She lifted the lantern to light the interior.

Before her was nothing but awful disarray. A tipped-over cradle, the rough-hewn one Clara had taken from her aunt's home. A torn swaddling was draped over one edge, and in front of her lay a cloak, bloodied and smelling of fear and loss.

Clara let out a cry. Rowena and her babe had been found and stolen away.

Quite unwillingly, too.

Chapter Nineteen

"Nay!" Clara cried out. She could do nothing more than that as she stood in the center of the hut, its ceiling barely above her head and its dark shadows revealing little but the proof of the raid. She turned slowly, her jaw hanging and her breath now stalling in her throat.

What had happened? Kenneth, barely able to stand in the low hut, took the lantern to hang on a hook. Then, still wordless, he righted the cradle. The scrap of swaddling dangling from it was part of the provisions she'd brought just before the stormy weather. Tufts of fresh moss used in the babe's nappy lay scattered behind it.

Clara lifted up the torn section of cloak and out fell a simple brooch. It had ripped from where the hood attached. Blood stained one side of it.

"Kenneth!" she exclaimed. "This blood has not yet dried!"

Bile rose in her throat as she blinked back tears. Her sweeping gaze rolled over to him where he stood, slightly stooped, at the entrance.

"Nay. Nay!" She thrust past him, tearing out into the

moonlight. She skidded to a stop and screamed, "Rowena! Where are you! Answer me!"

An owl took flight to her right, startled by her cries, and she spun, hopeful, only to sag a moment later.

A hand gripped her shoulder, making her jump. Kenneth was behind her, having stepped from the hut, his footfalls muffled by her screams and the soft, wet earth.

"Clara! She's not here."

"Nay! She has to be close." Clara pushed past him into the hut and returned a moment later with the lantern. Still as stone, she cocked her ear toward the bog. "Keep quiet. We may be able to hear the babe's cries."

Kenneth waited patiently as she leaned forward, straining to hear the babe, to hear anything at all in the night.

Nothing.

"She's gone, Clara. Not without a fight, but she's gone."

"Nay!"

Kenneth reached forward to touch her, but she smacked his hands away. "It's your fault! I trusted you. You've told Lord Taurin where Rowena was!"

"How? I didn't know where she was."

"You did! You guessed she was here by the way I reacted to your comments." She lit up with anger and her voice rose. "And the way I reacted to what the smithy said. You saw me at the corner of his house! When the smithy spoke of harvesting peat for his furnace, you saw my reaction. You saw it and guessed that was where I kept Rowena!"

"'Twas just a guess, Clara. I wasn't sure of it until I spoke to you after. Besides, I didn't even know how to get to this place! And I told no one of my suspicions."

He stopped. After muttering something under his breath, he carried on. "But Taurin learned of this peat bog from someone."

"From you! You told Taurin because you believe that the child should be with him. And I trusted you!"

"I have pledged to keep you safe from Taurin. Why would I turn around and tell him that? 'Twould risk him punishing you, also!"

"Rowena wasn't part and parcel of that promise! Oh, how you Normans can twist words and steal hearts to get what you want!"

"I didn't know where the bog was! I have no reason to harvest the peat or even guess its location. Wait! Steal hearts? What foolishness is that, Clara?"

She rushed on, ignoring his last question. "Then how did Taurin learn this location? He wasn't even there at the smithy's house, and that soldier arguing with the smithy paid me no mind. He had no idea who I was!"

"I did not say a word to anyone!"

"Then who did?" Her heart pounded, her skin crawled with fear for Rowena, a desperate, breath-stealing fear. "The villagers spoke to no one. Did one of your soldiers say something?"

"Nay, they were instructed to say nothing to Taurin's men."

She'd been spinning around, searching the bog and the woods that skirted it. Wobbly, she stopped and shook her head. "Then 'twould have to have been Lord Adrien."

"I cannot believe it!" His voice grew sharp. "Lord Adrien and I spoke of the difficult situation and that he was glad Taurin had left." Kenneth took a step toward her. "Adrien has grown to understand 'tis wrong to take a babe from its mother. He sees how 'twould hurt Lady Ediva and found he could not do so to Rowena, either."

She could feel the sodden earth soak her feet through her simple leather slippers. The hem of her cyrtel and cloak hung heavy with rainwater that had nowhere to go in this bog. Cold wicked up her feet and calves, but 'twas nothing to the burning anger that filled her heart. "Then who? There is no one left! You are the only one who disagreed with keeping Rowena away from Lord Taurin, so why wouldn't I suspect you?"

He stood there mutely, his mouth shut tight no doubt to seal himself against convicting himself. Clara's heart twisted anew. Oh, how painful betrayal felt!

She wet her lips and swallowed to heal her cracked and painful throat. "And should any of the villagers have revealed my identity, they still wouldn't know where Rowena was. *You* were the only one who had any idea where I'd hid her."

Clara turned away from him, pulling up her cloak's loose hood so he could not catch the quiet sobs she tried to muffle. But instead of leaving Kenneth and the hut, she strode back inside. There, with shaking hands, she coaxed the fire to return, throwing on some kindling set near the hearth.

She returned outside with the lantern and, after digging through the top layer of peat, found some drier bits underneath. She scraped at them, praying that this fuel would not smother the tender fire.

"What are you doing?"

She looked up at Kenneth. "I'm going to stay the night here, and as soon as the sun rises, I'll start searching for Rowena. Go back to the keep. You're not needed here."

"I won't leave you alone, Clara."

"Why not? You only protected me in order to discover Rowena's whereabouts. Well, neither of us knows where she is now, and Lord Taurin has gone. I expect he found her and dragged her out, stole the babe and left her for dead."

"If you believe she's dead, why stay to search for her?"

She lifted her chin and threw back her shoulders. "Because she may have survived, and if she didn't, and I find her body out here, I will bury her properly. It's the least I can do after failing her. Good night, Kenneth. You've done enough for me now."

She hefted up more of the peat, keeping her back to him and fighting the tears that blurred her vision. 'Twas dark enough out here without adding unshed tears to make her stumble and fall.

After a moment, as she was entering the hut, she peeked over her shoulder. Kenneth had turned and disappeared into the night. When she could no longer hear him pushing through the woods, she fell to her knees and began to cry.

Kenneth had reached the new road before his temper cooled enough for him to take a deep breath. By the time he'd reached the end of the forest, where the smithy's house introduced the village, he was cooled down sufficiently to think straight.

But fury still roiled inside of him. Clara had ordered him out of her sight and he'd obeyed like a whipped pup! 'Twould not be for long, though. She needed time to cool down, as he did. And, as she'd berated him, he'd formed an idea of what might have happened. He needed to confirm the theory first, though, and he wasn't prepared to leave Clara alone in the peat bog for long.

He strode past the smithy's house, stopping to think as he reached the shop front. On the day of the altercation between the smithy and Taurin's man, there were several Normans around the shop, not just the one who'd argued with the smithy. Was it possible that one had suspected Clara and seen her reaction when she'd heard the men discuss the peat bog?

But only a few would know the bog's location, so how would they know where to go?

Unless…

He strode up to the bailey gate. After pounding on it and shouting out his name, he shifted impatiently until the gate opened. There, he ordered one of the men to the bog, with strict instructions to guard Clara without revealing himself. Should she leave, he was to follow and protect her.

Then Kenneth charged into the keep.

The guard at the front door snapped to attention. Kenneth asked, "Is there anyone in Lord Adrien's office?" Kenneth usually slept there, but since Lord Adrien conducted business there, it didn't feel right calling it his own quarters.

"Aye, Sergeant. Harry and that addled boy, Rypan."

Kenneth nodded. Since Kenneth had taken on the task of guarding Clara, he knew Harry had snuck in to sleep there. He'd most likely coaxed Rypan into the misbehavior, as well.

The sounds of sleeping men filtered into the corridor from the Great Hall. The soldiers snored on tables and benches all set around the hearth. The unattended fire had waned, and no one appeared awake enough to rekindle it.

Beyond, in the kitchens, someone was beginning the day's work. Most likely the cook, who preferred to rise early and begin her baking. Kenneth moved past both the entrance to the hall and the kitchens, heading toward the office. He opened the door and strode over to turn up the lamp that hung at one side. Light bled into the room.

Rypan lifted his head from the far corner pallet. Harry was asleep on the table. Kenneth roused him. "Go share the pallet. I have need of this desk." Dutifully, Harry scampered down and fell onto the pallet.

Kenneth pulled up the box that contained the maps and banged it on the table. Rypan started at the noise, but Kenneth paid him no mind.

"What's wrong, Sergeant?" Harry asked in French.

"I have need of the maps."

"Why?"

Kenneth tossed a fast glare at him. "Never mind."

"I could help, as I did before."

Kenneth found the maps and spread them out. But the light was still too weak, so he turned up the lamp even more. "When did you ever help with the maps?"

"This evening. Before Lord Taurin left. One of his soldiers asked to see the way to Broad Oak. I was glad to show him."

He looked up at the boy. "This evening? Early?"

"Aye. Several soldiers came in, asking for maps."

"They only wanted to see the road to Broad Oak?"

"Nay. They also looked at the map of the road to Colchester."

Cold rushed through Kenneth. "And the new road?"

"'Tis on that map."

Of course! He snapped, "What did you say to them?"

"I told them 'twas nothing at the end of the new road save the peat bog. I haven't been there, but Rypan has helped the smithy carry peat out."

Beside him, Rypan nodded wordlessly.

"He has? When?"

"Lord Adrien ordered some metalwork to be done at Christmastime. The smithy asked for someone to help him carry peat."

Aah, 'twas so. Kenneth nodded to himself. He remembered that Lord Adrien had asked for a special stand made to dangle small toys over a babe as it lay in its bed. What was it called? A carousel of something? 'Twas a gift to Lady Ediva last Christmas.

Harry shrugged. "The soldier said he wanted peat so the smithy could reshoe Lord Taurin's courser, but they left without that getting done."

His mouth thin, Kenneth recognized the soldier's lie. But young Harry would not have seen what it really was.

Thankfully, Lord Taurin and his men were gone, and Clara was safe for now.

But not so Rowena. Was she even alive? He looked over at Harry. "Did they look at any other maps?"

"Just the one of Broad Oak Forest."

Kenneth wasn't familiar with the lands to the west. He rolled up the map before him and found Harry already unwrapping the one of the west. They spread it out on the table. Rypan played with the lamp a bit and then lit a candle he drew from the cupboard.

"I remember one of Taurin's soldiers saying they hoped to reach Broad Oak Forest by sunset," Kenneth mused out loud.

"'Twas a lofty plan, sir, and 'twill not happen."

He looked at Harry. "Because it's too far? Have you ever traveled it?"

"Only when I was a babe. I don't remember, but we came that way with Lady Ediva for her first wedding, and M'maw still talks of not liking that trip through the forest. She says it takes a full day of riding to reach the edge of Broad Oak Forest, and it is so vast, you have to spend the night in it."

"I remember someone speaking of Lady Ediva's birth home, Liedburgh. A place with more apple trees than anything else, they said." He looked down again at the map. Broad Oak Forest encompassed much of the west of Essex, while Liedburgh lay beyond that. He stretched his memory to recall who owned the majority of the county. Fitz Osborne? Regardless, Taurin held some land at the southern tip of the forest.

"He would have to travel past the abandoned watch-tower and past the mill," Kenneth said, thinking aloud. "His horse isn't shod on one hoof, and the blacksmith said at least one more shoe needed replacing. That would slow them down. Not to mention a babe and mother."

"'Twill take a full day to make it to Broad Oak," Harry warned ominously. "And 'twill make the horse lame."

Kenneth ignored his tone. "They'll only get halfway to the forest before sunup." He caught Harry's gaze with a penetrating look. "Assemble a pack of food for me. I will need good cider, some cheese, and bread and linens for bandages and swaddling." To Rypan, he said, "Saddle a horse, the fastest one, but not Lord Adrien's courser. 'Tis too loud when it runs. A fast, but quiet horse."

"What are you going to do, Sergeant?" Harry asked.

He paused, then drawing in a deep breath, he said, firmly to his own ears, "I'm going to prove to Clara that I am worthy of her trust."

Chapter Twenty

Too agitated to simply wait and unable to hurry dawn along, Clara cleaned up the peat cutter's hut as best she could in the dull firelight. She found the pot she'd brought Rowena early on, and heated some water she'd drawn from the nearest drainage channel. 'Twas necessary to boil the water for some time, for stagnant water made a person sick and this water was as brown as old tea. As it was coming to a boil with the small fire below it, she swept the floor and set aright the few bits of furniture.

She found another strip of swaddling and her throat closed sharply. *Please, Lord, save Rowena. I have not been able to do it and have failed her. I risked so many people here and in Colchester in my stubbornness.*

Scrunching up the cloth, she sank onto the old bench. Could Rowena really be dead? And what of her babe? He was such a sickly boy, and Clara's determination to keep them safe had forced mother and son into horrid conditions. Rowena had tried to survive, to do what she thought was best, but she was a young woman with no experience, barely out of childhood, discarded by her family.

Lord, all I wanted was to keep them safe.

And Kenneth? Hadn't he also wanted to do what he thought was right? Had he really believed the child was better off with its father?

She drew her hand to her face. Hadn't that very thought crossed her mind as she'd watched Lady Ediva rock her babe? The warmth of her solar, the good food and safety that came with wealth were the defining factors, weren't they? Was that what Kenneth felt all the time?

But he'd betrayed her. He'd risked their blossoming friendship to do what he thought was right. Yet, wouldn't she have done that, also? She, who would do anything to keep her pledge.

And then, as pinpricks of hot tears threatened, she swallowed her pride and added, *Please help me forgive Kenneth.*

Dawn could not arrive soon enough. With a need to hurry it along, Clara pulled together the edges of her cloak and stepped outside.

The air was warmer than the past few days, for the rain had pushed the colder air away. To the east, where the bog opened to a marsh, the sky was lightening, hinting at a fair day ahead.

She began her search, being careful to study the bog around her for signs of a struggle, working in circles around the hut until she found what she searched for.

Footprints, heavy and going in all directions, had scuffed the moss in many parts. 'Twas good that they'd cared not for the earth beneath their feet, for she wouldn't have spotted the marks in the forgiving moss had it not been for the scrapes.

Into the forest, she spied broken branches, a portion of torn material, dull in color and much like what Rowena wore, and the abrasions of sword blades as they scraped on the bark of many trees. Someone with a blade had opened a new trail.

Clara continued to scan back and forth as she followed the signs, hoping against hope that Rowena had been able to escape and that Taurin, more interested in the child, had abandoned her. She prayed that at least one of the two she'd vowed to protect would be safe.

But as the sun rose high, she found the markers of the struggles in the woods continuing off into the distance, and knew she wouldn't find Rowena close by. Despair added weight to her steps, and it hung heavily on her shoulders like a sodden wool cloak.

She staggered into a small clearing, and sadly, she scanned the ground. A horse had been here. Nay, several horses, for one set of hoofprints was bigger than the rest. Marks on the branches of one tree suggested that was where the horses had been tied. She looked again at the ground. During those years with her aunt, who lived beside a blacksmith, Clara had learned the prints of horses, both in need of shoeing and not. Taurin's courser had been here, and it still needed to be shod.

Looking up, she found dark red smeared on the bark of a tree. She leaned forward, gingerly touching the smear with her forefinger. Blood. And it was still damp. But whose blood?

Clara sank to her knees. *Lord, don't let it be Rowena's! Or the babe's!*

She looked heavenward, hoping for an answer in the

rays of early sunshine that split the tree branches and
glowed in the morning mist.

But all was silent. Heart-heavy and with her stomach clenched so tight it hurt, Clara struggled to her feet
and wiped her tears away with two harsh dashes of her
hands. She focused again on the ground and continued
to follow the prints. At least the blood was still moist.
That meant they'd left not so long ago.

Before the forest began again, she could see the
man's prints disappear abruptly—he'd mounted one of
the horses. Rowena's prints were nowhere to be found
since she'd stepped into the forest. Her feet were small
and slippered only in leather so thin they'd barely make
a dent in the soft moss.

"Rowena!" she called out, hoping that she was close,
but all that answered her was a pair of annoyed birds
that fluttered off.

She strained to hear more, and in the distance, she
could hear the regular strike of metal on metal, the sort
of noise a blacksmith might make. Though hidden in the
woods, she must be close to Little Dunmow.

And close to Kenneth, too, assuming that he'd returned to the keep. She should really fetch Brindi from
the kitchen, but would that increase her chances of meeting Kenneth?

Forget about your feelings. And forget about Kenneth.
This was about Rowena and the babe. Clara straightened.
She would go straight into the keep and demand an audience with Lord Adrien and Lady Ediva. They would
help her find Rowena. Surely they would know where
Lord Taurin was headed? She would remind them of
their promise, and then they could provide her with the
means to find Rowena.

She pushed through the thicket, hiking up her cyrtel and tossing back her thick hair to avoid getting it tangled with twigs and brush until she stepped free of the thick forest. She found herself between the blacksmith's shop and the second house along the road. Ahead was the lane to the keep, and to her left, the stables the smithy used to shelter horses before and after they were shod. For safety's sake, the smithy's home was set away from the shop. Yesterday, she'd slipped out of that home and yet had been hidden from the men who argued.

She frowned.

A doubt nibbled at her, something akin to eating a portion of food that soured her stomach. Deep within, she felt a warning, yet couldn't grasp it.

Pushing the feeling aside, she hurried into the bailey and came to a dead stop within its center. She glanced anxiously around, her eyes searching for Kenneth. But the tall, lean Norman couldn't be seen. Instead, she found people going briskly about their own business, the mood more relieved than she'd expected. Because Lord Taurin had left? Refusing to speculate, she trotted into the keep and spied young Harry peeking out from the lord's private chamber.

"Harry!" she cried as she rushed up to him. "I need to speak with Lord Adrien and Lady Ediva. Immediately!"

Shock fell onto his face. "Is there something wrong?"

"Aye. Please, find Lord Adrien for me!"

Harry galloped up the stairs to Lady Ediva's solar, leaving Clara in the corridor. The door Harry had slipped through eased open more. The young man Rypan peeked out. As soon as he spied her, he slammed the door again.

She wished she could help him. His aunt, one of the cooks, had said that Rypan had been given a dose of stink gum once a week. Clara knew the plant well, but used it only to ease stomach troubles when nothing else worked. She didn't feel it had an effect on brains and had told the boy so when he first came looking for a dose. 'Twas as if he expected her to feed him, also, but she'd had nothing to offer him that day, and he'd not come back since.

Footfalls on the stairs turned her attention, and she found herself watching Lord Adrien approach.

"Milord," she began, "I need to speak with you!"

"Into the hall, then." He strode into the Great Hall, ordering the soldiers who were there out to do a litany of exercises.

Sitting down, he indicated she should take a chair, also. She sat on a short bench nearby, but too agitated, she jumped up again. "Milord, Rowena has been kidnapped!"

"How?"

"Someone found the hut. There was a scuffle, and she's gone!"

Adrien frowned. "Your hut?"

"Nay, the one in the peat bog."

"Where is that?"

"Deep in the forest, past the new road."

He sat back. "'Tis a dangerous place that far into the forest." He paused. "There's a hut in there?"

"Aye. 'Tis old and abandoned, most likely once used by the man who cut and sold the peat. I took Rowena there when I discovered I was to come here. 'Tis closer to Little Dunmow than where she stayed before." She pulled in her breath. "I know you disapproved of me hiding her, but you understand my reasons, don't you?"

"Aye. But 'twas wrong of you to keep her hidden and

risk bringing Taurin's wrath on the town of Colchester, not to mention here. You should have trusted my brother. Lord Eudo would have kept her safe."

She stemmed her counterargument. Normally, she would have burst forth with a string of reasons without any thought. But Lord Eudo was Adrien's brother, and in retrospect, Clara was sure he would have intervened. "Lord Eudo is a good man and well liked in Colchester, but I did not know him, and I couldn't take the chance that he'd allow Lord Taurin's men to steal her away in the night. I'd pledged I would keep her safe. I didn't realize how much I'd endangered Colchester." She sank down on the bench again and let her head fall into her hands. "I see now that I endangered Little Dunmow, too. For that, I am truly sorry. It makes it worse that the people here did not do as those in Colchester did, but banded together to protect me."

Tears sprang into her eyes. "I pledged myself to healing and not hurting anyone, but I see I have done so much damage."

"Indeed you have."

She straightened to find Adrien folding his arms. With a quick glance around, she found them still alone in the hall. Odd that even Kenneth had not appeared. Where was he?

A pang of missing him punched her inside. "Then I must pledge anew to not hurt anyone. I have already asked God for forgiveness, and I promised it won't happen again. But Rowena has been kidnapped and her babe stolen! She could be dead!"

Adrien's expression grew grimmer. Clara bit her lip and swallowed. Was he preparing to punish her? She held her breath, then, unable to sit and wait for her much-deserved punishment, she rushed up to him. "Nay, please don't throw me in your dungeon again! Who would look for Rowena? If she's dead, who would give her the one last scrap of respect she deserves and bury her body? Nay, no one! We may not even find her body! I can't go to the dungeon without trying to find her! I won't!"

Adrien's look darkened. "'Twas Kenneth who threw you in there, not me."

"Kenneth was right to toss me down there, for I had endangered too many people. I don't hold that against him."

"What do you hold against him? Why did you come to me and not him?"

She paused, shocked by the questions. What did he know? Did he know that Kenneth had revealed where Rowena was hidden?

Or had he? Clara swallowed, feeling the doubt that had lingered out by the smithy's home return to her.

"Milord, I accused Kenneth of telling Taurin where I'd hidden Rowena, for he guessed the location. But how could he have told Taurin when he had promised me he'd protect them as he'd protected me? 'Twas not—"

"Be quiet, woman!" Adrien snapped, his frown deeper now as he rubbed his head.

A movement by the door caught their attention, and Clara spun. Lady Ediva walked into the hall. Behind her were Harry and Rypan, both hovering close in case their beloved lady felt faint.

Clara rushed forward, but was passed by Adrien, who took his wife's hand and led her to her seat. "Was it necessary for you to witness this meeting?" he asked her.

"The walls of the solar are closing in on me, Adrien. Harry and Rypan helped me down the stairs. I am healing well." She looked to Clara. "Is it true that Rowena has disappeared?"

"Aye, mistress," Clara answered, her voice cracking. "I have failed her. I couldn't keep her safe from Lord Taurin."

"Mayhap 'twas because you were doing it by yourself."

Clara frowned. "Nay, Brindi helped me."

Ediva waved her hand. "She's a child. You wouldn't even allow Kenneth to help you."

Clara stiffened. "He wanted to give the babe to Lord Taurin!"

Ediva turned to her husband. "Is this true? You said to me that you wouldn't allow that, so why allow Kenneth to think it could happen?"

Adrien shook his head. "Kenneth would never do so without my authority." He turned to Harry. "Where is your sergeant, boy? Bring him here."

Harry stepped up cautiously, with wide eyes. Rarely had Clara seen him so earnest. He was more a mischief maker and cheeky soul than this. He jerked his head side to side. "Milord, he's gone."

"Where?"

"To catch up with Lord Taurin."

"Alone?"

Harry nodded. "He said he has lost Clara's trust and must earn it back."

Ediva caught her husband's arm. Her words echoed Clara's own fears so very precisely. "Lord Taurin has ten men with him! Kenneth will not survive if he challenges them!"

Chapter Twenty-One

Clara rushed up to Lord Adrien and, without thinking, grabbed his hands to capture his attention. "I must go after them!"

"You! You won't catch them. Taurin left last night." He looked to Harry. "When did my sergeant leave?"

"Very early this morning, just before dawn."

Clara tightened her grip on Adrien. "I may be able to catch up with Kenneth. Mayhap talk him out of this addle-brained idea!"

Adrien turned to Harry. "Which horse did he take?"

Harry looked behind him at Rypan. Then, as if reading the older boy's thoughts, he said, "The fastest and quietest one. The one with the four white hooves."

Adrien nodded, as if knowing which mount it was. "Which way did he head?"

"Up past the watchtower on the way to Cogshale." Harry stepped closer. "My lord, he might easily catch them, for Lord Taurin's horse had one shoe missing and another loose. It won't run well with that. It may be lame by now."

"The horse's shoe was not replaced?"

"Nay, milord. The smithy didn't have a fire hot enough before the horse went missing."

Clara added, "Aye, and he refused to go to the peat bog because 'twould have been nearly dark when he arrived. The smithy also said he believed that someone was watching him the last time he was there, and—"

Adrien's face lit up. "'Twas Rowena, wasn't it?"

Clara dropped her gaze but still clung to Adrien. "Aye, 'twas her. He was afraid she was a thief who would attack him and leave him for dead. But all Rowena did was steal his lunch."

"How do you know this?"

"I went to the smithy's house after all of the women met here. The cook had sent Brindi to help his wife with their boys. Kenneth had already led Lord Taurin's courser down there, and I feared Taurin's men spotting Brindi or hearing the children use her name. I heard the smithy arguing with one of the Normans. It nearly came to blows."

Yanking back his hands, Adrien walked away. "I should throw you in my dungeon myself, woman, for being so reckless after all we did to thwart Taurin's plans! The Normans could have easily seen a wisp of hair escaping from your wimple, or have seen that your brows are red and deduced that your hair would be also!" Adrien thundered. "Someday you will not only put your life in danger, but others, also. Indeed, haven't you already done that? All to keep a promise you made to yourself! Aye, you are honorable to a fault, but 'tis a fault with that pride of yours!"

"I wouldn't be a good healer without some pledges!" she shouted back, then, realizing her foolhardy temper, clamped her mouth shut and lowered her gaze.

Ediva caught her husband's arm as he stepped toward Clara. "Nay, Adrien, her intentions are honorable, but her methods, not so much." To Clara, she said, "You are much like I was before you came. I had promised to keep my people here safe. 'Twas in part why I did so many foolish things. But I needed to learn that by doing it all by myself, I was pushing away God's chance to help me. God gave me Adrien. I've since learned to trust both my husband and the Lord. I was arrogant in thinking I was the only one who could keep my people safe."

Her expression softened. "We sometimes think we're too important to need others in our lives. Sometimes we even shut out God, thinking our problems are impossible for God to solve, so we must solve them ourselves."

Clara sniffed at Ediva's soft words. "But I can't sit here and do nothing! 'Tis my folly that has caused all of this danger, especially to Kenneth! How could he simply ride off thinking *he* could handle this?"

Ediva stepped down and walked close to Clara. "The same way you thought *you* could solve the problem by yourself. You hid Rowena, and you hid behind a pledge. Kenneth rode off to earn your trust again without thinking of the consequences. It appears he's learned that bad habit from you."

Clara fought back tears. Aye, he had. "But if he is wounded, he needs me to be there, not here, waiting for him to come home!"

Lady Ediva opened her mouth, but Lord Adrien spoke first, shooting a look at her. "I know another woman who felt the need to do something rather than wait at home. But I won't allow you to go alone. I will go with you. Mayhap my influence will convince Taurin to release Rowena and the babe."

She sagged. "My thanks, milord. But I need a fast horse to ride."

"You can take my mare," Ediva insisted quickly. "The good one that the king gave as a wedding gift. I cannot ride her, anyway."

Clara nodded. Ladies did not ride, but thankfully, she wasn't a member of nobility. She could easily handle that mare. "Thank you!"

She rushed out, not without hearing Ediva say, "You best catch up with her, Adrien, or she'll leave you behind. She may know that she must trust God, but she still has two fast legs."

Clara discovered that Rypan had anticipated her need and was already saddling the mare, the one everyone called the gift mare. She was thankful the beast was of good stock and able to go fast. No sooner had Rypan tightened the last strap than Clara mounted her. She cared not that her cyrtel rode up about her thighs. She wanted to be on her way.

As she galloped the mare through town, she heard Adrien coming up fast beside her. Refusing to allow him to take the lead, she urged her mount forward, and with the ease of many trips in the saddle, she kept him behind her for a time.

But not for long. His courser was a powerful beast.

As he came up beside her, Adrien held out his hand. "You will obey my orders, woman, and not ride ahead. This business is as much mine as it is yours." He threw her a hard look. "I can stop Taurin. You cannot."

"There are so many lives at risk. Rowena's, the babe's." Her voice hitched. "Even Kenneth's."

"All the more need to go safely. You won't do anyone any good riding recklessly. Though," he added as they slowed, "for an animal that allows only me on her, she is good under your command, I see. When we return to the keep after this business has settled, I expect you to teach my wife to ride her."

As she eased the mare to a slower pace, Clara smiled briefly and nodded.

Kenneth reined in his horse, peering at the ground below as it slipped past him. Several horses had already passed this way, including one large animal with a shoe missing.

He stopped and dismounted, trying to count the number of horses. There were eleven, and, he noted, one of the courser's other shoes was loose. 'Twas easy to tell in the soft, damp earth that it was slipping.

With disgust, Kenneth shook his head. Taurin was a fool to risk his courser's legs with one shoe missing and another loose.

Kenneth's mount snorted. The animal loved to run, he knew, and was anxious to continue. He peered ahead, to where the road dipped into a shallow valley and rose again to penetrate a large, dense forest. He peered hard at the wide, strong trees that edged it. 'Twas the leading edge of Broad Oak Forest, where Taurin had hoped to reach soonest. That cur was making better time than expected.

He looked down again at the prints Taurin's horses had made. They'd been galloping, and not too long ago, for the sun had risen and had not yet dried the wet ground.

Taurin had been pushing his mount hard, which meant he wanted to put as much distance as possible between him and Dunmow Keep. Out of Adrien's influence, Kenneth assumed.

But not out of mine. With a tight jaw, Kenneth mounted the horse again and spurred it to a trot. He would do right by Clara. He'd vowed to protect her and though she was safely ensconced in the bog, searching it for Rowena, his vow to her expanded into this mission. Clara's promise to the young mother was also his, for he'd disappointed Clara before and 'twas her pain and worry and disappointment that wrenched his heart. She'd been so incredibly hurt by what she thought was his betrayal.

He spurred the horse to a full gallop.

Half a league into Broad Oak Forest, Kenneth noted his mount sniff the air. When he sensed the horse's desire to join those of Taurin's men, he immediately stopped the animal and led him into an open patch beside one of the many oaks. Ivy, so prevalent here in England, had climbed and entwined itself throughout the branches, and even though 'twas early summer, it already hung low from the budding oak leaves and offered a place to tether.

He soothed his anxious horse with a soft word and a pat on the neck. And over his soothing, Kenneth could hear the sounds of other horses. They were stopped, probably by the stream that meandered to the road's right.

A babe's sharp cry rent the air, along with a shout to shut the child up.

Tensing, Kenneth led his horse deeper into the sheltered area close to the river so he could drink from the same stream. After refreshing the animal, Kenneth tied its reins to a low branch and began to ease slowly toward the others. Thankfully, the road bent and dipped to follow the stream, allowing Kenneth to come up behind the men. Crouching down behind a cobnut shrub, he spied the group ahead.

The sight sickened him. Rowena was tied at her ankles to a tree, with only enough of a leather lead to be able to sit and cradle her babe. She bore cuts and scrapes. Blood covered the side of her face.

She was fussing over her babe, trying to soothe it. But the poor thing was probably sensing his mother's tension and had begun to cry, further adding to her distress.

In front of her, several Normans sat, some dozing, some watching the road. But Kenneth's dun-colored clothing camouflaged him well. Taurin and one other Norman were inspecting his courser's hooves. As Kenneth had suspected, the mount was feeling the loss of its shoe and twitched and stamped its feet impatiently.

He eased back out of sight and, as slowly and quietly as possible, slowly drew his sword from its scabbard, all the while praying that the anxious courser in front of him couldn't hear it. He was a fighting horse, and such a sound would stir him to action, alerting the men around him.

Abruptly, the babe began to shriek. Kenneth heard Taurin shout at Rowena, demanding to know what was wrong.

"I don't know! He's upset over something. He must be hungry."

"Then feed him!" he shouted back over the screams.

"I'm trying!"

Abruptly, a sharp slap sounded, and Rowena's cry followed. "Don't talk to me like that, woman, or you won't see the end of this day!"

Kenneth used the infuriating noises to mask the sound of his sword finishing its release. The screech nearly matched the child's. He looked forward again. One of the horses sidestepped and neighed loudly, having been the only one in the crowd to recognize the different sound.

The nearest soldier reached out and patted the horse's head. "The babe is upsetting the horses, milord. Mayhap we should ride. It could soothe the child to sleep."

Taurin turned. "And have it screech even louder when we stop next? Nay, she needs to feed the brat now, so 'twill have a full belly when we get home. I have a healthy wet nurse ready there to feed it." He returned his attention to his horse.

The soldier shrugged before heading into the forest to Kenneth's right, obviously for some privacy. Kenneth clenched his jaw, hating how the numbers were against him. But, as if to remind him what was at stake, the babe let out an even more pitiful cry, followed by Rowena's soft, defeated whimper. He had to do something. The farther they traveled into this thick forest, the greater the chance that they would kill and discard Rowena.

She stroked her babe's head, revealing a crop of wild black curls, like his father's. This child resembled Taurin so strongly, 'twas as if the boy bore no part of his fair and delicate mother at all.

Kenneth stood and gripped his blade even more tightly as he spied the soldier facing a tree. The pommel at the end of the hilt could knock a man unconscious quite easily. Time to practice it.

Chapter Twenty-Two

One sharp blow, barely heard over another round of the child's anguished cries, and the soldier who'd disappeared into the woods dropped to the ground in front of Kenneth.

He needed to even the odds more, but 'twas a good beginning. If he could injure several before they knew what was happening, he would have a fighting chance to win.

A scuffle grew in the open area where Taurin was inspecting his horse's hooves. A long neigh from the mount now rent the air, and Kenneth scrambled down to peer through the trees.

Taurin was berating his courser filthily, all the while rubbing his thigh. It seemed the horse had kicked him. When the animal again turned to put his rump to Taurin, a sure sign another kick was to follow, the baron drew back and unsheathed his sword.

With another curse, as the horse's back leg floundered in open air, Taurin lashed out with his sword. The blade met the side of the animal, slicing it ruthlessly.

Kenneth flinched. No baron worth his salt would treat his mount so! The man must be insane.

The horse bolted away, disappearing around the road's next bend. Taurin blasted out orders to find it, and two of the men leaped onto their mounts to obey.

Thank You, Lord. For Taurin's cruel behavior had resulted in two men and three horses leaving.

The odds were better. More so if he acted quickly. He lunged forward, slicing a deep cut into the arm and shoulder of the one man lounging to his left. He then spun, kicking one of the other soldiers who leaped toward him. His well-placed boot drove the air from the man's lungs in one hard swoosh. He spun again, his blade arcing out to catch one soldier's knuckles as the man reached for his sword. On the follow-through, his blade caught another's knees.

Another soldier let out a growl and drew his sword from his scabbard, but Kenneth thrust forward. Norman mail was good, but 'twas no match for a sword's point. The man fell. Taurin raced across the road behind the falling soldier to grab Rowena.

Kenneth spun, preparing to intercept Taurin before he could use the girl as a shield.

But his rear flank was exposed. Two more soldiers lunged for Kenneth from the left. Their blades already free, they prepared to end this skirmish quickly.

Clara itched to leave Lord Adrien in her dust and push the big mare faster. She sensed the horse had the will and ability, not to mention the bloodline, to pass the heavier courser with ease.

She shot a furtive glance at Lord Adrien, but his

thoughts remained his own. He was most likely upset with his sergeant for running off without orders.

What had she caused? Kenneth was so determined to prove his innocence, he'd ignored his responsibilities to Lord Adrien and the keep. Did that mean he truly hadn't told Lord Taurin where Rowena was?

Sourness bit at her stomach and she found herself thinking of the smithy. Why? Because he'd told Taurin? Nay, he didn't have the time to go to the bog, and he certainly wouldn't have reported to Taurin that the person there could be the woman for whom Taurin searched. The smithy didn't care for Normans. Unless he said something to Taurin or his men by accident?

She and Adrien galloped along, and oddly, it felt good to be in the saddle again. The wind rushed past her face, freeing her hair, giving her a purposeful sense she was doing something, a sense she was getting closer to Kenneth.

In the distance, Broad Oak Forest loomed, swallowing the road. Yet, no sooner did they race into it, but Lord Adrien lifted his hand and pulled his horse to a stop. Clara did the same.

She walked her mount closer to Adrien. "What's wrong?" she whispered.

"I don't care to race through unknown woods. Broad Oak may belong to the king, but it's full of thieves and other dangers."

"Your horse is trained to fight back. I heard you did that on the new road when you were attacked."

"True, but your mount is untrained and she's been bred. I want a good foal from her next year."

"Riding fast is safer than walking slowly, Lord Adrien."

"Aye, but I don't want any sur—".

A whinny! Clara snapped up her head and listened intently. A horse was coming their way. A moment later, a horse with white feet trotted into view. Clara reached across the saddle and grabbed the dancing reins as the animal slowed past them. A switch with crushed leaves was caught in the knot at the end of the leather, and Clara untangled them. "'Tis Kenneth's mount. And look. Ivy and oak. This horse has been tied to one of the bigger oaks. Ivy takes many years to cover an oak, and 'tis deep into the forest where you find the bigger and older trees."

"Aye," Adrien added as he dismounted to take the reins and lead it behind his courser. Kenneth's horse was edgy, not wanting to be behind the bigger stallion. It took some turning for Adrien to quiet him and set him in line. Clara watched as he tied the pair in tandem.

Then, abruptly, she smacked the courser's hind end with the switch she'd untangled from Kenneth's mount, just enough to annoy it. Immediately, it broke into a gallop, forcing the other horse to follow.

"Clara!" Adrien shouted. But before he could add another word, she spurred her mare into action. She put Adrien out of sight, easily passing the startled horses as they bolted deeper along the forested road. Kenneth's mount broke free of its leather tie and turned immediately, while both the mare and Adrien's courser kept the same pace for a long stretch.

Only when Clara had ridden around several bends did she stop the mare. She gasped. A babe's screaming rent the air over the sounds of fighting, and Clara raced around yet another bend to find Kenneth pinned by two soldiers. To her right, Taurin gripped Rowena, his arm tight around her frame and his sword pressed against her neck. The babe wailed in Rowena's weakening embrace.

The remaining soldiers, those recovering from Kenneth's attack, whirled toward her with swords at the ready. Clara hesitated. Though mounted, she wasn't sure what she should do next.

Adrien's courser had followed her, and it had not survived the Battle of Hastings by being a foolish old cob. Immediately, agitated and sensing a good fight, it turned, driving both hind legs out behind it and drilling its powerful hooves into two of the soldiers. The men immediately fell.

In the next breath, the well-trained courser, used to fighting with little rein control, shoved hard sideways, then swung its strong hindquarters to knock down another man. The man in front of it received a powerful bite to the face, made worse because the soldier no longer wore his helmet. He also fell, screaming.

Caught up in the excitement, Clara's mare reared up. Clara slipped from the saddle and fell to the ground. The other horses bolted away.

Taurin spotted her, recognizing her by her hair. "You! Grab my son and set him aside! Now! I won't have his mother's blood spilled on him."

Horrified, and still slightly stunned by her fall, Clara scrambled to obey immediately, for Rowena looked as if she would surely faint, causing her son to drop. Quickly catching the babe, she stepped back, tripping on a large stone.

She stumbled backward into the trees but regained her balance quickly. Then she gasped. Beside her feet, one of the soldiers lay facedown, his head covered in blood. Had Kenneth ambushed him?

As she turned again, she peered back down at the rock she'd tripped over, wanting to move it. But with the babe in her arms, she could do nothing.

Kenneth spied Taurin wrenching sideways to control Rowena more fully, but the girl was barely conscious. He pressed his sword tighter against her throat. "Stand up straight, woman, or I'll slice open your throat!"

Immediately, Rowena stilled, though 'twas obvious she could hardly keep herself upright. Kenneth looked to his right and saw that Clara still held the child.

"And you, Sergeant?" Taurin growled out. "Did Lord Adrien send you in his stead? Is he now some fool fawning over his wife, under her thumb and unable to get away?"

Kenneth struggled against the men holding him. Adrien's angry courser had knocked out four soldiers, but two held him firmly. Two were out chasing Taurin's mount and one was half-dead in the woods. One more soldier stood near Taurin, who shifted sideways, closer to Adrien's still-agitated horse. Kenneth held his breath. He was one man against Taurin and three of his men.

"Release him." Taurin then shoved Rowena toward the remaining soldier. "And kill them all." In the next moment, he grabbed the babe from Clara's arms and swung up into the saddle of Adrien's courser.

Then he was gone.

Chapter Twenty-Three

Immediately, Kenneth swung his booted right foot hard to the left, connecting it with the soft inner thigh of the man beside him. Clara cringed. At the same time, he wrenched free of the other man and dived away from both. On the roll across the road, he caught Rowena's legs and pulled her free from the soldier who held her upright. She dropped like a rock.

Standing, he glanced at both his hands. Clara knew his thoughts. Where was his sword? Snatched from his hand when he was caught, no doubt. He jumped and kicked sideways at the man coming at him, but then, too late, found himself facing the last unharmed soldier. The man's sword lifted, readying to end Kenneth's life.

The man suddenly slumped and fell hard.

Clara gasped at what she'd done. She had used the rock she'd tripped over to hit the soldier's head on an angle that, she hoped and prayed, would only knock him out and cause him to drop the sword.

Horrified, Clara dropped the rock. Then, in that moment of revulsion, she scooped it up and flung it into the forest.

When she spied yet another sword, perhaps belonging to the unconscious man by the tree, she retrieved it and quickly hurled it into the trees, also. Then she looked up to find Adrien standing near Kenneth.

"I see I'm not as needed as I first thought."

"Nay, milord," Kenneth heaved out. "You're needed here." With that, he hefted up the sword nearest him and quickly mounted the mare that stood edgily nearby. He galloped off after Taurin.

Adrien threw a black glare at Clara. "Where's my courser?"

Ignoring him and suddenly shaking, she fell to her knees, fighting nausea. In front of her lay a man with his skull opened, an injury that could prove fatal. And, she noticed as she twisted about, others lay about with dangerous injuries from Adrien's horse, the one she'd driven here, while Rowena slumped nearby, half-unconscious.

"Rowena!" She struggled to her feet and staggered toward her friend. Pulling back the tangled mess of the younger woman's pale hair, Clara leaned forward. Rowena was still alive. Her lids fluttered, and her small, chapped lips formed a pair of soft words.

"My babe?"

Tears burst into her eyes, and she pulled her friend closer. "I'm so sorry! Taurin has taken him!"

The grunt of a man pulled Clara from her grief. She looked up just in time to see Lord Adrien mount one of the remaining horses and gallop away. Her heart squeezed. *'Tis too late, Lord Adrien. The babe is gone.*

"Dear God, are You there? I'm not in a church. Give me back my babe. Clara says You can do everything. Please?"

Clara gaped at Rowena. The woman was praying?

"Rowena? Are you a Christian?"

The woman's eyes fluttered open and she shrugged. "I don't know. I just want my babe back, and you told me once that God can do everything. I want Him to give me back my son. And make me more like you."

Shaking her head, Clara looked around at the carnage. "Nay, Rowena. You don't want to be more like me. For my pride was so great, I didn't even ask God for help."

She shuffled over to the nearest soldier. The crack on the back of the head she'd given him would ache, but the lump was not as bad as she'd first thought. Already he was rousing. She quickly spied the leather strips used to tie Rowena. They still dangled from her wrists and feet.

Clara hastily tied the rousing soldier's wrists at the back and did the same to the one she expected to awaken next. Her gaze returned to the first soldier, knowing that she'd seen him before, but unable to place him. She looked back at all the others.

She had pledged never to hurt anyone, and look what she'd been a party to! The least she could do was minister to them now and try to save their lives.

All the while asking God to forgive her prideful and stubborn ways.

When she was done, she returned to Rowena and lifted her up. "Come, we must leave. The men are all tied up, but Taurin may return at any moment."

"But my son?"

"We can't help him here, Rowena. All that I can say is that it's in God's hands now."

Rowena nodded. "Taurin won't hurt him. Not like he beat me. He has plans for my son, he said."

They wrapped themselves in Clara's cloak, and supporting each other, they began their journey home. Just as they were about to turn the bend and disappear from the soldiers, Clara glanced over her shoulder.

The first soldier was sitting up, tugging on the leather she'd used to bind him. His frowning profile edged clearly against the dark oak forest. *Something about him,* she thought. *I'm certain I've seen him before.* But she would not return to question him.

On Lady Ediva's gift mare, the one Clara had ridden, Kenneth easily caught up with Taurin. The evil man had been kicked twice by Adrien's courser and surely must find it hard to ride, and Lord Adrien's courser— accustomed only to his master—would not make it any easier for him.

Racing up beside Taurin, Kenneth reached out and grabbed the courser's reins, yanking them from Taurin's grip. Taurin struggled to stay seated until, when the courser stopped, he slid, babe held tight, to sit on the ground.

Taurin slipped down between the horses, and Kenneth was sure he was kicked anew for it.

Kenneth leaped off his mount and, with one hard jab, drove the blade of the weapon he'd found deep through the chain-mail hood, piercing the opposite side of where the babe was cradled. With a shove, Kenneth pushed Taurin back and impaled his blade fiercely into a felled log behind him.

Taurin struggled to yank the sword out, but his arms weren't long enough to get a good grip on it. He stopped after a few moments, chest heaving wildly and eyes glazed with pain.

"You deserve far more than being pinned like this, Taurin." Then, horror sweeping over him, he yanked at the scrap of cloth Taurin was holding. "Where is the babe? What have you done with him?"

Taurin laughed, then coughed before sinking back against the ground. "He's on his way to Normandy, where he belongs. You'll never catch my men."

"Normandy? Not your estate here? Why?"

"Here the brat will impress no one. But to my wife's family, he will be like the finest gold. Their only child, my wife, *God rest her soul,* has given them a son. And I will be given lands that will rival even those of the king himself."

Kenneth grabbed the slick and cold metal rings that made up the front of Taurin's chain mail. He pulled Taurin up as far as the embedded sword would allow. "That child is not your wife's!"

"He looks more like me than his mother." Taurin tried to laugh, but coughed weakly.

Cold washed through Kenneth. Then fury. Relenting to the rage surging within him, he pulled back his arm, preparing to punch the man. Taurin shut his eyes.

Kenneth staggered backward, horror rolling through him. He was about to do something Clara would despise. He *was* a violent man, designed to fight, to hurt and to do everything Clara had vowed *not* to do.

And the child was gone. Ripped from his mother, being taken across the channel for the gain of land and power.

Kenneth had failed in his mission and promise. He hadn't been able to save the little boy.

He looked around. Taurin must have caught up with the two men who bolted after his courser and handed over the babe to them. Where would they go first?

To collect a nurse needed for the journey, now that

Rowena had been left behind. Taurin's land lay to the south of here. Along the road that twisted like the letter *S*.

A thought, born of many hours spent updating Lord Adrien's maps, came to him. He yanked out his sword and mounted Adrien's courser just as the sound of thundering of hooves hit him.

Lord Adrien pulled his horse to a halt and looked down at Taurin, who still lay in a stupor. "Is he dead?"

"Nay. But part of me wishes so. He has handed over the babe to his men, to be sent to Normandy. His wife's family has promised him tracts of land to rival the king's in return for a babe from their beloved only child. But I suspect Taurin has murdered his wife and is passing Rowena's babe off as hers."

"We'll tie him up and I will send my men for him. King William can deal with this deceit."

The task done in short order, Kenneth looked out through the break in the trees, to see the land dip into a natural field.

"The men cannot travel fast with a small babe, especially a sickly one they want to survive until Normandy," Adrien commented.

Kenneth lit up. "Aye, and having updated your maps a hundredfold, I know a way to intercept them." With that, he remounted the stallion and galloped off. Not alone, he knew, for Adrien was close on his heels. He only hoped that they could intercept the men before it was too late.

Chapter Twenty-Four

The soldier was pacing his mount well, Kenneth noted immediately as he spied him approaching the edge of the forest in which Kenneth hid. The man knew the easy but unusual gait with less bounce would lull the babe in his arms. The Norman had swapped his mount wisely. This beast could pace for hours and not tire its rider.

Kenneth eased Lord Adrien's mount back and tensed his legs. When he drew out his sword, he tightened the reins, not wanting the courser to react too sharply.

The beast stilled, its whole body taut and ready to fight.

"Nay," he whispered to it softly. "I will decide when to go, not you."

Thanks to memorizing the maps, he knew this edge of the forest finished in a series of serpentine turns. Kenneth had cut across the field to bypass half the road.

The soldier's horse paced closer, its smooth, rolling gait slicing through a summer's growth of shrubbery along the roadside.

Ever closer.

Now! The soldier was nearly dead ahead and Kenneth pushed the courser forward to cut off the smaller animal.

It startled, skidded to a stop and turned away. But Lord Adrien's courser steered itself in front and around, blocking the horse further. Kenneth lunged and deftly caught the soldier's mail hood, keeping his sword high. Much higher than the babe's head. The man had neither time nor a free arm to draw his weapon.

"'Tis a bit foolish to travel alone," Kenneth growled. "And with a babe in your arm."

The soldier stilled, knowing any sudden movement might slice open his throat. He said nothing.

"Climb down."

Awkwardly, the soldier dismounted at the same time Kenneth did. Kenneth managed to keep the tip of his sword directly at the man's throat. "Now, soldier, put the babe behind the nearest tree."

Following the man, his sword still perilously close to the man's throat, Kenneth kept control as the man eased the babe down. As they both bent forward, Kenneth relieved him of his sword.

"Untie your thongs," he told him, indicating the strips of leather that held his leggings in place.

The soldier obeyed. Kenneth grabbed them and, in the same fluid motion, shoved the man to the ground and rammed the tip of his sword into the mail collar and then into the ground, similar to what he'd done to Taurin. Kneeing him in the back, he snatched the soldier's hands and swiftly tied them behind him.

Still, defeated and acquiescing, the man remained subservient, lying in the dirt of the road. Kenneth straightened, his mouth turning grim and yet satisfied. *Aye, 'tis finally over.*

A squall of protest rent the air and, his expression growing grimmer, Kenneth sighed and rose.

He walked over to the babe and scooped it up. Swaddled well, but as light a kitten and with face scrunched up, the babe fought and yelled for all he was worth.

Kenneth moved the outer cloth and freed the babe's arms. Then he opened his eyes. Blinking away his tears, the child stared up at Kenneth.

His lip quivered. His mouth opened. His eyes turned slightly cross-eyed as he tried to focus on Kenneth.

Kenneth had never before seen such a look of wonder and trust as he saw in this boy's dark eyes. And all the turmoil, the anger, the determination to treat this child as a thing to be dealt with according to law and justice and common sense, all fell from him.

'Twas no purse of coins to fight over, no parcel of land to barter. Not a cloth nor a cloak or even a fine piece of horseflesh.

Nay. This was a child, with a mouth parting and drool threatening to slip from of his lips. Kenneth brushed the babe's rosy cheek with his finger and the babe turned his head, opening his mouth as if he expected to be fed. Leaning forward, he rooted against Kenneth's callused hand, not minding the rough skin in his search for milk.

The knot forming in Kenneth's throat tightened further as he realized how close his sword had come to this babe.

What had he been thinking?

He had fought all his adult life, fought for a king older than he, rounder than he, and with power and control that stretched well past Normandy.

Yet, in this moment, this short, soft breath of time,

he would have surely disregarded all he knew and had protected to fight for this small babe.

He would die for this babe.

As Clara was willing to do.

A thrum of pounding hooves drew his gaze and he quickly recovered his sword. Around the corner came Lord Adrien, pulling the gift mare to a fast halt.

Kenneth could do nothing but try to straighten for his baron. But 'twas a weakened effort, one that elicited a grim snort from the man before him.

'Twould be a long ride home.

And, he thought, his breath sharp as he pulled it in, Lord Adrien was here, but…

"My lord, where are Clara and Rowena?"

"Clara is comforting Rowena. They're probably walking back to Dunmow."

Alarm shot through him, for the walk was long and dangerous and both had had difficult days up to now. "We left them!"

"Aye, for good reason. One I see you finally understand." Adrien dismounted. "When I first laid eyes on my own babe, I swore to myself I would do everything in my power to protect him. Even my duty to William is not that strong." He stepped over to peer down at the wide-eyed child tucked tight against Kenneth's chest. "And this child is not your own. Imagine what you will feel then."

"I have no wife."

"Then you should get back and see if you can't change that."

A need as strong as the one that had brought him here now surged through his blood and choked his words. Kenneth could not think. His baron stood beside him waiting for an answer, but Kenneth couldn't form one, for he knew not what to say.

But he did need to see Clara.

The downed soldier's pacing pony stood in the center of the road, ears tucked in fear, having backed away from the intimidating courser. He needed that mount for the babe's sake, but could only pray it would get him and the babe back to Clara in time.

"Clara. Clara?"

She could feel someone rearranging the furs around her face and fought the heavy pull of slumber. But with such sleep, her dreams had been harsh and cruel, mixed with Normans and horses and, oddly, the smithy. She began to cough and a warm, strong hand turned her from her back to her side.

Opening her eyes, Clara stared at the dark tunic of a man. When she was finished hacking, the man laid her back down again.

A man? The smithy? Nay, not him, but a profile of the man she'd bound in Broad Oak Forest. She gasped, shrinking away even as she sat up quickly. Now she knew where she'd seen him before. That man had been standing outside of the shop, watching her! "You! You were at the smithy's shop! And you saw me there!"

"Nay, Clara. 'Tis me, Kenneth."

From the blur of sleep, she focused on the man leaning over her. Kenneth! She sagged. "I thought you were the first man I tied up, the one I hit with the rock. I'd seen his profile before, at the smithy's shop. He was there, coming up behind me!"

Kenneth turned up the lamp. "Aye. I'd venture a guess that he saw a wisp of that red hair of yours. Remember when you said the wimple was too small for your thick hair? I suspect a small lock escaped or he noticed your eyebrows. I know I heard you gasp when the smithy mentioned the bog, so I imagine he did, also. He knew you were the midwife. Like me, that gasp told him exactly what he needed to know."

"But he didn't grab me and take me to Taurin!"

"Nay, he probably wanted to check the bog first. In fact, he sought out Harry and looked at the maps to find where it was."

Clara shut her eyes. Kenneth pulled her closer and she gripped him back. "I have been so unfair to you! 'Twas *that* man who saw me and guessed the truth! And I blamed you for telling Taurin!"

"'Twas reasonable to think," he whispered back into her hair. "But you must lie down. You've caught a fever from your walk."

Clara let him ease her to the pallet. There, she looked around. She was back in her home in Dunmow.

Home? How was this possible? She and Rowena had been walking. 'Twas the last she remembered.

She cried out. Rowena? Nay, had she—

"Clara, what's wrong?"

She swiped away her eyes. "Everything. Where is Rowena? We lost her babe, for Taurin snatched it and everything we worked for was for naught."

"Rowena is up in the keep and is quite safe. We left the cook in charge of her, and she's resting in the maids' room *with* her babe."

"Her babe?" A shocked smile danced across her lips. "How?"

"'Tis a long story and you need some hot broth in you first. Your walk back to Dunmow was difficult, and you and Rowena were both feverish when the miller found you. He brought you back."

Kenneth stood and left her small chamber. A hearty fire crackled, warming the entire room, but Clara refused to remove the heavy furs covering her. A moment later, he returned with a steaming bowl on a long wooden platter.

The offer of food coaxed her to push the furs from her face. Clara spied a soft, delicious trencher of bread beside the bowl. She tried to sniff, but her nose felt stopped with rags.

"I'm full of cold," she said.

"You had a fever, also," Kenneth added, setting the food down on a low table. "You tossed and turned all night."

She sat up woozily. "How long have I been here?"

"Only a day, but you and Rowena were barely conscious when you arrived."

She threw off the furs. "I must go to her!"

"Nay." Kenneth gently pushed her back. "The cook found another mother to help her. I told you that she and the babe are fine."

Falling back, Clara shook her head. "I pledged never to hurt anyone, and I hurt Rowena, and that man when I hit him with the rock…."

Kenneth sat beside her on the edge of her pallet and poured a small amount of broth into a cup. "Your pledge was an honorable gesture. But 'twas not proper as a Christian to take all of that burden solely onto yourself." He placed the cup into her hands. "You believed you could do it all without His help."

"I prayed all the time that He would keep Rowena safe and help me."

"There were many around you, given to you to help with that very task, but you wouldn't let us."

She set the cup down. "You wanted to hand her over to Lord Taurin!"

Kenneth frowned, his lips tightening. "Aye, 'tis true, and for that I owe both of you my deepest regrets. I was wrong. I realized that when I took him in my arms."

"You held him?"

"Aye. And 'twas as if my stomach twisted and turned like an acrobat. I can't explain it. But I knew, deep down, that how I felt before was very wrong."

"What was Taurin going to do with the babe? A child is a big responsibility."

"Aye. But Taurin wasn't that honorable. He wanted the babe, but not for anything noble."

"Not for anything noble?" She echoed his words. "What do you mean?"

"His wife's family had promised him great tracts of land should his wife bear a son. She was their only child and well loved. When she couldn't conceive, he bought Rowena because her family convinced him she would bear him a son. He planned to take her son, kill his wife and present the babe to his in-laws as their grandson. The land they'd have given him would have rivaled King William's, for they are quite wealthy and related to King William's father, Duke Robert."

"How do you know this?"

"Taurin is in the keep's dungeon, separated from his men and awaiting word from the king. He has admitted a lot of this, but is saying that he did it to relieve his in-laws of the land so he could present it to the king. They threatened William's control in southern Normandy because their lands lie in Brittany and Maine. But I suspect the king will see through Taurin's lies."

"It has worked out for the best, then, despite all my efforts."

"God has a plan for everyone, even Rowena. 'Tis coming to fruition, for she has given her life to Him."

"And the worst of it all was when I accused you!"

He toyed with her hair, for it was loose, shooting out in all directions. "I'm not a child, Clara, to bear a grudge over words spoken hastily in anger. Aye, your words hurt me, but I also needed them to learn that I'm not always right, either. When I learned Taurin had arrived here and I took you out of the village, I was just doing what you did. I assumed I could fix everything."

"And now?"

"Now I know that I have to trust in the Lord and His plan. And finally I understand what I truly want." He buried his fingers deep in her hair and lowered his face closer to hers. Their noses nearly touched. Her heart pounded.

"What do you want?"

He paused. A noise in the outer room caught their attention. Someone was entering the hut. Brindi called out, "Kenneth? Are you here?"

He looked back at Clara, and she wished that Brindi had waited a few more moments. "Here isn't the best place for us to talk. There's so much to say."

He called out to Brindi to come into the chamber. Clara forced a smile as her sister bounced into the little room.

Clara felt much better after eating, and rose to find the day half-gone. With Kenneth and Brindi close on her heels, Clara visited Rowena at the keep. The young woman glowed when she told Clara she would be given a home in a nearby village, near an estate belonging to a friend of Lord Adrien's. Several of the villagers, and even Lady Ediva, had rallied behind the new mother, showering her with gifts and foodstuffs enough to ensure a good start in their new life. Clara returned to her home satisfied the babe was stronger than he'd ever been.

Later, reported by Brindi, Lord Eudo had arrived with a platoon of men. Kenneth then excused himself to return to the keep.

Even later still, a knock sounded at the door. Clara's heart leaped. She'd not seen or spoken to Kenneth since he'd become busy with the logistics of providing a welcome to the baron's brother and his men.

Brindi skipped over to the door. Since seeing Rowena's child, she was as happy as summer flowers, laughing now as she threw open the door.

Kenneth. His expression was cool and distant as he stepped into their hut. "Brindi, I need to speak with Clara alone."

The air around Clara chilled. Was it possible that he had rethought his actions and decided that the time they'd spent together was best forgotten? That they were an ill-matched pair and 'twas no use encouraging a relationship?

Brindi, head down, slipped outside.

"Don't go far!" Clara warned.

Kenneth closed the door firmly behind him.

"Lord Eudo has brought a platoon of men to accompany Lord Taurin to London. He also sent a missive ahead to the king about Taurin's disgraceful behavior."

"And Taurin's wife? Did he really kill her?"

"Thankfully, nay. He had not yet placed that part of his plan into action. She will return to Normandy, however."

Clara bit her lip. The woman would surely face disgrace and shame and be forced to live out her life like a spinster daughter.

"How could he have believed he'd succeed? There were too many people who knew the truth."

"Only here in England. He had enough influence over his staff that they would lie for him. And once he had possession of the lands from his in-laws, he would have felt even more secure."

"'Twas a bold and dangerous plan."

"Aye. Taurin planned to say that his wife died birthing the babe, and since his staff here in England would never go to Normandy, he felt sure that her parents would never learn the truth. But the king will not be impressed with this treachery."

Kenneth stepped closer to her. "Clara, you would have been the only one who knew with certainty that Rowena birthed that babe. And you were the only one who had no loyalty to him. He not only sought out the child, but hoped to kill you and Rowena, also."

She nodded. All of this explanation, all this was simple reporting of the end of the story. 'Twas why he came here. Not to see her. Not to continue their earlier talk. Her heart wrenched in her chest. She straightened, determined not to show her hurt.

"But you're safe now, Clara."

"Oh." *Is this all he's come for?* Her heart confirmed her worst fear. She was too stubborn, not thinking of anyone but herself. This was God's way of telling her not to charge through life.

Kenneth paused, then with a small shake of his head, he pulled a doll from his inner pocket. With her wizened face and rope hair, she looked like an old hag, but somehow he'd carved a smile into it and shoved bits of bone in for teeth. The body was soft and the dress was a lovely blue, sewn with care.

"For Brindi. Margaret finished the body, though it doesn't match the head much."

Clara swallowed, remembering her foolish jealousy that day in the bailey when Kenneth spoke to Margaret. "Brindi will treasure it."

He set the doll on the table. "Clara, there is much to discuss."

She lifted her hand to interrupt him. "I need to think on all you've said about me doing things on my own. I've been charging along in my life." She heaved a sigh. "You see, I took in Rowena because 'twas right and proper to do so, but 'twas not my only reason. I did it because I was determined to show that I knew what was right. I was arrogant. I must learn not to be so."

"True."

She tamped down on her sudden indignation. Oh, she had so much to learn. "And also, Kenneth, you must learn that sometimes the right way is *not* your way, either." She shook her head. "Wait, 'tis not meant as a slur against you." She rushed out her words before her bravery dissolved. "I want you in my life, but unless I ask God what He wants, I'm just returning to my old ways, something I do not want to do."

She stood resolute before him. Finally, he nodded. "This must be God's will for us, and since you haven't felt led to be with…" He trailed away.

Then, without another word, he spun on his heel and left her home.

She slumped onto the bench and dropped her head to her hands. Oh, how easy 'twas for him to let her go. Were they meant to be together? Or were the emotions in her heart, those trappings of his honor and duty, fooling her into thinking 'twas for love he'd stayed with her, even after Taurin left?

Lord, show me what You really want for my life.

Chapter Twenty-Five

Kenneth's patience stretched thin the next few days. Attempting to respect her wishes, he'd avoided Clara as one avoided a deadly fever. He prayed at chapel services, at the back, away from all the others and buried deep in the ranks of soldiers who stood apart from the Saxon villagers. He stared at the priest to prevent his eyes searching for Clara, until he was surprised the old chaplain didn't have a hole burned right through his forehead.

He threw himself wholly into training, taking the initiative of ensuring all the men knew how to capture and incarcerate men of all rankings. He ensured all the horses were shod properly and ordered a stockpile of peat to be stacked behind the smithy's shop. He worked morning to dark, then retired early, even before the men he worked so hard.

Anything and everything to avoid thinking of Clara.

But always thinking of her.

Later, at the bog where they were harvesting the last of the best-quality peat, he stepped into that hut again and was sure he caught the light scent of herbs that was uniquely Clara. He stooped to retrieve the pot she'd left by the small fire pit, and he considered returning it to her.

Nay. She'd said 'twas not God's will for them. What would be the point in torturing himself? He'd seen her enough, also, as she went about her duties with smiles for all whom she met. Lady Ediva and her new babe were strong, mostly due to Clara's daily devotion to them. When she wasn't there in the solar, she was with milady's maid, Margaret, who took over the duties of seeing to the health of all the village children. Like him, Clara had thrown herself into her work and was obviously enjoying it.

Still clutching the pot, Kenneth shut his eyes. *But still, Lord, if it be Your will, give me Clara, the willing, loving Clara that I have seen so much of.*

All he heard in response was the men working outside.

A week later, Harry reported to him that Lord Adrien was ordering him into his office. There, Adrien sat at his desk, a long missive in one hand, a map Kenneth had not seen before in the other. His expression was grim as he told Kenneth to shut the door.

Rowena was to be dispatched to a village to the north, and Clara was to help her settle in. Lord Adrien had asked a fellow Norman there to allow her to start her life again under his protection. Clara had heard that this Norman was a fair man, loyal to the king and put there to protect royal lands in an area near Ely, a seat of much unrest. The man would assign the hut to her. After Rowena was settled and had learned as much as possible for her, Clara would return to Little Dunmow. She and Rowena would say their goodbyes with tears and prayers, but all would work out for Rowena.

Meanwhile, the week had been quiet for Clara. She had been given a pregnant rabbit for payment for a healing. 'Twas a grand gift, for only landowners had rabbit warrens, and no one was allowed to hunt them in the king's forest.

Brindi was thrilled with the animal. For a time, Clara kept the rabbit with the hens, knowing that she needed to build another coop soon, for the hens would kill the litter as soon as they were born.

The sun had begun to dip lower to the trees by the time Clara and Brindi had fashioned a decent cage. "Won't the mama rabbit chew through the netting, Clara? She eats everything we put in front of her."

"Nay, not this netting. I have used the strongest rope and soaked it in stink gum. 'Tis a decent use for the foul stuff. See, the mama rabbit isn't touching it. 'Tis far too bitter for her." They watched the mother sniff around and then begin to build a nest, probably relieved to be out of the henhouse.

"I'm glad we have her. She's pretty," Brindi announced. "I asked God for a kitten because the cat down the road had some, but they all died. I like our rabbit better. Funny how God didn't give me what I asked for, but showed me what I really wanted all along." She peered deeper into the cage. "We need more hay, not the stinky stuff from the henhouse. Can we get some now? Rypan took some from the fields for the stables today. He showed me where it was."

Clara agreed, thinking how good it would be to walk to the distant field and collect what they needed for the rest of the week. Anything to stop Brindi from chatting about how her prayers for a kitten had been answered in an even better way.

Lord, am I just to ask You?

Soon, they were headed around the keep, passing the bailey gate. Her heart sank. Kenneth stood outside. How long he'd been there, she couldn't tell, but she knew one thing.

Her heart wanted him in her life so very much.

Lord, I love him. What am I supposed to do? Just ask?

She slowed her pace, her gaze fixed on Kenneth's and her heart thrilled that his fixed on hers. Brindi called out a greeting, thanking him for the doll and announcing that she had a new pet and they were off to get hay for it. Then she began the long, convoluted explanation about how she'd asked for a kitten, but got a mama rabbit instead. Clara groaned. The girl must simply stop telling the world their business.

Kenneth smiled down at her, but the smile was smaller, more cautious than usual, she thought. Today, he wore a longer tunic, cinched at the waist and trimmed with embroidery she recognized as Lady Ediva's unique style. 'Twas dark blue, a color she'd not seen on Kenneth before, but the expensive clothing suited him well.

He'd abandoned his cloak, for the day was warm and fair. And he didn't carry his sword, either. What had instigated this change? To the north there was such unrest, and yet here it was so peaceful that no sword was needed?

He playfully tugged on one of Brindi's braids. She'd forgotten her kerchief so often that her hair had begun to lighten to a warm golden color. At Kenneth's simple gesture, Clara's heart twisted.

Lord, what is happening here? Do not jest with me, please. Tell me exactly what to do.

Kenneth walked straight up to Clara, greeting her politely. Brindi asked if they may take a bit of the new hay from the field. "Of course. May I escort you there?"

Her heart pounding, Clara nodded. She dared not breathe for fear this was but a dream. Why was he talking to her? Why was she finding herself praying fervently?

With Brindi skipping on ahead, Clara and Kenneth walked more sedately to the upper field. The last cutting of hay for the year was finished and the air was still filled with the fresh scent.

"Clara," Kenneth began.

She stopped him, unable to curtail the thoughts roiling within her. "Do not say anything that will hurt me, Kenneth, please! You know I weep at the drop of a hat and it has been worse than ever lately, especially since I left Rowena!"

His brows shot up. "I never did understand why you were like that. You were firm and unyielding to me from the moment we met."

"I have to be. If I give in to this weepiness, I would never be able to work."

"Have you asked God for strength?"

She looked away. "Nay, I have asked for nothing."

He touched his finger to her chin and guided her attention back to him. "Nothing at all? God wants to give you good gifts."

"But if they don't include what I want?"

"Which is?"

She held her breath, then blurted out, "You! I want you! I don't want just to see you in the bailey, doing exercises or training men or standing in the back of the chapel with the other soldiers. I want you! But you were so quick to agree with me that we should not be together the day you brought the doll, I tried to tell myself 'twas for the best."

He smiled, and fear and annoyance and hurt all rolled into one lump of something caught in her throat. "Stop laughing at me. I know I am but a silly maid sometimes, but I won't ask for something that will be denied me!"

"Will it? You seem to know all God's answers without asking."

She stiffened her shoulders.

"Ask Him. I did."

"What did you ask Him?"

"I asked for you. And I have been given so much more."

Clara frowned. "I don't understand."

"King William has given me Lord Taurin's estates. He's made me the baron there. What Taurin tried to do was akin to treason and he will be tried for it in Normandy. He has a home there and is ordered to remain at it though all other lands have been taken from him."

"A sad end."

"And us? Do we have a sad end? I see you every day, busy about your work, and those around me say you look at me when I turn away. They say your look is filled with love. And you say you want me."

Heat flooded into her face.

Kenneth took her hands. "Clara, marry me. Come with me. The estate is not as lavish as Colchester nor does it have as strong a keep as Dunmow, but 'tis a good place, with fine land and a warm house. I want you to be my baroness."

Her soul leaped within her, and she found herself wordless.

Kenneth continued, "Brindi asked for a kitten and received a pregnant rabbit. I asked for you, that you'd accept a sergeant at arms who had been made a steward and that we'd find some way of making a life together within Dunmow Keep. Just as God increased the blessing He's given Brindi, He has increased our blessing. These days away from you have taught me that my heart belongs with you, Clara. And I know yours belongs with me. Say you will be my wife."

"But what of my work here?"

"Margaret has learned a lot, I'm told. And so has the cook. My new estate has no one and needs someone with good knowledge of birthing and healing." He drew her closer. "Marry me, Clara. I love you. I want us to be together, always."

She stared hard into his eyes, but found her stare dissolving into a soft gaze. "I will be your wife."

He kissed her soundly, interrupted only when Brindi pushed herself between them. "Can we take the rabbit, too?"

"Aye. She will have a grand pen, and we'll let her litter go free in the forest to make our own warren of them." He looked into Clara's eyes. "We'll make our family bigger, too."

She laughed, seeing him through blurring tears and through the love God had given her.

* * * * *

Dear Reader,

Thank you for choosing my book. I hope you enjoyed it. We met some of the characters in this book in my first medieval, _Bound to the Warrior_. But it was great fun to flesh out their lives, their thoughts and their personalities. In doing so, I discovered that Clara has a stubborn streak not unlike my own. I think we all have one, especially when it comes to something that is important to us, and sometimes it's not a bad trait. But we must all learn to bend that will to God, and that's where it gets hard. So as we ponder this book and continue in our lives, let's consider how we can have the strength to do what's right in God's eyes and still be the wonderful, diverse creations He made us to be.

I hope you will continue reading this series, as I give you Rowena's story next.

Blessings,

Barbara Phinney

Questions for Discussion

1. What did you think of Clara hiding Rowena? Would you have done the same or trusted that God would keep her safe wherever she was?

2. At the beginning of the book, did you get the sense that Clara refused to seek God's will in all things?

3. Kenneth was introduced in the previous story, *Bound to the Warrior*. If you read that one, did you feel he differed in that story?

4. Did Kenneth's personality ring true to you?

5. Clara was stubborn, but weepy. Did that make sense? Has God softened your heart to the point of being weepy?

6. Who was your favorite character? Why?

7. Did you learn something from this story that you didn't know before? What was it?

8. When Adrien ordered all the women into the Great Hall, did you think he was deceiving Taurin? Why or why not? Was it right?

9. Have you ever deliberately not asked God for something because you were afraid of the answer?

10. Did you ever just go ahead and do something because you felt it was the best thing to do, without praying first?

11. Did Taurin's personality make sense to you? Have you ever known someone who would do anything to achieve their desired goal?

12. In the beginning, while in the dungeon, Clara says a prayer for Lady Ediva's safety. Do you feel it was a matter of "too little too late" or "praying after the deed was done"?

13. Clara knew little of God, but had faith in Him. Would you say this faith is true, like a child's? How would you describe your faith?

14. Do you think that Rowena became a Christian? She prayed for her son, saying she wanted to be more like Clara. What would you have suggested to her?

COMING NEXT MONTH FROM
Love Inspired® Historical

Available September 2, 2014

HIS MOST SUITABLE BRIDE
Charity House
by Renee Ryan
When Callie Mitchell is asked to help widower Reese Bennett find a prospective bride, she finds the idea of Reese marrying anyone but her simply unthinkable....

COWBOY TO THE RESCUE
Four Stones Ranch
by Louise M. Gouge
When a handsome cowboy rescues her father and takes them to his ranch, Southern belle Susanna Anders begins to fall for the exact opposite of all she'd thought she wanted.

THE GIFT OF A CHILD
by Laura Abbot
To help an abandoned child, Rose Kellogg and Seth Montgomery enter into a marriage of convenience. But can an agreement between friends lead to true love?

A HOME FOR HER HEART
Boardinghouse Betrothals
by Janet Lee Barton
Reporter John Talbot thinks he's found the story of his career. But when the truth he uncovers threatens to expose the father of the woman he's come to love, will he sacrifice his dreams for her happiness?

REQUEST YOUR FREE BOOKS!

2 FREE INSPIRATIONAL NOVELS
PLUS 2
FREE
MYSTERY GIFTS

Love Inspired.
HISTORICAL
INSPIRATIONAL HISTORICAL ROMANCE

YES! Please send me 2 FREE Love Inspired® Historical novels and my 2 FREE mystery gifts (gifts are worth about $10). After receiving them, if I don't wish to receive any more books, I can return the shipping statement marked "cancel." If I don't cancel, I will receive 4 brand-new novels every month and be billed just $4.74 per book in the U.S. or $5.24 per book in Canada. That's a saving of at least 21% off the cover price. It's quite a bargain! Shipping and handling is just 50¢ per book in the U.S. and 75¢ per book in Canada.* I understand that accepting the 2 free books and gifts places me under no obligation to buy anything. I can always return a shipment and cancel at any time. Even if I never buy another book, the two free books and gifts are mine to keep forever.

102/302 IDN F5CN

Name _____ (PLEASE PRINT) _____

Address _____ Apt. # _____

City _____ State/Prov. _____ Zip/Postal Code _____

Signature (if under 18, a parent or guardian must sign) _____

Mail to the Harlequin® Reader Service:
IN U.S.A.: P.O. Box 1867, Buffalo, NY 14240-1867
IN CANADA: P.O. Box 609, Fort Erie, Ontario L2A 5X3

Want to try two free books from another series?
Call 1-800-873-8635 or visit www.ReaderService.com.

* Terms and prices subject to change without notice. Prices do not include applicable taxes. Sales tax applicable in N.Y. Canadian residents will be charged applicable taxes. Offer not valid in Quebec. This offer is limited to one order per household. Not valid for current subscribers to Love Inspired Historical books. All orders subject to credit approval. Credit or debit balances in a customer's account(s) may be offset by any other outstanding balance owed by or to the customer. Please allow 4 to 6 weeks for delivery. Offer available while quantities last.

Your Privacy—The Harlequin® Reader Service is committed to protecting your privacy. Our Privacy Policy is available online at www.ReaderService.com or upon request from the Harlequin Reader Service.

We make a portion of our mailing list available to reputable third parties that offer products we believe may interest you. If you prefer that we not exchange your name with third parties, or if you wish to clarify or modify your communication preferences, please visit us at www.ReaderService.com/consumerchoice or write to us at Harlequin Reader Service Preference Service, P.O. Box 9062, Buffalo, NY 14269. Include your complete name and address.

LIHI3R

SPECIAL EXCERPT FROM

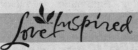

Don't miss a single book in the
BIG SKY CENTENNIAL miniseries!
Here's a sneak peek at
HER MONTANA TWINS
by Carolyne Aarsen:

"They're so cute," Brody said.

"Who can't like kittens?" Hannah scooped up another one and held it close, rubbing her nose over the tiny head.

"I meant your kids are cute."

Hannah looked up at him, the kitten still cuddled against her face, appearing surprisingly childlike. Her features were relaxed and she didn't seem as tense as when he'd met her the first time. Her smile dived into his heart. "Well, you're talking to the wrong person about them. I think my kids are adorable, even when they've got chocolate pudding smeared all over their mouths."

He felt a gentle contentment easing into his soul and he wanted to touch her again. To connect with her.

Chrissy patted the kitten and then pushed it away, lurching to her feet.

"Chrissy. Gentle," Hannah admonished her.

"The kitten is fine," Brody said, rescuing the kitten as Chrissy tottered a moment, trying to get her balance on the bunched-up blanket. "Here you go," he said to the mother cat, laying her baby beside her.

Hannah also put her kitten back. She took a moment to stroke Loco's head as if assuring her, then picked up her son and swung him into her arms. "Thanks for taking Corey out on the horse. I know I sounded…irrational, but my reaction was the result of a combination of factors. Ever since the twins were born, I've felt overly protective of them."

"I'm guessing much of that has to do with David's death."

"Partly. Losing David made me realize how fragile life is and, like I told your mother, it also made me feel more vulnerable."

"I wouldn't have done anything to hurt Corey." Brody felt he needed to assure her of that. "You can trust me."

Hannah looked over at him and then gave him a careful smile. "I know that."

Her quiet affirmation created an answering warmth and a faint hope.

Once again he held her gaze. Once again he wanted to touch her. To make a connection beyond the eye contact they seemed to be indulging in over the past few days.

Will Hannah Douglas find love again with handsome rancher and firefighter Brody Harcourt?
Find out in
HER MONTANA TWINS
by Carolyne Aarsen,
available September 2014 from Love Inspired® Books.

*Brave men and women work to protect
the U.S.-Canadian Border.
Read on for a preview of the first book in the new
NORTHERN BORDER PATROL series,
DANGER AT THE BORDER by Terri Reed.*

Biologist Dr. Tessa Cleary shielded her eyes against the late summer sun. She surveyed her surroundings and filled her lungs with the sweet scent of fresh mountain air. Tall conifers dominated the forest, but she detected many deciduous trees as well, which surrounded the sparkling shores of the reservoir lake.

A hidden paradise. One to be enjoyed by those willing to venture to the middle of the Pacific Northwest.

The lake should be filled with boats and swimmers, laughing children, fishing poles and water skis.

But all was still.

Silent.

The seemingly benign water filled with something toxic harming both the wildlife and humans.

Her office had received a distressing call yesterday that dead trout had washed ashore and recreational swimmers were presenting with respiratory distress after swimming in the lake.

As a field biologist for the U.S. Forestry Service Fish and Aquatics Unit, her job was to determine what exactly that "something" was as quickly as possible and stop it.

"Here she is!" a booming voice full of anticipation rang out.

A mixed group of civilians and uniformed personnel gathered on the wide, wooden porch of the ranger station.

All eyes were trained on her. All except one man's.

Tall, with dark hair, he stood in profile talking to the sheriff. Too many people blocked him from full view for her to see an agency logo on his forest-green uniform.

Tessa turned her attention to Ranger Harris. "Do you have any idea where the contamination is originating?"

He shook his head. "We haven't come across the source. At least not on our side of the lake. I'm not sure what's happening across the border." George ran a hand through his graying hair as his gaze strayed to the lake. "Whatever this is, it isn't coming from our side."

"Let's not go casting aspersions on our friends to the north until we know more. Okay, George?"

The deep baritone voice came from Tessa's right. She turned to find herself confronted by a set of midnight-blue eyes. Curiosity lurked in the deep depths of the attractive man towering over her.

Answering curiosity rose within her. Who was he? And why was he here?

For more, pick up DANGER AT THE BORDER.
Available September 2014
wherever Love Inspired books are sold.

Love Inspired HISTORICAL

His Most Suitable Bride

by

RENEE RYAN

No one in Denver knows how close Callie Mitchell once came to ruin. Dowdy dresses and severe hairstyles hide evidence of the pretty, trusting girl she used to be. Now her matchmaking employer wants Callie to find a wife for the one man who sees through her careful facade.

For his business's sake, Reese Bennett Jr. plans on making a sensible marriage. Preferably one without the unpredictable emotions that spring to life around Callie. Yet no matter how many candidates she presents to Reese, none compare with the vibrant, intelligent woman who is right under his nose—and quickly invading his heart.

**Offering an oasis of hope, faith and love
on the rugged Colorado frontier**

*Available September 2014
wherever Love Inspired books and ebooks are sold.*

Love Inspired

Her Hometown Hero
by
Margaret Daley

In a split second, a tragic accident ends Kathleen Somers's ballet career. Her dreams shattered, she returns home to the Soaring S ranch…and her first love. Suddenly the local veterinarian, Dr. Nate Sterling, goes from her ex to her champion. With the help of a lively poodle therapy dog, the cowboy vet sets out to challenge Kathleen's strength and heal her heart. He'll show her there's life beyond dance, even if it means she leaves town again. But maybe, just maybe, he'll convince her there's only one thing in life worth having… and he's standing right in front of her.

Loving and loyal, these dogs mend hearts.

Available September 2014
wherever Love Inspired books and ebooks are sold.

LI87908